W9-BJA-515

COURAGEOUS HEART

The young man took a quick stride across the the room and flung himself in a comfortable chair.

"The point is this, Jen: you can't possibly stay here and run this house with all these children. I've spoken to your aunts and they assure me they've made plans to provide for them."

Jennifer looked up with angry eyes, her lips closed in a thin line, but she said nothing, and Peter Willis went smoothly on.

"Now my idea is this, Jen. I decided we should get married right away, then take a run over to Europe for a while . . ."

"I'm not planning to marry anyone at present."

A swift look of anger passed over the handsome young man's face.

"I've been considering you mine for a long time," he protested. "I've always expected to make you my wife."

"Oh, *really?*" Jennifer retreated a step towards the hill, and there was the utmost contempt in her face.

"Well, *I* wasn't just looking around for someone to marry me. And I'm sure of one thing. If ever I do marry anyone, *it won't be you!*"

Bantam Books by Grace Livingston Hill
Ask your bookseller for books you have missed

1 WHERE TWO WAYS MET
3 A GIRL TO COME HOME TO
4 AMORELLE
7 THE BEST MAN
12 HEAD OF THE HOUSE
14 STRANGER WITHIN THE GATES
16 RAINBOW COTTAGE
19 DAPHNE DEANE
20 THE SUBSTITUTE GUEST
24 BY WAY OF THE SILVERTHORNS
27 APRIL GOLD
31 THE STRANGE PROPOSAL
34 THE PATCH OF BLUE
38 SPICE BOX
39 THE SEARCH
41 BLUE RUIN
42 A NEW NAME
43 DAWN OF THE MORNING
44 THE BELOVED STRANGER
45 THE GOLD SHOE
46 THROUGH THESE FIRES
47 THE STREET OF THE CITY
48 BEAUTY FOR ASHES
49 THE ENCHANTED BARN
50 THE FINDING OF JASPER HOLT
51 THE RED SIGNAL
52 TOMORROW ABOUT THIS TIME
53 JOB'S NIECE

GRACE LIVINGSTON HILL

HEAD OF THE HOUSE

BANTAM BOOKS
TORONTO · NEW YORK · LONDON

This low-priced Bantam Book has been completely reset in a type face designed for easy reading, and was printed from new plates. It contains the complete text of the original hard-cover edition.
NOT ONE WORD HAS BEEN OMITTED.

HEAD OF THE HOUSE

A Bantam Book / published by arrangement with J. B. Lippincott Company

PRINTING HISTORY
Lippincott edition published 1940
Bantam edition / May 1969

2nd printing .... June 1969
3rd printing .... June 1969
4th printing .... October 1969
5th printing .... April 1970
6th printing .... September 1970
7th printing .. September 1970
8th printing .... August 1971
9th printing .. November 1971
10th printing .... October 1972
11th printing .... February 1973
12th printing .. November 1973
13th printing .. November 1974
14th printing .... October 1975
15th printing .. November 1978

All rights reserved.
Copyright © 1940 by Grace Livingston Hill.
This book may not be reproduced in whole or in part, by mimeograph or any other means, without permission.
For information address: J. B. Lippincott Company, 521 Fifth Ave., New York, N.Y. 10017.

ISBN 0-553-12222-3

Published simultaneously in the United States and Canada

Bantam Books are published by Bantam Books, Inc. Its trademark, consisting of the words "Bantam Books" and the portrayal of a bantam, is registered in the United States Patent Office and in other countries. Marca Registrada. Bantam Books, Inc., 666 Fifth Avenue, New York, New York 10019.

PRINTED IN THE UNITED STATES OF AMERICA

HEAD OF THE HOUSE

1

The house was wide and low and charming, built of rough gray stone with ivy climbing about the terrace walls, creeping up the rambling solid chimneys, and about the stone bay windows. It had a homelike look, as if it were a place beloved where happy living went on, and joy echoed from its solid walls, a place whose every spot was enjoyed to the full, a place where friends and neighbors loved to come.

But that morning it seemed to be standing aghast in the early summer sunshine, its bright frill of daffodils that edged the terrace walls gazing with fixed yellow stare at a world that overnight had changed. The whole house seemed stunned with the sudden catastrophe that had befallen, like a beloved dog wagging his lonely plumy tail, wistfully, grievedly, to an unresponsive relative.

Two cars were parked on the wide drive near the front entrance and a third drove hastily up as if it feared it was late. A lady in the back seat leaned forward looking up at the house speculatively, with an almost possessive glance, critically taking in all its features. She stepped out of the limousine as her chauffeur opened the door for her, and hastened up the broad low steps, noting a flower that hung down from its stalk over the walk, reminding herself to speak to the gardener about picking the flowers and sending them over to her house.

She was a large lady, imposing in her bearing, sharp of glance, firm of chin and thin of lip, a great aunt on the mother's side who had always considered it her business to set the whole family right and keep them so. Her name was Petra Holbrook, Aunt Pet for short, disrespectfully called by the children sometimes, "Aunt Petunia."

At the threshold she paused with her hand on the doorknob and identified the two cars that were parked at the right of the drive, side by side as if a procession were expected and they were the first. She sniffed as she recognized them. The first would be Adrian Graeme's car. Of course he would come first and try to act as though he was the most important member of the family, just because his name was Graeme and he was the oldest relative on the Graeme side. But he surely didn't expect to have anything to say about matters. He was only a second cousin and had never been generous. But then of course the notice had been sent to them all. That was certainly a shabby car he was driving. His second best likely. It didn't seem very respectful to come to such an important engagement in a car like that, but then his flibbertigibbet wife Lutie likely had the other off somewhere shopping. Wasn't she coming? Probably she was going to try to get out of any responsibility. Perhaps she would be late, and come fluttering in after everything was all arranged. Lutie Graeme! Such a silly name for a grown woman. Well, she for one intended to see that Cousin Lutie had a task set for her that would make her wish she had come earlier.

And the next car was Jim Delaney's. Jim had been a half-brother of John Graeme and would likely think he had a say. And of course he was pretty well fixed, and ought to be able to shoulder some of the responsibility. But he needn't think he was going to choose what it should be. After all he was only a half, and a man at that. And a man wouldn't know rightly what was good for children suddenly left without father or mother. Jim's wife was dead so she would not be there to complicate matters.

She swept the driveway with another glance that glimpsed the side toward the garage. Apparently the lawyer hadn't come yet. Well, that was just as well. She would have a good opportunity to talk things out with Adrian Graeme and Jim Delaney before he arrived.

Great Aunt Petra turned the knob and tried to open the door. It was her habit to open her relatives' doors and walk right in as if she owned them herself, when she could. But in this case the door was locked.

"Utterly absurd!" she murmured annoyedly as she petulantly rang the bell.

A man servant appeared and opened the door for her with respectful formality, as Miriam Graeme had taught him to do.

"The gentlemen are in the living room, Mrs. Holbrook," the man said.

Aunt Petra made no comment, but turned on him with orders.

"Stanton, why don't you take the night latch off that door?" she said dictatorially. "It's absurd to keep running back and forth to open the door when you know there are a number of people coming!"

"I'm going according to my orders, ma'am," said Stanton.

She reached out and snapped the latch off herself. "Now," she said with authority, "you needn't come when the bell rings. Let them walk right in!"

Then she turned and sailed into the great beautiful living room.

Stanton stood at one side waiting until she had paused an instant to take in the situation and turned to the right toward the far end where the two men were sitting. Then he reached a swift hand and snapped the latch on once more, disappearing silently into the recesses of the back hall, alert and prepared for the next ring of the bell. His mistress who had laid this responsibility upon him was lying in a new-made grave, but as long as he was in this position he would continue to do as she had taught him.

Aunt Petra took her leisurely way down the room, noting with appraising eye several articles in the room that she had long admired, a priceless painting on the wall that well might adorn her own wall now, if she should feel it wise to take over one of the children and look after her. Jennifer, perhaps, because she would soon marry and be off her hands. A tall lamp with a unique arrangement of indirect lights. A lovely jardiniere she had long coveted. And those marvelous rugs! But there wasn't a room in her house that was large enough for them, and they would likely have to be sold anyway. What a pity!

The two men had arisen as she drew near, though they still continued their talk until she was opposite them. Then they turned.

"Good morning, Mrs. Holbrook," said Jim Delaney. "Won't you have this chair?"

"Thank you, I prefer a straighter one," said Aunt Petra perversely. "Good morning, Adrian. I'm surprised you're able to be out. I heard Lutie telling someone yesterday at the funeral that you were feeling quite miserable and really ought to be in bed. I didn't expect to see you this morning."

"H'm? Ah! Why, I'm feeling quite well, Mrs. Holbrook, thank you. It is a sad occasion of course, but I'm in my usual health. Perhaps you'd like this chair."

"No," said Aunt Petra sharply, "I'll take this straight chair. Hasn't the lawyer come yet? I thought he was always ahead of time." She glanced at her watch severely as if it were somehow to blame.

"H'm, no, not yet," murmured Adrian. "It's just as well, as we aren't all here anyway."

"Oh, who else is coming?"

"I really couldn't say," said Adrian. "All of them, I suppose. Ah, I think I hear footsteps. Someone else has arrived."

Stanton had arranged the bell with a muffler so that it sounded with a subdued bur-r-r back in the hall, and he was at the door before Aunt Petra could even know anyone had come. They all looked up, however, as a shadow crossed the sunlight from the front windows and portly Majesta Best walked in, followed, a pace or two behind, by her thin apologetic husband, Uncle Pemberton

Best. Majesta Best was a younger sister of Petra Holbrook and her rival in every way.

"Oh," said Petra, somewhat haughtily, "Pemberton, Majesta, I didn't suppose you'd be able to get away this morning, you took home so many of the cousins from back in the country after the funeral yesterday. Have they gone so soon? I was hoping some of them could come to dinner."

"Oh, no," said Majesta sinking comfortably into an ample armchair, "they're staying over the week-end. You'll have plenty of time to invite them, Petra. But I know my duty and I told them frankly I'd have to be over here and do what I could to look after my dear dead niece's children."

"You needn't have felt that way, Majesta," said Petra, "there are plenty of us here to plan for the children, and we would all have understood that you were taking care of the cousins. But, we're all here now, aren't we? I mean of course the more active ones. The uncles are all here, at least, aren't they, Adrian?"

Adrian looked about him.

"Why, no, I believe Blakefield hasn't come yet."

"Blakefield!" chorused the aunts. And then Petra, "But what does he matter? Of course he wouldn't have a voice in saying what should be done with the children!"

"You must remember, Petra," said Adrian, "that Blakefield is an uncle of John Graeme, and one might almost say a favorite uncle," he added in a half-offended tone. "Of course I never have felt that Blakefield was practical. Still we have to give him the courtesy of an invitation. John always did think a great deal of his Uncle Blakefield. Perhaps because he was John's father's twin brother."

"Yes," sighed Aunt Petra, "of course John always was quite sentimental about everything, and his father dying so young and all, I suppose he felt that Blake was a little nearer to him than any of the others. And of course it's all right for Blakefield to be here and sit in on this conference, but he can't be expected to really do anything. He hasn't been so awfully successful in business, has he? And now being an unmarried man he couldn't be expected to give any of the children a home. But I did expect Agatha Lane to be here. She has plenty of money, and room, and servants, and no husband to interfere, and being Miriam's only wealthy relative ought to do something handsome. She ought to be depended upon to take over the two younger children. She's nothing in the world to do but amuse herself and she always pretended to think the world and all of her niece Miriam. There! Didn't I hear another horn? Isn't that her car, Adrian?" Great Aunt Petra got up and sailed to the front window. "Yes, it is! There's Agatha now! Well, I'm glad she's come. Now, if the lawyer were only here we could get started at once."

Aunt Agatha Lane entered languidly, slim, youngish, elegant, inclined her graceful body in a bow that included them all and dropped dramatically to the end of a couch. She was a widow, well made-up, with a threadlike eyebrows, delicately flushed complexion, and a cloud of golden hair, done in a long golden bob that gave her the appearance of at least half her age.

"Well, I'm glad you've come, Agatha," said Great Aunt Petra, raising her deep voice so that it could be clearly heard over the large room and penetrated even to the adjoining library. The library opened in a vista from one end of the living room, and Jennifer Graeme had taken refuge there behind heavy drawn curtains. She had been weeping her young heart out for her adored parents, and was miserable now over what she considered the intrusion of all these relatives. Why did they want to come here at this time when she wanted to be alone? What right had they, she asked herself pitifully, as she curled more deeply into a great leather chair and stuffed her little damp handkerchief into her mouth to still her sobs.

But Great Aunt Petra's voice came sharply through the curtains.

"Yes, Agatha, I certainly am glad you are here! For you see you will have to play quite an important part in the plans we have to make. It has seemed to me from the very first that you would be the ideal one to take over the two youngest children, or one of them at least. You have more leisure than anyone else, and it would be just a pleasure for you to bring them up and plan their future."

"Oh, *mercy!*" said Agatha Lane, suddenly rousing from her languor. "*I? Bring up* the *children?* And such *terrible* children! Why, Petra, the last time I was here I went home utterly exhausted from the strain of having them come pelting into the room every few minutes, as dirty as two little pigs, and howling! That little Robin is positively disgusting when he eats chocolate, and smears it all over himself and the chairs. He actually wanted to get into my lap! At least his nurse suggested that he do so, and eat his chocolate dog *in my lap!* Fancy it! And that little Karen is unspeakable! She climbed up on the lattice outside the back terrace and swung there before the window until I thought I should lose my senses! No, Petra, you'll have to leave me out of any plans like that. I haven't the strength to stand it. I've just come from my doctor's, and he thinks I should have a long sea voyage, and a little time of resting abroad in some resort where I can have baths and treatments. Of course I could take Jennifer with me for a few months perhaps. She is old enough to look after herself I should think, although I'm afraid I should lose my mind, she is so peculiar and unexpected in her reactions. I just couldn't stand it to have to watch out for her on shipboard. One has to be so careful about whom a young girl meets, you know. At that age! There are so many ineligibles about, too, especially when a girl might be thought to have money."

"I don't think you need worry very much about Jennifer," said Aunt Majesta dryly. "*I* think she's pretty well provided for, isn't she, Petra? I've seen her going about a great deal with that Peter Willis, and he's enormously rich. I imagine she'll be marrying him before long and then she'll be off our hands!"

"Jennifer is a little young to be married off yet, isn't she? Do you all realize she isn't of age?"

They all looked up startled, and there in the doorway

stood Uncle Blakefield, gray-haired, somewhat bald, kindly-faced, but grim just now.

"Oh, is that you, Blakefield?" said Great Aunt Petra. "I didn't hear you come in. I don't suppose you realize that Jennifer wouldn't be counted young to be married in these days. But do come in and sit down and let's get to work. Why doesn't that lawyer come?"

"By the way," said Agatha Lane, in a clear voice that dominated the room at once, "I wonder if you all realize that there's a perfectly good way to settle these matters without the least bit of trouble to any of us? Why don't we just put Cousin Abigail Storm in here and let her run the house and take care of them all, at least until Jennifer marries? That will kill two birds with one stone. Cousin Abigail is in abject despair. She's lost every atom of her money and she can't find a job anywhere, she's too old. I had a most forlorn letter from her this morning, and I felt that it just came in the nick of time. Here we'll have Abigail on our hands if we don't do something about it pretty soon, and it strikes me that this will be a perfectly lovely arrangement."

"Well, *I* think it would be perfectly ruinous," said Petra with scornful eyes. "It might be a lovely arrangement for you, Agatha, saving you from any responsibility at all, but it would be disastrous for the family! Simply disastrous! Those children need to be dealt with strenuously, and they *mustn't* be allowed to stay together! No one woman could deal with them adequately if they were left in a bunch. Those children have been allowed to run wild, and we've got to separate them, or we'll have a set of criminals on our hands before long. I tell you they have *got* to be *separated!* You can't ever do a thing with them if they are left together for they will protect each other. Haven't I seen them? They are little devils. I know what I'm talking about—"

"They ought *not* to be separated!" declared Uncle Blakefield's quiet stubborn voice.

"Well, really, Blakefield, what have *you* to say about it?" demanded Aunt Majesta grandly.

And then the fight was on.

Blakefield stood his ground amazingly, unaccustomedly, saying little except when the others seemed to consider that their arguments were about to prevail, and then he would utter a single sentence, cryptically, which would startle them into a momentary silence.

"Well, I think it's ideal, having Cousin Abigail come and keep them together just as their Uncle Blake says," stated Agatha Lane happily in one of the brief intervals of silence. "That would take care of Abigail so beautifully, and give Blake his way. We could allow Abigail a reasonable salary, and a certain sum for running the house. Then let her train the children to help. That would save money for them when they get older."

Agatha Lane just loved to get up plans and elaborate them in finished little sentences.

"You will never put that selfish, hard-eyed, unloving woman over those dear children with *my* consent!" said Uncle Blake.

"Well, it isn't in the least likely that *your* consent will be necessary, Blake," said Aunt Petra dryly. "It would naturally be the women of the family, especially the women belonging to the *mother* of the children, who would arrange those matters."

"That remains to be seen," said Uncle Blake quietly, and said no more, sitting down in a far corner in front of the great bookcase that lined the wall from floor to ceiling, and from window to window. He looked quite at home and insignificant, there among his nephew's gorgeously bound books, just a plain old man with an unexpectedly firm set of lips, meddling in affairs that really did not concern him in the least. So thought Aunt Petra, studying him with annoyance, amazed to catch a sudden passing likeness to the dead John Graeme in that firmness of jaw. Could it be that just Blakefield was going to make delay and trouble for them?

Meantime the others chattered on, discussing various plans, each apparently trying to shunt the weight of responsibility upon someone else.

"Of course we shall have no trouble with the boys. That is, the older boys. Jeremy will naturally go back to college. Or prep school, which was it?" said Uncle Adrian thoughtfully.

"*Prep* school! I think, wasn't it?" said Aunt Petra sharply. "I doubt if he ever gets far enough to enter college, and you don't know what you're talking about, Adrian. If he once does enter college you'll have more troubles than you can shake a stick at. That boy will go from one scrape to another, or I'll miss my guess."

"I shall talk to him," said Uncle Adrian. "I shall let him understand that we will have no nonsense. That he will have to go out and fend for himself if he dares to get expelled from college. And I think he'll understand when I get through with him that the time has come for him to brace up and try to be a man who will bring credit to his family name. At least he will see that someone is looking after him who will take no excuses from him. I don't really anticipate much trouble from Jeremy. Of course I don't know him so very well. I doubt if I've seen him since he was ten or twelve, but I fancy he will see life from a different angle after I am through with him. Then if you ladies can take Jennifer and give her a good dressing down and let her understand what is expected of her from now on, I should think you could count on her making a good marriage within a reasonable time, and that's two of them disposed of. Now, how many more are there?"

"Five!" said Majesta Best laconically. "Robin, and Karen, and Heather, and Tryon, and Hazel!"

"Mercy! What names! Every one of them *queer!*" said Aunt Petra. "Whatever did Miriam and John mean lumbering their children up with such awful names? If I were in their place I'd change my name, every one of them. Think of handicapping a boy with that queer old-fashioned name of Jeremy! It sounds as if it came out of the Bible. And as for Jennifer, it's heathenish, I think. I should be ashamed to introduce her to my friends by that name. I shall call her Jennie. Or Jane. That's very popular now, Jane! I'll begin calling her that right away. It suits her very well. Jane Graeme!"

And all the time Jennifer Graeme lay cramped in that deep leather chair in the far corner of the library, boiling with rage at her relatives.

"Well," said Aunt Lutie, who arrived just then in the best car, and entered with a flutter and a flourish, "did I hear you criticizing the children's names as I came in? You must admit there is one that is well named. Tryon. Tryon Graeme. He's the most 'tryin' ' Graeme I've ever come across! The last time I was here his mother was away, and he was acting like a young hyena. I really had to speak to him. Yes, I did! He was prancing across the room and mimicking everything I did, and when I told him to stop he ran out in the hall and I heard him singing at the top of his lungs, "Oh, Lutie, Lutie, ain't she cutie!" and he got his two little sisters laughing so they couldn't answer me. I certainly should have turned him over my knee and spanked him if his nurse hadn't come along just then. Well, are you all here? The lawyer hasn't come and gone already, has he? I didn't want to miss the reading of the will, of course, though I really had my hands quite full without coming here. What have you done?"

"Oh, nothing at all," said Agatha Lane coldly, "that is nothing that need worry you. We've just been talking—disagreeing as usual." She lifted her chin disdainfully.

"Well," said Lutie vivaciously, "*I* think the first question to settle is whether John Graeme had lost his money. If he hadn't, if there's plenty of money, of course the whole matter is quite simple. Simply ship the whole lot of them off to good schools where they will be brought up to be a credit to the family, finished and all that. Even little Robin isn't too young. There are kindergarten boarding schools, I understand, where they are looked after and brought up just as well, or even better than they could be brought up in the usual home. Personally I think all these Graeme children are badly spoiled and need to be taken in hand at once. As for Jennifer, she can be sent abroad for a couple of years on a trip with a good chaperone, who will see that she doesn't get too intimate with the wrong young man. There! I think I've arranged the whole affair nicely, don't you?"

Jennifer in her dark refuge behind the library curtain suddenly sat up very straight and very angry, her eyes blazing, her tear-wet lashes starring them, her face white and drawn with a sort of righteous fury. Almost, for an instant, she was on the point of darting out among them and smiting them with bitter words. Then caution came upon her suddenly like a calm hand on her forehead and warned her to hold her peace, and not manifest opposition too soon. Let them make their plans. She would see that they were not carried out! She would do something, *anything* to prevent them. Trips to Europe for herself might be all very well sometime, but not at *their* will, not by force, sugar-coated as if they were doing her a favor. Not with her little brothers and sisters parked here and there, anywhere, as if they were all a part of the furnishing of the house.

Then an interruption occurred in the entrance of the lawyer and his assistant, and there was a general hush, and a stir while the chairs were rearranged, and the lawyer took a seat by a little table which Jim Delaney cleared of bric-a-brac for his use.

While the lawyers were bringing forth sheaves of papers from their brief cases, and talking in low monosyllables to each other, the whole company subsided for an instant or two, and then the ladies began to converse again, in low cultured whispers, Majesta loftily telling Lutie what had been said and suggested so far, and adding some of her own comments, her tones gradually waxing clearer, so that her words were quite distinct on the other side of the library portiere. Jennifer caught her breath softly and clenched her small hands tensely. She wished with all her heart that her beloved father could come back for just one minute at least, from the far place to which the fallen airplane had sent him, and tell those horrible relatives where to get off. "Where to get off." That was just the way she knew he would have phrased it if he had been here and heard their preposterous plans. Separating his children! Sending them off to suit their will, as if they belonged to all of them! Oh, how terrible! Could dad ever have dreamed that he would leave them in danger of such things?

But of course he wouldn't have expected, when he thought of it at all, that he and mother would both be taken away, not at once. Of course he would have expected mother to do the planning.

The tears streamed forth again and pelted down the frightened young face, stern in its anger. And now she, *she* was the only one left to take her mother's place. Well, of course, there was Jerry, but he was only a year out of prep school. They wouldn't feel that he had authority. They knew nothing about him. Thought him still in prep school! But she would be of age in a little over three months, and she must somehow protect the rest, just as father or mother would have done if either one of them had been left behind from the horrible disaster that had taken them both in one swift stroke. She, she must do it alone! She would have to get them all away out of harm's reach!

Then a sentence from the whispered conversation beyond the curtain reached her. It was Aunt Lutie's chipper little voice, trivial even in a whisper:

"Aren't you going to have trouble with that Jennifer? She's rather headstrong, I think. Her parents allowed her too much leeway. If she doesn't want to go your way she'll take a stand."

"Nonsense!" hissed Aunt Majesta. "She'll find that we aren't treating her that way. When we say a thing we mean it! Besides, she's only a frivolous little thing. Give her a new dress and a trip to Europe and get her mind off her own way. As for the rest, our word will be law. I'm not so sure myself but Agatha's idea about Abigail Storm might be a good thing after all."

"What do you mean? Keep up this great house just for those children? That would be ridiculous!" said Lutie. "I thought perhaps one of us would take it over, pay rent to the estate of course—not much, for it ought to be worth something to have it lived in and looked after. But those children, just children, living all alone in this great house with Abigail would be absurd! A great waste, I should say. I wouldn't mind living here myself."

"After all, it's their house, of course," said Majesta loftily. "I don't see myself why *you* should live here any more than the rest of us. However, I presume it will likely be the consensus of opinion that the house should be sold and the money invested. The furnishings sold too, I suppose. We could each bid in some of the best things, at a nominal price. I've always fancied this rug, but I'd have to see if it fits my room. I have considered taking out that back partition between the library and the living room. I'm sure it would fit then. You don't get antique rugs of this type often nowadays."

"Oh, I guess you can get plenty if you know where to look!" said Lutie indifferently. "But if the house were sold where would Cousin Abbey and the children live?"

"Why couldn't they go up to the old farm? Most of them would be off at school a good deal of the time, anyway."

"Oh, I hadn't thought of that. Well, perhaps I could get Adrian to bid in this house for us. It really isn't bad, though I'd hate to leave our own house, small as it is compared with this one. But one could really entertain here, it is so spacious!"

Jennifer in the back room stealthily slipped out of her chair and rose, her eyes snapping fire. What she wanted to do was to rush right in through that curtain and tell those two old hawks to get out. It was not their house and none of their business what became of the rugs and pictures and things. Surely nobody could sell their home and its furnishings right out of hand that way without their consent! Oh, if they would only go away, out of the house, she would lock all the doors and never let them in again!

She stood there trembling with young fury. How angry her mother and father would have been to know that these cormorants were daring to talk this way about the precious home things! Actually planning which things they wanted themselves! Oh, how much power did they have? Surely, *surely* dad would have fixed things so they couldn't do this!

It was with difficulty that she restrained herself to listen as she heard the lawyer clear his throat and begin to talk. She must be quiet and careful. She must not let them know that she had heard their conniving. She must listen and know just what they were going to try to do, so that she would know how to work against them.

Quietly she subsided into her chair again, but she did not relax. She was alert, frightened, her heart beating so fast that she almost feared the aunts outside the curtain would hear it. She held her breath and listened.

The lawyer was reading the will. She took a deep breath. Then daddy had left a will. Of course he would. Of course he would not leave them all at the mercy of these unfeeling relatives! She began to listen again through all the maze of legal phrases. Some of it she understood, and some was not even lucid to her, but she sat there with her brown curls bobbing, and her eyes like two great angry stars shining from the gloom of the room.

There were long involved paragraphs that seemed utterly unnecessary to her when all she wanted to know was what her father had planned for them. But as the phrases rolled on in the other room concerning stocks and bonds and properties, and the time of the coming of age of each of them, she gathered enough here and there to calm her troubled spirit. It was evident, gloriously evident, that their father had planned for them no such shunting off into the world of boarding schools and European trips and marriage as the relatives had suggested, and she meant to foil them in any attempt to spoil her father's plans.

Gradually a purpose began to form in her own mind. If those combative aunts and uncles, who were even now interrupting the lawyer with questions designed to clear the way for their own ideas, had but glanced behind them into the next room, and caught the gleam of those bright angry eyes, the set of those determined red lips, they would have been startled to see how much Jennifer Graeme looked like her dead father, in spite of the fact that she had inherited a great deal of the beauty of her dead mother.

It was Aunt Majesta who finally cleared her throat and broke in upon Lawyer Hemmingway's monotonous listing of special bequests under which the women of the conclave were growing restive.

"Really, Mr. Hemmingway, we aren't especially interested in those trifling bequests that John left to his servants and henchmen. Couldn't you just excuse the ladies of the party? We want to talk over what we are to do about the children, and arrange for their welfare at once. It seems to me that is the important thing now. We can just step into this next room, the library, and be close at hand if anything important should come up for which we are needed. Come, Petra, come Agatha! And Lutie, would you care to come?"

Aunt Majesta had risen and taken hold of the heavy portiere that separated the rooms, drawing it firmly back for a few inches, so that Jennifer's hiding place was in full range if any had been looking.

The lawyer gave Aunt Majesta a sharp reproving glance and said coldly: "That will scarcely be necessary, Mrs. Best. That can all be left to the children's guardian. If he needs your advice he will doubtless ask you. I am coming to that soon, if you will kindly be seated and be a little patient."

"Guardian?" ejaculated Majesta Best hoarsely. *"He!"* and she slumped heavily back into her chair.

"As if any mere *man* would be able to cope with those children!" fairly snorted Petra Holbrook, rearing up in her chair.

But Jennifer did not hear any of this. At the moving of the curtain she had uncurled herself in a flash from the big chair and vanished out into the hall.

And just at that minute the doorbell rang and Stanton answering it came back toward Jennifer with a telegram in his hand.

There had been so many telegrams and letters of condolence that Jennifer naturally supposed this was just another, somewhat belated. She held out her hand for it.

"I'll attend to that, Stanton," she said in a whisper, and taking it fled lightly up the stairs to her room. She didn't want even Stanton to know that she had been hiding in the library.

She tore open the envelope idly, scarcely knowing why she thought it necessary to read it, just another expression of sympathy of course! Then she caught her breath, her eyes grew frightened, her little white even teeth came down tensely on the pretty under lip, as she read the name signed to the message.

"Oh!" She read the whole message slowly.

> "Shall be delighted to come and stay indefinitely with John's children. Will arrange to start as soon as you say. Abigail Storm."

Her face grew dark and her lips set in a determined line. She turned and stood staring out the window toward the lovely garden, and the wide hedged playground for the children.

She could see them out there now, Tryon and Heather over at one side on the tennis court idly playing a set of tennis, with the attitude of killing time. Hazel curled in a hammock under a tree with a book. Karen swinging Robin in one of the big swings hung from a tall elm. And Jeremy. Where was Jeremy? And what was she going to do about it all?

She gave another despairing glance down at the telegram that trembled in her hand, and then swung about and fled down the back stairs. Jeremy would likely be in the garage, or the stables. His pony and his car, those would be his only two interests for refuge at a time like this when life was in chaos. And she must have Jeremy. He was next in age.

2

Jennifer found Jeremy in the stable, lovingly grooming his black satin pony whose coat was already shining with care and rippling over the quivering muscles with nervous energy.

She arrived silently before her absorbed brother, the telegram still crumpled in her tense young hand.

"Jerry, do you want to be separated?" she asked in a dramatic voice.

Jeremy straightened up from his task and looked at his sister bewildered.

"Separated?" he echoed. "Whaddaya mean, separated? Heck, Jen, you scared the life out of me. What's happened?"

"Plenty!" said Jennifer lowering her voice. "Don't talk too loud, somebody might hear. Where's the chauffeur, or the stable boy?"

"Both away," said the boy. "Cook sent the stable boy on an errand, and the chauffeur asked me if he might go to the village for an hour. Why, did you want him?"

"Mercy no! I just want to be sure nobody will hear."

"Well, there's nobody around here but my horse and I guess he won't do anything about it. What's up?"

"Oh!" said Jennifer, wide-eyed, and white to the lips, "the whole outfit of relatives are hot on our trail. They want to separate us, send me off to Europe, or marry me off, send you to college, and park the rest around among 'em while they sell the house and snitch all our nice pretty home things!"

"Creeping catfish! Nobody can do that to us, can they? Who wants to do that?"

"Practically all our aunts, except Agatha Lane, and what do you think she's got up her sleeve? She wants to park us up at the old farm with Cousin Abigail Storm as our overseer. And I'm not sure but she'll win them all over to her plan! Look there!" and Jennifer held out the crumpled telegram.

Jeremy put down his grooming implements and smoothed out the telegram, reading it with startled eyes.

"Where did you get this?" he asked, looking up at his sister accusingly. "It wasn't sent to *you*, was it?"

"Why, I didn't look," said Jennifer. "Oh, my goodness! It was sent to Agatha Lane. I supposed it was just one of the telegrams that have been coming in every day—" She stopped appalled. "Say, Jerry, Aunt Agatha must have been sounding out Cousin Abigail Storm or she never would have sent that telegram!"

"Well, maybe not," said the boy speculatively. "Still, you know the Storm was always one of those who rush in where angels fear to tread. She might have thought it was a good way to feather her nest. But say, Aunt Agatha's going to be sore as a boil when she finds out you opened her telegram. Especially if she's been expecting an answer. Must be she gave our address, or Gay-Abby would never have sent Agatha's telegram *here!* Old Ag sure will be furious at you!"

"Well, she's not going to have the chance!" said Jennifer snatching the telegram, tearing it across into little bits, and stuffing them into a minute pocket of her blouse. "But say, Jerry, what are we going to do about it? You don't want to be separated, do you? And you certainly don't want the Storm to be our policeman?"

"I should say not!" said Jeremy. "Before that I'd beat it and go round the world or something. Abby Storm isn't going to tell me where to get off."

"Oh, you would, would you? You'd go off alone and have a good time, and leave your family to suffer whatever came to them, would you? Well, if that's the way you feel, it isn't worth while to waste my time talking to you, for there isn't much time to waste, I'm telling you!"

Jennifer held her head high and turning on her heel walked crisply out of the stable and up the driveway.

Jeremy stared after her in dismay.

"Hey! Jen! Come back here!" he called. "Come on back! Oh heck! Whaddaya haveta get up in the air for? Come on back! I didn't mean that!"

But Jennifer walked swiftly on around the drive toward the high hedge where the children were playing, and Jeremy presently started after her full tilt, catching up with her and striding along by her side.

"What's eating ya, Jen?" he said. "I didn't mean I'd go away and leave ya all. Of course I wouldn't! What d'ya think we ought ta do? D'ya want me ta go in there where the lawyer's supposed ta be and tell them all where ta get off?"

"No," said Jennifer. "That would be the worst thing you could do. They've got a bad enough opinion of us all now. You ought to hear them talk! But I haven't time to tell you here. We've got to get busy, and we've got to do it on the q.t. If they once suspect we're onto them our goose is cooked and no mistake!"

"I suppose so," said Jeremy dejectedly. "With all that outfit against us we sure won't have very smooth sailing. Say, Jen, what if I hunt up Uncle Blake—"

"No!" said Jennifer sharply. "Uncle Blake's all right in his place, but he can't do a thing. Not if those aunts get started. You let me manage, Jerry. I've got a plan, only you've got to go the whole show or I won't count you in."

"Aw! Whaddaya mean, Jen? I'm with ya of course. I'm the man of the house, only they won't think so. If I was only a few years older I'd make 'em all stand around and tell 'em all ta get out of our house and let us alone."

They were coming toward the house now and the voices

of the cook and waitress could be heard in animated discussion.

"You'd better turn off here, Jerry," whispered his sister. "Go around the other side of the house and slide up to your room by way of the balcony. Get a pencil and paper and all the money you have, and then after a minute or two you go up to the old playroom and wait there till I come. But don't let anybody see you go!"

"Okay," said Jeremy watching her keenly, and then turning off briskly as he was bidden. His sister fairly flew across the grass and entered the shelter of the tall hedge around the playground.

She went first to the hammock and whispered to Hazel.

"Hazel, take your book and slip up the backstairs to the playroom, but don't let one of the aunts see you, or know where you are going. If they come around just slip into your own room and wait there till they are gone. Hurry! And don't tell anyone I told you to go. I'll be up in a minute or two."

"Okay."

Hazel arose slowly, apathetically from her hammock, her eyes still on her book, and went dawdling down across the grass, reading as she walked. The story was so absorbing that she hadn't noticed the suppressed earnestness in Jennifer's voice. She thought it was only some bid to get dressed for dinner, or to go somewhere, and she was much more interested in her story than in going anywhere. Probably to visit some old relative or something, she thought contemptuously as she sauntered languidly along.

Jennifer went over to the tennis court and signaled her young brother, Tryon, and of course Heather promptly came over to the conference also.

"I want to see you two up in the playroom in about five minutes," she said in a low tone, casting a swift look toward the house. "You don't want anybody to know anything about it either, see? Just play on here for another game or two, and then act as if you were tired, and walk slowly toward the house. Don't come together, either. Go around the other side of the house so the servants won't see you, and go up the back stairs. Go one of you at a time! Heather, you go first, and Tryon, you go hang around the garage a minute or two. Not too long, and then slip up quietly. Do you understand?"

"What's doing, Jen?" asked the boy.

"Never mind, I'll tell you all together. Don't for anything tell anybody, not even the servants, that I told you to come upstairs. Just go up as if you were going to your own room. You can manage it. I don't want any of those relatives to know where we are, see?"

"Sure thing!" said Tryon, and turned immediately back to his game. Not that the rest of the game was very well played, but they played, those two, with eager young determined faces, and busy wondering minds. There was a look of their dead father in their faces as they accepted their role and went forward in this program that their sister had set for them. She didn't usually have much time any more to interest herself in them, but now sorrow had leveled their lives together as when they were small children, and Jennifer was the nearest to mother that was left.

With a matter of fact manner Jennifer went to the other end of the enclosure and watched the other two children for an instant, then walked firmly over to them.

"Karen, Robin, come on upstairs with me. I've got something to talk to you about."

"I isn't been doing nussin' naughty!" said Robin with suddenly alarmed eyes. "Did my nurse say I had?"

"No, of course not, honey. I haven't seen your nurse. But I want you all upstairs a few minutes. It's something nice, so you needn't worry. I think perhaps I've got a few pieces of candy up in my room. Do you want some?"

"Wes!" said Robin delightedly hopping down from the swing. "Is we going to your room?"

"No, we're going up in the playroom, but I'll get the candy and bring it up. Come on."

She held out a hand to each and they came happily enough. Their older sister hadn't been noticing them much of late. They had a forlorn feeling that the world was made up of nurses and cooks and they must walk carefully alone to escape getting in the way of any of them. Nobody had had time to realize how desolate the two youngest had been since the accident.

Jennifer had a sudden feeling of joy in the warm little hands that were nestled in her own, a sense that they were her special care now, and it was to her they must look. She was surprised that it brought a tender pleasurable thrill to her sad fierce young heart. She squeezed the two confiding young hands and Karen and Robin looked up at her and smiled with a sudden light like new sunshine in their apathetic little faces.

"I like you, Jennifer," said Karen wistfully. "I wish you would stay home with us always."

"Wes!" said Robin. "I viss you vass our nurse. I don't wike hers wery much. She makes me vash my hands too much."

"Well, that's too bad!" said the sister sympathetically, "but you don't want to have dirty hands, do you?"

"No, but I don't wike her. I wiked my ovver nurse better."

"Well, that's too bad, too," said Jennifer, giving a little gasp at the thought of all the questions that must be waiting ahead for her to settle, things her father and mother used to manage.

"Now," she said briskly, "I'll tell you what I want. I want to get you both upstairs to the playroom just as quietly as possible. You know there are a lot of aunts and other people down in the living room, and we don't want to disturb them while they are talking, so we are going up the kitchen stairs. See how very quietly you two can walk, so you won't make the least bit of sound on the stairs. Robin, where is your nurse?"

"Her is down to the postoffice to get a 'tamp to put on her letter. Her told me to stay wif Karen in the praygwound till her getted back. Her said she would pwank me if I goed avay."

He stopped short in his tracks at the memory.

"That's all right, Robin, I'll see she doesn't spank you. Karen, you run to the kitchen, and tell cook to let nurse know I took Robin upstairs. And then you come out the side door and meet us around the other side of the house. Understand?"

Karen nodded and sped away on her errand. Jennifer led Robin around to the door at the other side of the house, and stealthily they stole up the back stairs.

"Softly!" she warned in a whisper. "Don't talk!"

"Aw wight!" he whispered back, and a look of compliance came brightly into the eager little face. This was fun. This was a game. He gripped his sister's hand, and took slow careful steps, with a great flourish of caution, stealing from one stair to another, lifting his fat legs up one at a time with great effort.

Jennifer had a sudden vision of what that sight would have been to the baby's mother, and quick tears blurred into her eyes. She stooped and brushed her lips over the small gold curl at the back of the little boy's neck, and felt a deep rush of love such as she had never realized before. Her little motherless brother!

Karen was behind them now, stealing up with exaggerated caution.

At the head of the stairs they stole along the back hall to the third story back stairs which went straight up to the playroom.

"Now, you slip softly up there and wait at the top of the stairs for me while I get that candy!" whispered Jennifer.

They nodded delightedly and then she sped down the hall to her own room, and was back like a flash with a large beautiful box of bonbons, as yet unopened, the quite recent gift of Peter Willis. It had come while she was too immersed in sudden sorrow to care for anything pleasant like that. And now in the light of what Aunt Majesta had said, it was almost revolting to her. Better get it out of her sight.

Up in the big playroom, bright from a splendid skylight, Jennifer led her young brother and sister to the far corner where their toys had special place on broad low shelves.

"Now," said Jennifer, placing two small chairs conveniently, "you may each choose one piece and sit down and eat it. Then you may take out some of your blocks, or any toy you choose that you can play with quietly. Remember, we have to be very quiet! We don't want any people coming up here to interrupt us. We've got something very important to talk about."

The children settled down on the small chairs and surveyed the handsome box of bonbons with seraphic smiles, lingering, uncertain fingers hovering from one bright luring piece of sweetness to another. They finally settled down with possessiveness on their choice, eyes wide with awe at such privilege.

Before they were fairly taking the first delirious lick, Hazel, her book still in her hand, came light-footed, settled down on the big old denim-covered lounge with a lovely dormer window just over her shoulder and went on reading.

Jennifer stepped softly over beside her and plumped a bonbon in her mouth.

"Mm-mm-m-! Thanks!" she murmured and went on with her reading.

Jeremy came up the stairs so silently that they were not aware of his presence until he was among them, reaching over to his sister's box of confectionery and helping himself.

Then came Tryon, with Heather just a moment behind. They were a bit out of breath and carrying their shoes in their hands, having made as much as possible out of the dramatic side of the situation. They seated themselves cross-legged on the floor, and then suddenly rose with outstretched hands for some of the candy.

Jennifer passed the box around again, and while their mouths were well filled she began to talk.

"Now, listen! You mustn't make any noise no matter what I say, not one of you! If you want to speak raise your hand!"

They sat petrified, even their jaws ceasing action temporarily.

"How many of you want to be separated? Raise your hand if you do."

The little huddled family sat quivering with horror at the thought that was presented. Not a hand was raised. Their wide-eyed attention culminated in a hoarse whisper from Tryon.

"Whaddaya mean, separated? D'you mean have a noperation?"

Hazel stopped reading long enough to giggle at that, but Jeremy looked grave, and slid down on the floor beside his younger brother with a protective attitude.

"No, kid, she just means taken away from the rest of us!"

"Oh! Not on yer life I don't!" said Tryon, a frightened look coming into his eyes. "Do we havta?"

By this time Robin's lip was puckered, and two great tears were gathering in his eyes.

"I—don't—vantta!" he burst forth. "I don't vantta go avay fum you-all!"

"No, of course not!" said Karen crossly. "We *won't* go!"

"Who wants us to?" burst forth Heather. "Some aunts? What right have they?"

"They haven't any!" said Hazel sitting up sharply and letting her book fall on the floor! "They shan't get me, I know that, old bossy things!" There was young fury in her face.

"There, now, don't get noisy!" said Jennifer sharply. "I just wanted to find out how you feel about it. And here's another question. How many of you would like to stay here and have Cousin Abigail Storm come and take care of you?"

There was another awful silence, while the Graeme children stared at one another in consternation.

"Not on yer life!" ejaculated Tryon.

"I'd wun avay!" declared Robin with belligerent eyes and trembling lip. "I'd take my Karen and wun avay!"

"I'd put pins and tacks in her bed!" declared Heather.

"Well, that would be the only thing that would make me willing to go away to boarding school!" declared Hazel, who dearly loved home.

"Well," said Jennifer with satisfaction, "I thought you'd feel that way, so we're not going to let either of those things happen. But you've all got to promise to be just as good as good can be, and help us, so Jerry and I can work things. We mustn't let the aunts or uncles suspect. And we mustn't let the servants get onto it at all. How many are willing to be good and do just what they are told?"

Their hands came up eagerly.

"All right! Then we're all set. And the first thing is to stay right here in this room and keep very quiet for a while. We can't do much till those relatives are done with their meeting downstairs. But you've got to keep so quiet they'll forget all about you, so they won't come nosing around. I suspect they'll be around to take some of us home for the night or something, but if any of them come up here hunting you you just be sitting here quietly playing or reading."

"Jerry too?" asked Tryon.

"No, Jerry and I have a lot of things to do, if we're going to work this thing, so you mustn't ask any questions, just play along, or look at picture books or read, and act as if you were having a perfectly lovely time, and if they ask you if you want to go home with them you just say, No thank you, you'd rather stay with sister!"

"Aw wight!" said Robin. "But aren't we going to have any wunch? Course we could eat candy!" and he eyed the candy box wistfully.

"Yes," said Jennifer looking at her watch, "you're going to have lunch pretty soon. I think I'll have it brought up here, just sandwiches and cocoa, and you can pass the candy box afterward twice for dessert."

"Nat's nice!" smiled Robin.

"All right, then Karen and Heather can get out the doll's table and dishes and set the table. You can play that Hazel and Tryon and Robin are your guests coming to lunch. And when the tray comes you can serve everybody. But don't get into any fights, or make any noise, for if you do maybe Aunt Pet or Aunt Majesta will come up and take you right away home with them, and then all our plans will be spoiled. Now, will you all promise to be good?"

They all promised solemnly.

"All right then. Go on playing for a few minutes while Jerry and I make plans. Remember if anybody slips up on his promise we'll maybe not be able to work things, and we might have to be separated after all."

Robin bowed solemnly and answered for them all:

"Wes. Ve vill!"

Then Jennifer and Jeremy retired to the top of the stairs and sat down speaking in low tones.

"Jerry, I've been thinking. We've got to *run away!*"

"Run away!" said the boy catching a startled breath. "You mean all of us?"

"Of course!" she said coolly. "We've got to. It's the only way."

"But *how?*" He drew his brows in puzzled thought. "Where would we run?"

"*Where* isn't so important just now. The thing is to *go,* and get off before anybody has any idea we're going, don't you see?"

"Well, but—with all these kids, how could we? Somebody would be sure to tell those nosy aunts, and we'd have the whole town on us."

"Listen, Jerry! We've got to get them *all* away where they won't find us till I'm of age. When I'm of age I can do something, and they can't stop me. It's only three months and I guess we can hide ourselves that long. But it's got to be snappy or they'll tie our hands and make a mess of things. I haven't thought it all out yet, but we've got to get away first, and then work it out step by step."

"But they'll set up a howl and send all the police in the nation after us," said Jeremy wisely.

"No," said Jennifer. "I'll write a note to Uncle Blake and tell him we are all safe and will come back as soon as I'm of age and that there is no use looking for us for they won't find us."

"They'll *look!*"

"Maybe. But we've got to fix it so they can't find us. We'll think about that after we get away."

"But we'd have to have money."

"Yes," said Jennifer. "I'd thought about that. I've got a little over a hundred in the bank, I've been saving up. A lucky thing I hadn't spent it yet. I'll scout around and see what else I can find. Maybe dad left some in the safe. He taught me the combination. I'll see. Of course if there isn't any there we'll have to sell something, but not tonight. The thing is to get away. How much have you got? Any?"

"Not much. Ten or twelve. Got some new golf clubs the other day. This was left and dad said keep it. Maybe I could get them to take the clubs back. I haven't used them yet."

"Well, you could try. But you'll have to see about the car. We'll have to have one of the big ones, and not the new one either, I should think. That would be the one the relatives would try to trace. They wouldn't know about the big old sedan, the one the servants use, would they?"

"No, but the servants would. That chauffeur knows everything about the cars of course. You can't put anything over on him."

"We'll have to find some way to get rid of all the servants," said Jennifer with a puzzled frown. "I guess that's my job. I hadn't realized before."

"Well, say, that reminds me," said the boy. "I just met the chauffeur down by the side door. He got back from wherever it was he went, and he asked me did I know what we were going to do, were we intending to stay here at the place? I told him we hadn't had a chance to make plans yet, and he said did I know where you were, he wanted to see you, so I told him I'd send you down there as soon as I could."

"Yes?" said Jennifer thoughtfully. "Well, I guess I'd better go right down and see if there isn't some way I can get rid of him without making him suspicious."

"He's a good scout," said Jeremy thoughtfully.

"Yes, I know he is, but we can't stop on that now. Besides, the aunts are hot on the warpath and they won't let him stay here. And we don't need him now anyway. You and I can both drive. And we've *got* to run away. I'll go right down and talk to him a minute and you stay here and see that the children keep quiet, and try to think out how we can get away from town without our license plates being read. Get a map and figure it out."

"Okay," said Jeremy, and Jennifer went swiftly and silently down the stairs and out toward the garage.

3

The chauffeur wasn't hard to find. He was hovering anxiously outside the garage with a troubled eye toward the house, and he looked greatly relieved when he saw her coming.

"Thank you, Miss Jennifer, I'm sorry to have to trouble you," he said as he came to meet her. "I just thought perhaps you could tell me how things are going to be. You see, something has come up, and I was anxious to know whether you folks would go on living here at the house, and would be wanting to keep a chauffeur? I know it's a little soon for me to be putting such questions, and I'm not sure you're the one I should ask, only you are the oldest, and I thought perhaps you would be able to give me some idea. You see I've heard of a man who wants a chauffeur bad, wants him right away, and it's a good place with an all-right wage, and I thought if 'twas all right with you I'd snap it up before it was gone. But of course, if it isn't, I wouldn't want to do anything to cause you inconvenience. Your father was all right, and treated me fine as silk, and I wouldn't want to do anything to his family that wasn't right."

Jennifer looked up with a pleasant smile, tempered by the sorrow in her young eyes.

"Now, that's nice of you, Phillips. I appreciate that," she said. "I know my father trusted you a lot, and we all have felt that you sort of belong to us. But as a matter of fact I don't believe we are going to need a chauffeur just now, not for a while anyway, and if you've found a place where you think you would be happy I think you ought to take it. When do these people want you, Phillips?"

"Well," said Phillips with downcast glance, working an embarrassed toe back and forth in the gravel of the drive, "of course they wanted me right away. You see, they're from out west, and they come here visiting. Their own chauffeur got drunk and they wanted to get another one to take his place permanently. My cousin happened to hear about it. She works at the house where the man is visiting and told 'em about me, knowing my employer was dead. But of course, Miss Jennifer, if you want me to stay awhile, I'll manage somehow. There'll be other jobs."

Jennifer smiled.

"No, that's all right, Phillips. We'll be sorry to lose you of course, but I'm glad if you've found a good place right away. I know father would have said so too. Do they want you today?"

The chauffeur looked ashamed.

"Why yes, Miss Jennifer, if I could be spared. They wanted to start on their way today, this afternoon if possible."

"I see. Well, could you pack up and get ready to go by afternoon?"

"Oh, yes, Miss Jennifer. It doesn't take me long to pack. But I don't want to leave you in a hole."

"That's quite all right," said Jennifer. "Jerry and I can both drive. But how about your pay, Phillips? Did father owe you anything?"

"No, Miss Jennifer. He paid us all off the day he—the day—it happened." Phillips choked and looked embarrassed. "But is this all that is necessary, or should I speak to one of your uncles first?"

"No, Phillips. Don't say anything to anybody else about it. It's all in my hands of course. Are the cars in order?"

"Yes, everything is okay. I went over 'em all last night, just in case I got a chance to speak about going."

"Well then, go, Phillips, and I hope you will find it a nice place. Perhaps some day we'll send for you to come back again. Be sure to leave me your address. Good-bye."

Jennifer fled back into the house quickly. Somehow bidding a trusted servant good-bye so definitely, and feeling that her own act had done it, was like realizing all over again the terrible disaster that had made all this necessary. She wanted to fly upstairs at once and tell Jerry, but then she remembered the children's lunch, and went instead into the kitchen.

"I'm amusing the children up in the playroom," she said to the cook quite calmly, "and I've promised them a teaparty on a tray. I didn't want them to make a noise while the relatives are here. Please make us some sandwiches, lots of them, a pot of chocolate and bring up some fruit and cake or tarts or whatever you have. Make enough for us all. Jeremy is up there too. And if the aunts ask where we are just say we are looking after the children."

"Why, hasn't that nurse come back yet?" asked the cook astonished.

"I haven't seen her," said Jennifer. "Where did she go? She wasn't upstairs when I was up there."

"Why, she said she had an errand at the store to get some garters for young Master Robin, but she's been gone ever since breakfast. She ought to come down and help carry up, ef you're going to make all that trouble for lunch."

Jennifer gave the cook an astonished look. It wasn't like her to be so cross.

"Why, I'll try and find her," said she, "but anyway Jeremy and I will help carry up. I thought it was better to keep the children quiet till the aunts were gone."

"All right, Miss Jennifer," said the cook, "I don't mind, only I don't like that Mrs. Holbrook coming out and telling me what to cook. Ef she's goin' to butt in like that I'll be givin' notice before long."

"Oh, did she do that, Maggie?"

"Yes, she come right out here ta get a drink of water, and she snoops around and pries inta every corner, and she seen me gettin' the chickens ready fer dinner an' she ups and says she shouldn't think it was fitten to have chicken on week-days when it's just you childers, an' no comp'ny. The money by rights should be saved for you childers when you come of age, an' not feedin' a 'pack o' servants,' she says, just like that, Miss Jennifer. *'Pack o' servants!'* An' leavin' you all poor an' dependent on your relatives. That's what she said, just like that! An' I'm not one to be talked to like that, Miss Jennifer. Your blessed mamma never talked to me that wise, an' I'm not standin' for it!"

"Oh," said Jennifer, "she had no right at all to talk to you like that, Maggie. Don't you pay any attention to her. She doesn't belong here."

"Well, that's all right ef she don't butt in an' think she does, but if she does I'm leavin,' and that's the truth! I can't bear no back-talk from one that ain't a missus."

"Well, I'll try to see that that doesn't happen again, Maggie, but if she comes out again just don't pay any attention to her at all. Tell her you are following my orders. Of course I don't just know what we are going to do about anything yet, but I'll agree to see that Aunt Petra doesn't try to order you around. So, please, if you'll get us a nice little lunch, Jerry and I will carry it up. Or if the nurse comes in you might send her up with the trays."

"All right, Miss Jennifer, I don't mind going out of my way to do *you* a favor. You're like your blessed mamma. But I ain't pleasin' the likes of that nosy Holbrook woman."

Jennifer went on her way upstairs again thoughtfully. The servant problem was pressing upon her perplexedly. That had been a good opening to get rid of Maggie, but it wouldn't do to suggest it until those relatives were out of the house. How was she going to do it anyway? For it was certain they couldn't run away and leave a lot of servants in the house. The way was clear so far as the car was concerned, now the chauffeur was gone, but how was she going to get rid of the other four servants? And do it in time to run away before morning? Stanton would be the worst. He had been so devoted to daddy and mother! He wouldn't understand. How could she ever get rid of Stanton so that he would not suspect? And then there was the nurse! How could she possibly make her understand that she didn't want her any more? It wasn't done, to dismiss servants without any notice, was it? But this nurse was a comparatively new institution. The old nurse who had taken care of Robin since he was born had got married, and moved to the South, and this one was only on trial. Jennifer had a strange lingering feeling that she couldn't quite trust her.

But where was she? Certainly not on her job.

Jennifer went down the servants' hall and tapped at the door of the nurse's room, but there was no answer, and after another tap or two she tried the door but found it locked! That was strange!

With an uneasy feeling she went on to her own room, intending to hover around until that tray was ready for her to carry. If they went away tonight there was a great deal to be done before they left and not a moment must be wasted.

With her mind busy with possibilities she opened her bureau drawers, and gathered up the few valuable trinkets that she felt she ought to take with her, stowed them in a convenient box, then went through the other drawers and laid in quick piles the garments that she would need. Nothing fancy, just the plainest things she owned. Her own personal needs were simple. The difficulty would be to remember everything the children ought to have. If only she could trust the nurse! But she didn't! And the nurse wasn't here, anyway. Where in the world was she?

Then she heard footsteps, a clink of dishes on a tray, and she flew toward the back hall. Ah! It was Stanton bringing the tray. How faithful and good Stanton was! How was she going to manage that they would get away without his knowledge? Almost she could trust him not to tell the relatives, but it would put him in a very awkward position. No, and he would think he *ought* to tell, perhaps, to protect her and the children.

But how was she ever going to approach the subject with him? She would have to leave him till the last. If she could get rid of the rest maybe there would be a way to deal with him. But he was such a perfect servant, so utterly trustworthy, that she was almost a little afraid of him, as if he would use the spirits of her dead mother and father as a weapon to hold over her head.

"Oh, Stanton, I'm sorry to have made you extra trouble."

"It's all right, Miss Jennifer. I'm glad to help you. And I think you are quite wise to keep the children quiet. I think the presence of—of—" he cleared his throat and searched for the right word—"of outsiders," he went on hastily, "seems to excite them."

"Yes, that's right," said Jennifer with relief. "I thought you would understand."

Quietly he arranged the dishes on the little table, deftly he placed the cocoa pot where the little girls could pour it for themselves, teaparty-fashion, and withdrew.

When he came back with the dessert tray Jennifer had the emptied dishes on the tray at the head of the stairs, and stood there smiling to thank him as he went away again.

Then she saw he was hesitating, and looking keenly at him she saw a shadow of trouble in his eyes.

"What is the matter, Stanton, has something happened?" she asked quickly, her heart contracting suddenly with unnamed apprehension.

"Well, nothing that need trouble you, Miss Jennifer," he said apologetically. "It's just that I had a rather disturbing letter from my sister. It just came special delivery. She tells me that my old mother is very ill indeed, and she's been asking for me. My sister wants me to come at once. But of course she doesn't know what has been happening in this house, and of course I would not be asking to be released just now when you might be wanting me special, you know. Only if there would be a time, a day or two, when you would not be needing me so much, you know, I'd be glad to get off and see my dear old mother before she goes on—"

He hesitated, and a mist gathered in his eyes. Suddenly Jennifer felt very sorry indeed for Stanton.

"Why, of course, Stanton. You ought to go at once! You musn't think of staying."

"Oh, but Miss Jennifer, I wouldn't be asking for anything like that. Not just in the midst of the day's work as it were—"

"That's perfectly all right, Stanton. Just drop everything and go at once. You see, really, I'm thinking of going away myself. In fact we all may go, only I haven't told them yet, so you won't say anything about it, please."

"Of course not, Miss Jennifer."

"You see, I was just wondering what to do about you all," went on Jennifer. "You've been especially kind and faithful. I don't like the idea of sending you away. But it will be certainly all right for you to go at once and stay just as long as you want to, Stanton. The aunts have spoken about our coming to them. But anyway we shall not be needing you for a time, and if I were you I'd go right away before any of them come around and go to trying to manage things. I'll be of age in three months, Stanton, and then I'll know better what we are going to do. But you are welcome to go now, and stay as long as you like."

"Thank you, Miss Jennifer, that's very nice of you and I do appreciate your kindness, but of course I'll stay till the work is done. You might find that some of the relatives would be staying to dinner, and I might be needed."

"No, they'll not be staying to dinner, Stanton! I'll see to that. And I'll make everybody understand that *I* sent you away. They'll think I sent you on an errand, if they know anything about it at all. Just you get ready right at once and *go*. Do you need any money? I don't know just how much I have but—"

"No, Miss Jennifer, oh no! Your father paid me with all the others, paid us a week ahead, just before he left on that trip! You don't owe us a thing. Your father was always so nice and thoughtful like that. If he was going to be away on our regular pay day he always paid us ahead. He was a rare man, he was."

"Yes," said Jennifer with a catch like a sob in her breath. "Well, then, Stanton, you just go right away. And perhaps you'd better take your things with you, because you might need to stay some time, and you wouldn't want anybody else bothering with your things. I don't know that they would, but I think you'd feel happier to have your things with you, in case the house should be closed up for a while, or anything, and you couldn't get something you wanted."

"Yes, Miss Jennifer, I'll do that. You're very thoughtful. I'd not care to have some of the other servants going over my things."

"I understand," said Jennifer. "Besides, some of the relatives might think they had the right to go in and look things over. Aunt Petra always thinks she owns the universe."

Stanton's face lit up with a kind of satisfaction, but he only said:

"You're very kind, Miss Jennifer. You're very understanding."

"And Stanton," went on Jennifer, "do you know where the nurse is? If you find her won't you send her to me? Maggie says she went on an errand early this morning, but I tried her door and it's locked. You don't suppose she's sick, do you?"

"No, I scarcely think so. I saw her when she started. She looked quite spruce and well. But she was carrying a suitcase. I thought at the time it was queer. Maybe I'd better find a key and open her door, if you say."

"I wish you would."

He set down the tray and hurried down the servants' hall, Jennifer following. He pulled out a bunch of keys and selected a master key. After a minute he unlocked the door and swung it back, and they went into the room together. But it was evident at once that the occupant had fled. There were papers and trash in a pile on the floor, and the closet door was flung wide and empty. There wasn't a sign of a trunk or anything about. The nurse was gone.

"Well, that settles it, Miss Jennifer, if the nurse has left you in the lurch I'll stay till you're satisfied. I couldn't leave you that way. I was afraid when you spoke about her that she had gone. You see, she and Mrs. Holbrook had words last night about how to manage Master Robin, and I heard her say she wouldn't run any risks of having that woman tell her again what to do."

"Oh," said Jennifer with an enlightened look. "I didn't know that. I'm glad you told me. I'm going to take care of the children myself for a while, anyway. You know they miss father and mother terribly. So you don't need to worry. And you must go right along to your mother, Stanton. I really shall not need you. Just give me your address before you leave."

"That I will, Miss Jennifer. And if you need me, you've only to let me know and I'll come at once. And now I'll just take my bags and trunk down to the side entrance and get the express to come after them. I know the chauffeur is gone. He told me before he left how kind you had been."

"Why, no, Stanton, I'm sure Jerry would love to take you down. Wait, I'll speak to him."

Jeremy came willingly. This was going to give him a chance to put the old car in condition to travel. So presently Stanton had his baggage ready, and was off.

At the last he did not wait to go into the kitchen, and so it was Jennifer who announced his departure to Maggie the cook and Letty the waitress.

"Stanton had to go away in a great hurry," she said. "He got a message that his mother was very sick and wanted to see him at once, and I made him go immediately." She said it with a smile.

"Poor mon," said Maggie wistfully, "he's that fond of his mother. But he never stops to see what a hole that leaves the rest of us in, and we with funeral company still on our hands!"

Maggie was still grumpy. She had a vision of Petra Holbrook and her sharp tongue.

"No," said Jennifer quietly, "no company! I'm going to tell them all that we are very tired and want to rest. Anyway, I'm sure they are all going home at once. I listened from the upper hall just now and Aunt Petra and Aunt Majesta are just leaving. I don't believe anybody is expecting to stay here to lunch, and I heard them say they were going to invite us home to the different houses for a few days, so I thought it would be a good chance for you all to have a little vacation and get rested up from the extra work. How about it? Would you and Letty like to take a week-end off, or perhaps a little longer if we don't get right back?"

Maggie brightened up.

"Why, yes, Miss Jennifer, I wouldn't mind," said Maggie. "I been talking about running up in the country to my cousin's for a few days if you thought you could spare me, and I really would enjoy a bit of rest if you think you won't need me."

"No, I shan't need you, probably for several days, perhaps longer. I'm not just sure what we are going to do right away. We have to talk it over and decide. So, if you would just leave me the address where I could reach you, I can let you know."

"Why sure!" beamed Maggie. "You're like your blessed mamma, Miss Jennifer. And now, what about the dinner? I've got the chickens on cooking. It would be a pity to throw them away. I put in a few extra potatoes lest some of the relatives might stay."

"That's all right," said Jennifer blithely, "just go on with your dinner preparations. We won't have any company, at least I hope not, but I would like to have dinner a little early, say five-thirty, then if we're asked anywhere we can say we've had dinner, for the children are much too tired and excited to behave as visitors tonight. You needn't have any special fuss. You'll want to be getting ready to go. You can take the evening train if you like. Just wash up the dishes and go. And Maggie, if any of the aunts come out here to give orders, don't tell them you are going away. You needn't set the table till they are all gone, anyway, or if they ask you any questions send them to me."

"Yes, Miss Jennifer," beamed Maggie.

"And how about you, Letty? Is it all right with you to go away a few days?"

"I'll say it is," chirped Letty. "I got a date to go somewheres every night for a week, and I didn't suppose I could get off. And my cousin that's a nurse wants me to stay in her room in the city with her whenever I can. She's lonesome."

"Well, that's all right, then," said Jennifer with relief. "Now I must go and see that those children take naps. They are all worn out with excitement."

4

Astonishingly the relatives had all disappeared without coming in contact with any of the family.

It happened rather suddenly. Uncle Blake had an appointment at twelve-thirty, and slipped away without attracting much attention from the rest. The lawyer, when he had finished the reading of the will, put his papers away hastily, in a hurry to make a train. The aunts rose as one man and discovered that it was lunch time and they should be at home. With surreptitious glances at one another they made good their escape, all of them so angry at the final clauses of the will that they would fain have lingered to cast aspersions upon the judgment of the dead, only they couldn't do so until they were sure there was no one around to listen. So they whispered tentative appointments to meet at their own houses and talk the matter over together, to see what could be done. "It was ridiculous!" they said. "John and Miriam just hadn't exercised any sense at all, and something must be done. Those *poor* children!"

And then they all hurried off and left "those poor children" to their own devices—intending of course to call up later and offer a consolation or two before evening.

Jennifer listened from the back hall for a moment and then went stealthily into the front of the house and watched them go. Then, drawing a long breath, she went to the front door and made sure that the night latch was on. Now, she need not fear their interference!

But this freedom could not be counted on for long. Aunt Petra was not one to let the grass grow under her feet.

Jennifer sped up the stairs to her young prisoners, and with the promise of more candy for the first one asleep she persuaded them to their beds.

Her next thought was of money. She must have enough to finance this exodus.

Had her father left money in the safe? He usually did leave a little, a few dollars anyway, when he was going to to be gone a few days. For that reason he had told her the combination not long ago. But he had never left much. Probably there would not be enough to help them substantially now.

However, she recalled that her father had been waiting anxiously for a couple of hours before he left, for the coming of a man with whom he had an appointment. Wasn't it something about the sale of some property, a small house the man was buying? She could not remember definitely. She hadn't been interested. But just at the last minute, before they left for the flying field, he came. She remembered it was at least half past three, too late to put anything in the bank, if it was money the man was bringing. She remembered, too, that her father had rushed up to his room while his car waited for him at the door. Could it be possible that it had been money and he had left it in the safe? And oh, if it was money, would there be enough for her need now?

The meager hundred dollars in her personal account would not go far for seven of them in running away for three months.

Quietly she stole into the big lovely master bedroom which had always been the real center of their home, and where the presence of her father and mother still seemed to linger. Every wall and picture and rug, even the small personal things, seemed to remind of the lost dear ones so keenly that Jennifer paused in the doorway and caught her breath. Then she turned her eyes to the large photographs of the two who were gone. They stood on the mantel, and her eyes met their pictured ones. It was as if a promise passed between them, that Jennifer, the eldest of their children, would pledge herself to protect the rest.

The thought steadied her, and she brushed away the blinding tears that came unbidden, and set herself to find whatever would help her carry out her plans.

"You know, mother, daddy, I'm going to try to do my best, and I'll just have to take whatever I can find that will help us get away before those aunts try to separate us."

It was a sort of an apology, in place of the prayer that some girls in like situation would have put up. Then she went to the panel that hid the wall safe, pushed it aside, and her eager trembling fingers began to swing the little bright knob from number to number as she thought she remembered the combination. Oh, that it might be right!

And suddenly, the last turn—! The door swung open!

"Oh!" she uttered, and there was thanksgiving in her heart. Now, if there was anything—!

Carefully she went through the contents of that safe, compartment by compartment, her heart swelling with tears she had not time to shed, as she came upon jewels and a few rare treasures that reminded strongly of her mother and father. Some of them could be left there, but there were two or three rings and pins that she wouldn't like to feel were left in the house, in case of fire. And it was too late to take them to the bank. She would have to take them with her. She would have to wear them in her mother's little jewel case that she pinned inside of her dress when she was going on a journey and had small valuables to carry.

She opened another compartment and found only papers, apparently having to do with business matters. Still another contained bonds with coupons that had to be clipped off at regular intervals. Her father had once explained them to her.

Last she twirled a tiny knob of another inner compartment, where her father used frequently to put money when he was to be away over night. To her joy it swung open and there were bills inside, yes, and a little drawer with silver change! Wonderful!

She gathered them out. Across the whole bundle was scribbled in her father's writing, "Cash payment from Mr. Smith for deposit Monday." All but a few of the top bills were crisp and new, and done into small bundles some of which were labeled with the amount. As she fluttered them over she estimated that there must be somewhere around a thousand dollars altogether, perhaps a little more. She hadn't time to count them carefully now. There was too much to be done before night.

She hadn't an idea how much she would need to keep the seven of her family for three months, but certainly a thousand was better than nothing.

Much relieved she put away the papers and other things she did not mean to take with her, whirled the combination carefully, closed the panel, and replaced the picture that hung over it. Then she searched for her mother's jewel pocket, and taking them all retired to her own room behind a locked door to put her capital into safety for the journey, taking the precaution to save out a nice little sum for Jeremy to carry. She must get something to put it in, or he would stick it in his hip pocket and laugh at her fears. But she did not intend that they should take any risks with their tiny fortune. There would be many needs in three months if they were to stay hidden safely until she was of age. One of them might be sick. There would be board to pay. They couldn't live in the car continually, not with children.

As these thoughts flitted through her mind her young soul quaked within her. What was she daring to do? Take the whole family into an unknown world, and be responsible for all of them? Oh, was she doing right? But it was too late now, and there was no time to think of any other plan. She must get them all away before Aunt Petra and Aunt Majesta got to work and separated them.

Frantically she folded Jeremy's portion into a plain envelope. She would hunt among father's things for a money belt. She was sure he had one.

She hurried back to her father's chiffonier and found the money belt. Now, the money part was all arranged for the journey. That was a big thing off her mind.

Jennifer sat down at her own desk and wrote a list of things she must do before she left. There were letters to write, first and foremost, one to Uncle Blake. Then one to the gardener who lived in a little street not far away and must be asked to keep on caring for the place, the garden and lawn, etc. There was a note also to the local police, asking them to keep guard over the house during their absence, telling them that the gardener would be keeping things in order, and that they were to report any irregularities to Uncle Blakefield. Jennifer chose Uncle Blakefield to refer to because she liked him best of all her uncles. There might have been a guardian appointed, of course, who had power to lord it over him, Jennifer had not stayed in the library long enough to find out, but Uncle Blake would at least see that all was as it should be. A guardian didn't bulk very large in Jennifer's mind at that moment. She intended to be guardian herself before she came back to the family rooftree.

Her letters were crisp and to the point. She did not waste much time on them. To her uncle she wrote:

"Dear Uncle Blake:

I was in the library while the relatives were talking, and heard their plans.

We don't intend to be separated, so we are running away until I am of age and have a right to look after the family. That will be October 5th.

I am not telling anybody but you about it, because, even if there is a guardian appointed, I couldn't trust *anybody* else.

Sorry we had to do it this way, but we couldn't see having Aunt Petunia and Aunt Maje run us.

We've got some money, so we shan't suffer, and if we need anything we'll telegraph you.

If you need to get in touch with us after next Thursday, you can put a "Personal" in the New York *Times*, addressed to J.J. and we'll find a way to see it within a few days. Sign your own initials.

Now, give us a break, and don't tell the rest till you have to. And don't let them hunt for us if you can help it.

I've asked the police to keep an eye on the house and report to you if anything happens. And the gardener will look after the place. I've dismissed the servants for the present.

We're going to a safe quiet place. Don't worry! Three months isn't long.

Lovingly,
Jen."

The other notes were to Emil the gardener, and to the police.

She read her letters over carefully, satisfied that she had done her best. Was there anything else about the house that ought to be attended to?

Then she heard a car coming into the drive. Was that Jerry? She hurried down to the side door and met him as he came from the garage.

They spoke guardedly as they stood at the side entrance.

"Jerry! Your pony! Had you thought about that?"

"Sure! I told the stable boy to take him up to the farm, and I just phoned the farmer. He said it was okay, they'd look after him till we were ready for him again. And the boy can stay up there and work. He's pleased all right."

"Fine. Now what else is there to do? How about the car?"

"It's all ready. Had it filled down at Piper's filling station. Nobody would ever recognize it there. The chauffeur always took it to the stations up this way. Now, what do you want of me? Where can I help best? What's become of the kids?"

"They're all sound asleep," said Jennifer. "They were just worn out."

"Good work, Jen, we can get more done with them parked for awhile. What about the servants now? What's the next act?"

"Maggie and Letty are going on a vacation. We're having dinner at five-thirty. They'll wash the dishes and be ready to leave. I told Maggie you would take her to the seven o'clock train. Take her in your little car, so the other won't be seen going out again until after dark."

"Okay, Miss Graeme. You've got quite a head on you for a girl, if you are my sister. How about Letty?"

"She's taking the bus to the city. I told her you would help her on with her bags. Her young man meets her in town. So she's all right. She'll leave a little before Maggie. They think we are being invited out somewhere among the relatives. I promised to send them word when we wanted them back."

"Well, things seem to be working our way, don't they? But how about the relatives? Haven't any of the aunts turned up yet? You know any one of them could wreck our plans in less than a minute."

"Yes, I know. There! Wasn't that the phone? Oh, dear!"

Jennifer flew into the house and went to the telephone booth under the front stairs.

5

"Hello!" she said in an excited young voice. "Oh, is that you, Aunt Petra? Yes, thank you, we're all right. The children are all sound asleep. They were worn out with excitement, you know. They need to get calmed down. What's that? Dinner? Tonight? Oh, thank you, Aunt Petra, but I don't think I ought to leave the children. Besides, I'm quite worn out myself. I don't seem to want to go anywhere. No, I'm not going to brood. I want to keep cheerful for the children's sake. Stay all night? No thank you. Not at present. We're quite all right, Aunt Petra. No, you don't need to come over and stay with us. We really don't need anybody. We'd rather be very quiet for a while, you know. Yes, it was kind of you to call. No, we'll be better eating dinner here. Maggie has it all cooking for us, and it would be foolish for us to run away somewhere when all is ready here. No indeed, we're not afraid. Yes, I know you have other company. I understand perfectly, Aunt Petra, and it was sweet of you to call, but we're better off at home just at present."

Aunt Petra ceased talking at last, and Jennifer hung up with relief, hoping she hadn't said anything that wasn't true. The family had always been very particular about speaking the absolute truth, and she didn't want to overstep the rules she had been taught.

Jeremy appeared at her side as she turned away from the telephone.

"You got by that ordeal pretty well," he said grinning.

"I don't fancy it hurt her much that we wouldn't come. She never was keen on inviting any of us. I don't think she'll grieve! But that's only the beginning. You'll see, the other aunts will all call up pretty soon. Aunt Pet will tell them we've declined her invitation, so they'll dare try."

Then the telephone rang again.

"There!" said Jerry. "What did I tell you? But Aunt Petunia certainly got in her work good and quick."

"Oh, that's Aunt Majesta, I suppose. They went home together perhaps, or else they stopped down town together, and it didn't take Aunt Petra long to report," said Jennifer as she hurried back to the telephone booth.

She came out smiling a minute later.

"That's just what it was! Aunt Majesta wanted to go on record quickly before I changed my mind. She said she'd love to take two of the little girls for all night, but I told her we were staying together tonight, and couldn't accept any invitations. She even suggested *you* might like to come to dinner. She said Uncle Pemberton wanted to give you a little advice, and this would be a good time. But I told her no, we needed you!"

"Okay with me," said Jeremy. "*Advice!* H'm! Bologny! I don't care for any of his advice! Thunder! There goes the doorbell! Now who do you suppose that could be?"

They listened, and a shade of annoyance passed over Jennifer's face as she recognized a voice. Jeremy didn't miss her expression.

"Good *night!*" he said crossly. "Is that Pete Willis? Who does he think he is? Now I suppose you'll duck and run and leave us all up a tree! For goodness' sake tell me what to do while he's here."

Jennifer with a very determined look on her young face patted his arm.

"Don't you worry, kid! He won't stay long! I'll settle him."

But the boy drew his brows in a dubious frown.

"Aw, *you!*" he exclaimed. "You won't be able to get away! I know him! Why'n't ya have Letty tell him you can't see him t'day?"

"Because he would only come back tonight, just when we don't want him!" she said. "You go get your clothes together. Everything you'll need while we're gone. Nothing fancy, you know. One good plain suit for emergencies. Don't make a noise to wake those children. We can work better while they are asleep."

Then she turned and hurried out to the hall, intercepting Letty who was just going upstairs in search of her.

She came over to the doorway where the young man stood waiting for her. He was a handsome fellow, well groomed, with a pleasantly-subdued smile on his face.

"Hello, Jen!" he called breezily and took both of her hands in a big possessive clasp. "Say, this is hard lines, you to have to go through all this ghastly business. Sorry I couldn't have been here to help somehow, but I was way off in the wilds in the mountains on a fishing trip, and we didn't get the word till late last night, too late to get back and try for a plane. I knew the funeral must be over. But say, I certainly was sorry! Tough luck and all that for you! I'm glad you're looking sort of cheerful! I do hate long faces, and of course they don't do any good. Things like that are just as well forgotten as soon as possible. And after all your father and mother had had a good life, and it's probably all for the best! But I certainly am sorry as the dickens. I didn't even know in time to send flowers!"

Jennifer looked at him with strange quiet eyes. Somehow he seemed alien to her new world. The cut-and-dried, half-embarrassed phrases he was rattling off fell on her sore young heart like hard smooth pebbles, and had no tender message for her at all. He didn't really feel badly about the sudden taking away of her precious mother and father. He was only saying those conventional words because it was the thing to do and he must get it over with as soon as possible. He had been her companion in many a gay frolic, a nice escort to have, always ready with bright repartee, always sending delightful flowers, and ready for any wild episode that might be suggested. A little over-inclined, perhaps, to urge her to do anything that came along, to lead her into questionable situations that her mother afterwards seriously disapproved when she happened to find them out. But still nice, and a lot of fun, awfully good-looking, and richer than any of the other young men. Long ago he would have bestowed upon her elegant trifles that were fairly priceless, if her parents had not objected.

But now, suddenly, he seemed alien, and she did not know why.

A little conventional smile trembled on her lips.

"It doesn't matter," she murmured. "It was kind of you to think of it." Her voice had a sad little grown-up sound, and he looked at her keenly.

"Poor little kid!" he said in his big superior voice. "Come and sit down. You look tired to death. Sit over here beside me," and he sat down on a big luxurious couch and tried to catch her hand and pull her down beside him.

But Jennifer drew away from him and sat instead on a straight little chair almost in front of him, her pretty chin lifted with the least suggestion of aloofness about her, ignoring his request that she sit beside him.

"Why, I'm not really so tired," she said coolly. "Of course I've been pretty busy. There have been a great many things to think of, and it's rather hard to get adjusted to the situation. Did you have a pleasant time in the mountains?"

"Oh, sure! I always have a swell time when I go fishing. Made a record catch, and was the envy of all the older men. Took a lot of snapshots too. I want to show them to you as soon as I can get them developed. Say, how about coming up to the house to dinner with me tonight? The mater said there wouldn't be anybody there but dad and herself, and it wouldn't be a social affair, so you needn't feel there is anything out of place in coming, even if it is rather soon for you to go out. You know us all so well that it won't count. I've got something to talk over with you, and we can do it better there than here."

Jennifer's expression hardened, and her lips went into a thin line. "That's very kind, I'm sure," she said, her tone a bit haughty, "but I couldn't think of leaving the children tonight."

"Oh, say now, Jen, don't get that way! You aren't going to tie yourself to those kids, are you? Why, that's ridiculous! There are surely servants enough to look after them, and outside of that there are relatives enough. Your Aunt Lutie told me a few minutes ago that they were all going to be invited out tonight to dinner, anyway."

"They are not going out to dinner," said Jennifer with firmness. "You forget that they are only children, and that they have had a great shock, and feel that I am the one to turn to now that mother is gone!"

"Well, you surely are not going to encourage them in sentimental wailings. Sob stuff! I never thought you were like that!"

Jennifer stared at him coldly.

"I'm afraid I don't know what you mean," she said haughtily. "I love my brothers and sisters of course, and at a time like this we do not care to be away from each other."

"Well, you're making a great mistake, Jen," said the young man with a superior smile. "If you begin like that you'll find it will hamper you endlessly, and I don't see having you hampered this winter. I have a great many plans for the season, and you're not to be tied up so you will spoil them."

"Oh, really?" said Jennifer indifferently. "I'm afraid you'll have to find someone else, or else change your plans. I intend to look after my family! I'm in place of their mother, now, you know!"

Peter Willis stared at her with almost a shade of contempt on his face.

"What utter rot!" he said. "Your brothers and sisters will be shipped off to boarding schools till they are grown up and ready to shift for themselves, and you've nothing whatever to do with the matter. It wouldn't be at all wise for you to start in even for a few days to coddle them and make them softies. Just make trouble for them when they go away. Be sensible! Come on to dinner with me. I really have something important to tell you, and I can't possibly do it here with a lot of kids racing in and out. It has to do with you and me, and our future, Jen!"

Jennifer suddenly rose and glanced down at her wrist watch.

"Sorry!" she said with a lift of her chin and a level look at the young man. "It wouldn't matter what it had to do with, would it? I'm not interested to that extent."

"Now Jen, snap out of it! I really have got awfully important things to say to you."

"Well, you'll have to say them quickly, then," said Jennifer, "for I have awfully important duties just now and I can't give you but five minutes." She gave another glance at her watch with a soft little frown on her smooth brows.

"My word, Jen, what's the matter with you? I never saw you act like this before!"

"Perhaps not," said Jennifer. "You never saw me with a lot of responsibilities on me before. What is it that is so important? Why can't you tell me quickly? I really am in a great hurry just now. Don't waste time. Get to the point!"

The young man took a quick stride across the room, glanced out the door, looking up and down the hall, and then came back and seated himself in a chair opposite her with an annoyed fling, crossing one well-tailored knee over the other, and glaring at her disapprovingly.

"The point is," he said haughtily, "that I came here with the intention of planning something for you that I thought would be a help. I wanted you to come to dinner so that we might have the evening by ourselves, uninterrupted. But it seems you are trying to be difficult, so of course there is nothing for it but to tell you in a few words. Perhaps then you will come to your senses and be willing to go with me after all. The whole thing is this, Jen: you can't possibly stay here and run this house and deal with these kids. Somebody else will have to take that burden from you. And I understand there are plenty of relatives quite ready to do so. I have just been talking with your aunt, Mrs. Holbrook, and your aunt Mrs. Best, and they assure me that they have plans whereby all the children are to be provided for, and you will have no obligations whatever. There is no reason in the world why you will not be free to go your own way and do just as you please."

Jennifer looked up with angry eyes, her lips closed in a thin line, but she said nothing, and Peter Willis went smoothly on.

"Now my idea is this, Jen: I decided that the thing for us to do is to get married right away, and take a run over to Europe for a while till this thing here is all arranged, and then you will have no further obligation. Your aunts both assured me that none of them would offer any objections to such a course, and there was no reason why we shouldn't go straight ahead and make our plans for an early marriage. Of course I would understand that under the circumstances you would want a quiet wedding, and I would be quite willing for that. Everyone would understand, of course. And it isn't as if people hadn't all understood for some time what was coming off. Now, Jen, do you see why I want you to come to our house to dinner tonight, where we can have plenty of time and quiet to make our plans?"

He paused and eyed her rebukingly. Jennifer gave him a steady quiet look and then she arose.

"Why, yes, I suppose I do get your viewpoint now, but you see I have no plans to make. I am not expecting to marry anyone at present, and I have obligations here. Sorry, Pete, but my time is up and I simply *must* go. There are household matters that demand my attention at once. You really will have to excuse me."

"Nonsense!" said the young man sharply. "What about your obligations to me?"

"To *you? Obligations?*" Jennifer lifted her eyebrows just the least little bit. "I didn't know I had any obligations to you. Just what are they, Pete?"

A look of swift anger passed over the handsome face of the young man.

"The obligations of a girl who has accepted constant attentions from a man, and seemed quite willing to accept them. The obligations of a girl who has allowed her name to be coupled with a man's name until practically everybody in town considers them engaged!"

He flung the words at her like darts that he was aiming straight at her with a look of utmost contempt on his face.

"Oh! Really? Why Pete, I haven't been with you any oftener than I have with Chic Warrener, or Mont Martin, or Harold Fulton, or Rance Carroll, and I'm quite sure people wouldn't consider that I was engaged to all of them. I don't believe that people are saying or thinking that about us."

"And yet both of your aunts spoke as if they had thought for some time that our marriage was a foregone conclusion."

"Oh, *my aunts!*" laughed Jennifer. "I'm afraid they don't count. But really, Pete, this talk is absurd. You never asked me to marry you, and I never really considered the matter. But even if I had, even if we had been engaged, I would feel now that circumstances were greatly changed. I would not think of considering marriage with *any*body, and especially not with anyone who has just expressed such outrageous ideas about my brothers and sisters. You see, Pete, it happens that I love them all."

The young man looked astonished.

"Why, naturally. Of course," he said easily. "But I don't see what *that's* got to do with it. You've always loved them, haven't you? But you always had time to go around with me."

"That was a different thing," said the girl sharply. "They had mother and father. But now they haven't anybody."

"Oh, yes they have. They have a whole slew of aunts and uncles just aching to get hold of them and bring them up. They'll have no end of a good time and won't miss you in the least!"

Jennifer sprang to her feet furiously.

"That'll be enough!" she said. "They're my brothers and sisters and they're not going to be thrown out into the world! We're going to stick together, and that's *final!* And now I guess you'll have to excuse me. I have something that I must do at once. I really can't talk any more about that or anything else."

"Now look here, Jen! Don't get hot under the collar. You always were an awful little pepper pot!"

Peter Willis reached out a long strong arm and caught her wrists.

"Let go of me, Peter!" demanded Jennifer, quelling him with a cold glance.

"Now, now, *now,* Jen!" he said in his imperious tone. "Don't get excited. Let's get a little calm. Just quiet down and let me explain. You and I've been pretty good pals for a long time, haven't we?"

"Let go of my wrists and I'll answer you," said Jennifer coldly.

He dropped her wrists but continued to hold her glance steadily.

"Haven't we, Jen?"

"We've been playmates," said Jennifer steadily, "nothing more. It hadn't occurred to me that anything else was necessary at present. I hadn't got to the place where I even *wanted* anything more, and I don't believe you had either."

She gave him a steady look, and he colored a trifle annoyedly.

"I thought so," said Jennifer. "I was pretty sure all this nonsense was put into your head by my kind, benevolent aunts."

"Oh, no," he said easily. "I've been considering you as mine for a long time. I've always expected to make you my wife."

The girl's face took on several fine shades of indignation.

"Oh, *really?"* she said haughtily. "Just what right did you have to expect that? Kindly cancel that expectation at once! If I ever would have thought of you in that light in the past I certainly wouldn't now. I could never marry a man who thought of my family as lightly and casually as you have shown today that you think."

"Now Jen, don't be difficult. You certainly know that no man wants to marry a whole raft of howling irrational children. You won't find anyone to fill your ideal if you expect that. You'll be left high and dry, a lonely old maid, out in the cold, you know, and you would never enjoy that, I'm sure."

Jennifer retreated a step or two toward the hall, and there was utmost contempt in her face.

"I wasn't just looking around for someone to marry me at the present time, and I don't know but an old maid could have quite a pleasant life. I'm very sure of one thing, however. If I ever do marry anyone it *won't be you!* But I don't care to talk any more about this now. My mind has been occupied with so many sorrowful things that marriage doesn't seem to belong in the scheme of things, and I really must ask you to excuse me now. Thank your mother, please, for her kind invitation. I'm sure she meant to be very sweet. But tell her it is quite impossible for me to visit anywhere at present."

Jennifer drew herself up with a sweet young dignity, and stood waiting for him to take his leave, when suddenly there came a tremendous jarring sound as if something heavy had fallen on the floor, and Jennifer lifted a quick questioning glance above, trying to identify that sound, anxiety, perplexity in her eyes. There was a breathless instant when Peter too stood looking up to the ceiling with wonder. Then there came a quivering gasp from above, followed by an awful wail of a frightened baby, and a howl of anguish.

"I—v-v-vants my muvver!"

But by this time Jennifer was half way up the stairs, flying as if wings were on her feet. That was Robin! What had happened?

She found him lying on the floor before the bed where

he had been so sweetly asleep a little while ago, sobbing as if his heart would break. She gathered him quickly into her arms and sat down on the edge of the bed, holding him close, her lips on his soft baby lips, and kissing his wet closed eyelids.

"I v-v-vants my muvver! I vants my bootiful muvver!" he wailed, with quivering lip.

Jennifer's tears were falling now, mingling with his. She was not aware that Peter Willis had followed her upstairs to see what catastrophe had occurred, and that he was standing in the doorway witnessing a new Jennifer, a Jennifer he had never known before. A Jennifer all maternal sweetness and gentle comfort. Something strange twinged in the place he had for a heart, as he saw the rareness of the girl who had just turned him down so completely.

Not that he believed for an instant that she meant it. She was only angry of course. But what a girl she was! What would it be when he had her for *his own,* and that gentleness and sweetness, and tender comfort should be for *his* mishaps, and annoyances.

But the little boy was continuing to wail.

"I *vants* my *muv*ver!"

"But she isn't here just now, Robin-boy," said the controlled voice of the young sister.

Robin sat up and looked around the room, anxiously.

"Wes, she *vas* here. She vas standing wight beside my bed, and I twied to weach her and kiss her, and I wolled out of bed on the floor! Vare *is* she? I *vant* her."

"Listen, Robin," said the sister, drawing a deep breath, and suddenly looking quite mature and dependable, "don't you remember mother and daddy have gone to Heaven for a little while? I'm sorry I can't get mother for you, but she isn't here, precious."

"But I *seed* her. I weally *did,* sister!" The little boy's eyes were big and earnest now, the tears still trembling on his round pink cheek.

Jennifer looked earnestly into his eyes.

"No, dear, that was just a lovely dream of mother you had. Perhaps mother asked God to send it down to you to comfort you. Wasn't that nice to have a lovely dream of mother?"

Jennifer through her own tears was smiling at her little brother. He looked at her with a great questioning in his eyes, and then he suddenly broke into a sweet child smile.

"Wes!" he said happily, and his face was like the sunshine on a rain cloud, full of little rainbows.

"Will *you* have a pwetty dweam of muvver, too, Jenniver?" he asked earnestly.

"Perhaps," said Jennifer with a wistful tenderness in her eyes.

"And daddy too?"

"Perhaps. And now, Robin, have you forgotten how good and quiet you were going to be, and how there was a piece of candy for everybody after the nap, and three pieces for the one who went to sleep first? And do you know that *you* were the one who won the prize? You were asleep a whole minute ahead of Karen."

"Vas I?" Robin smiled delightedly.

"Yes, come on now, and let's go very softly to see if the rest have waked up yet."

She put him down with his bare pink feet on the floor, taking his warm little hand in hers, and not till then did she notice that Peter Willis was standing in the door watching her.

She gave him a dreamy absent smile and went on past him, only taking in the significance of his presence when she reached the hall.

"I'm sorry, Peter," she said pleasantly, distantly, "but you can see I am very busy just now."

He suppressed a quick thundercloud in his eyes, and nodded condescendingly. "This evening, then," he said with a kind of authority in his voice. "I'll be over about eight. The circus will certainly be over by that time, won't it?"

"No!" said Jennifer sharply. "Not this evening! Please

Peter, let me alone, won't you? I can't stand any more tonight! Can—you let yourself out?"

"Oh, certainly!" said Peter, in a displeased tone, but he watched her leading Robin away to have his face washed, and in spite of himself he saw something lovely in it all that he had not dreamed of in connection with the gay bright young Jennifer. So he set his determined lips in a firmer line than ever.

6

By the time Jennifer had Robin bathed and suitably clothed for the journey she had completely forgotten the existence of Peter Willis. She heard the great hall clock downstairs chiming four o'clock, and knew she had very little time in which to do a great deal. She had no time for erstwhile lovers. And marriage? What was marriage compared to the exciting adventure on which she was about to embark?

She settled Robin on the seat in his bedroom baywindow, with a comparatively new picture book, on his honor not to stir till she came back, and then she hurried to Jeremy's room.

That young man was just snapping shut the second suitcase.

"All packed!" he announced. "I knew you wouldn't get away from that chump as soon as you thought you would, so I went into Tryon's room and got his things."

"Oh," said Jennifer. "That's wonderful! But—are you sure you got everything he needs? Did you remember underwear, plenty of it, and socks? You know we may have very little opportunity to get laundry work done. We may have to stop at a stream somewhere and wash things out. We don't dare go to hotels, not for a while yet, anyway. Because, Jerry, I don't *intend* to get caught!"

"Of course not!" said the young man shortly. "What do you think I am? A babe in arms? Don't you think I have a mind? I ask you! Did you think I'd be packing nothing but dress suits?"

Jennifer laughed.

"No, of course not. But I didn't think you'd realize about laundry."

"Well, I did! Got plenty! Remembered bath robes for us both, too, and bathing suits. We'll have to take baths swimming in streams, probably."

Jennifer's eyes brightened.

"Of course," she said eagerly. "Bright child! I hadn't thought of that! And we'll have to have a lot of bath towels along! Mercy! I don't see how we're ever going to get everything we need into one car with the whole seven of us. And we'll simply have to take a blanket or two, for naps, and in case some of us get sick."

"Sure, we'll manage," said Jeremy nonchalantly. "I've got that contraption fixed on one running board, and we can get two or three big boxes or suitcases in that!"

"Wonderful!" said Jennifer. "I think I've been worrying in the back of my mind about how we could get all the baggage we need into the back of the car."

"Well, there's the car trunk, you know, besides quite a big place under the back seat. Now, say, Jen, what time do we aim to start? I thought I heard that poor fish yell back he'd be here this evening. Is that right?"

"I told him not to," said Jennifer with a worried brow. "I don't think he'll come."

"Well, if he does you'd better have an awful headache or something. Send me to the door. I'll get rid of him. There! There goes the phone. That's the other aunts, I'll wager. Let me answer!" and he strode to the upper extension in the master bedroom. Jennifer stole anxiously after him. There was no telling what he might say if they were disagreeable. He might spoil the whole affair. But as she listened her face relaxed, and she eased herself into a chair by the door, and gradually a twinkly smile began to creep around her mouth.

"Hello! Oh, hello, Aunt Agatha! This is Jeremy. No,

Jennifer is busy right now. At least, I'm not sure where she is, but I'll go hunt her up if you say so. A message? Oh, sure I'll give her a message. She'll be around at dinner time. Sorry you didn't see her this afternoon? Oh, I'm sure she'll understand. You had a bad headache and had to go right home to bed! Say now, that's tough luck! You take care of yourself, Aunt Agatha. Oh, sure, I'll tell Jen. She'll understand. Thanks a lot, Aunt Ag! Yep! We're all right! Right's we can be under the circumstances! Oh, sure, Aunt Ag. We knew we had your sympathy! It means a lot and all that, you understand. Yes, I'll take care of Jen. She's doing fine. She's getting the kids inta line now fer a bath and dinner! Oh, sure! I'll tell her. No, she wouldn't expect you ta come. So long, Aunt Ag! See you subse."

Jeremy hung up and turned grinning, repeating a few of Aunt Agatha's sentences, mimicking her little affected accents.

"She's 'just ahf-ly sorry she cawn't come over this evening and chee-ah you up!' " Then suddenly Jeremy lifted his eyes and his gaze fell upon the picture of his mother there on the chiffonier before him and his voice failed him. An unbidden mist came into his eyes. He was standing there making fun of his mother's sister! Of course if mother had been there she would only have laughed merrily over his clever imitation of the affectation which she had always acknowledged herself, but somehow it got him for the moment, and he had to go over to the window and get out his handkerchief, and blow his nose hard. And then, right into the midst of that the telephone rang again, and he whirled around quickly and took down the receiver again.

"Yes, Aunt Lutie!" His voice was a bit hoarse and his tone grave now. "Oh, yes, Aunt Lutie. It was nice of you to call. Yes, this is Jerry. Well, that's kind of you, but I guess you'll have to excuse us tonight, Aunt Lutie. I don't think Jen feels up to it and neither do I. Roast duck? Oh, *I say!* That sounds *swell!* But I guess you'll have to excuse us tonight. Jen and I are about all in. Oh, yes, the kids are all right. They've had a good long nap this afternoon, and I expect they'll go to sleep again early tonight! Thank you for calling, Aunt Lutie."

"Oh!" sighed Jennifer, "you're swell! I'll send you to the phone every time. And now, I guess we'd better get to work again. I've got a money belt for you to wear, and you had better put it on right now." She stepped nearer and whispered.

The brother nodded.

"Okay!" he said. "Say, that was great dad left that money! Looks almost as if he knew we were going to need it!" His voice was husky again with feeling. "There! Isn't that Karen calling? Say, are you going to tell the kids what we're going to do?"

"Not till Maggie and Letty are gone," said Jennifer decidedly. "One of them would be sure to forget and yell out something and then our goose would be cooked. If either of those two women found it out they wouldn't go! They would think it was their duty to stay and stop us, or else go and tell Aunt Petra. No, we'll do as much as we can before dark, and have everything all ready to put together and leave as soon as you get back from the station. It doesn't take long to put that trunk on the back of the car, does it?"

"Trunk's already on," said Jeremy laconically. "The car's away back in the garage behind my runabout."

"Well, but won't the servants see the trunk on when you take them to the station?"

"No, for I'm taking cook in my runabout, so she won't even know we are thinking about the other car. And as for Letty, she fell all over her tongue just now telling me her young man was calling for her at six-thirty, so she'll be out of the way, and we haven't that to consider."

"Jerry," said Jennifer with a grave sweet look of appreciation, "I really begin to think you are almost more grown-up than I am, and certainly much more thoughtful!"

"Thanks, awfully, sister, I'd have to be going some ever to catch up with your class. The way you've managed this servant question, and the matter of finances, can't be beat!

There! I hear Robin calling. Can't you get him out and let him run a little so he won't get restless tonight?"

"Yes, I'm going to send them all out to the playground."

Jennifer hurried to Robin.

"Just sit still till I get Karen ready," she said, "and then you two can go out and play hide and seek."

Robin smiled sweetly.

"Awright!" he said contentedly. "I wike you better'n my nurse!" he vouchsafed irrelevantly.

"That's nice," said Jennifer, and stepped into Karen's room, for she could hear her stirring now.

"Now, Karen, get up and get into your play clothes. You and Robin are going out to the playground and have a lovely time until I call you in to dinner. Be quick about dressing. Robin is waiting for you."

"Okay!" said Karen springing up. "I don't have to wait for that old nurse, do I? I like to dress myself."

"Don't you like the nurse either?" said Jennifer.

"I sure do not," said the little girl. "She never lets me do a thing. She says I don't know how, and I *like* to dress myself."

"Well, don't be long. I want you to get out before the sunshine is all gone and have a good time running in the fresh air."

"And are we going to do something after dinner, too? We don't have to go right to bed again, do we?"

"Not right away," said the sister. "I guess we'll have a nice time after dinner, if you are all good."

"Oh, we'll be good!" promised the young cherub.

In the next room Heather and Hazel were both wide-eyed.

"We don't have to stay here in bed any longer, do we?" pleaded Heather. "I certainly am sick of lying still."

"Come over here on Hazel's bed," said Jennifer in a low voice. "I want to tell you something."

Heather sprang up and snuggled in beside her sister. Jennifer sat down on the edge of the bed.

"Now," she said in almost a whisper, "I'm going to take you both into my confidence."

"Well, it's about time," said Hazel. "I think I at least ought to understand." Both their heads were snuggled closer and two pairs of eager eyes were fixed on her face.

"Now listen, girls, you're not to tell a soul now anything about this. It's a secret. We're going away tonight after dinner, after Maggie and Letty are gone."

"Forever?" asked Hazel aghast, her eyes casting a quick fond glance about her room.

"Oh no!" reassured Jennifer, "but I've told the servants we have been invited out for tonight—we were, you know, to several places—and I thought we might be away for a little while."

"But Jennifer!" said Heather aghast. "We aren't going to any of the aunts, are we? Oh, *please* Jennifer, not to the aunts! They'll separate us! I *know* they will! And you *promised* we shouldn't be separated!"

Then suddenly Jennifer to her amazement found that both the girls were crying. Her heart went out to them with a quick warm love of which she had never been so conscious before. She came closer and enfolded them in a sudden big hug and kissed one tear-wet face and then the other.

"No, no, no! You dear things! Of course you shan't be separated! Didn't I promise you? That's what we're going away for, so they can't separate us. You know I'm not of age yet, and if we stayed here they would say I wasn't old enough to manage things, and they would all jump in with both feet and make an awful time for us, so we're not going to give them the chance. Now, will you sit up and mop up your faces and get to work? We've a lot to do, and we haven't time to talk about it, or even to think about it. Do you think you both are grown-up enough, and have strength of mind enough to put this out of your thoughts entirely, and work like lightning? I want thoughtful work too, the kind that doesn't have to be done over, and checked up on afterwards. Can you do it?"

Two bright faces were suddenly lifted with hope shining like a rainbow behind the shed tears.

"We can! We *can!*" they cried. "What shall we do?"

"You can get ready to go," said Jennifer. "You know we've got to take clothes enough along so we won't have to buy any until we get back, and we've got to have the right kind of clothes, to keep either cool or warm in, according to the weather, so you've got to think as you pack, and not forget a thing you may need very badly when you are away, and haven't much money to buy things with."

The girl's eyes were round with the wonder of it all.

"Why, it'll be kind of fun, won't it, sister?" said Heather, who had scarcely smiled since she knew of the death of her beloved parents.

"Perhaps," said Jennifer, with a wistful look in her eyes. "I surely hope it will. Let's make it fun. That will help us not to feel sad about all that has happened. Now get to work! You'll want your very plainest clothes. Nothing fancy. Do you understand?"

The girls nodded, their eyes shining intelligently.

"Won't there be any parties?" asked Heather thoughtfully.

"No parties!" said Jennifer. "Now go!"

The children sprang into action, and Jennifer went down to be sure the front door was locked and no relative could walk in on her unawares.

Through the dining room door she glimpsed the table set. The odor of chicken getting itself to the finished stage was pleasantly obvious. Then Maggie stuck her head out of the pantry door and saw her going toward the stairs.

"Miss Jennifer, is that you? Well, Miss Jennifer, I was just coming up to ask you. Would I defrost the refrigerator? Or should I leave it going to keep things? Will you be coming back that soon? Today is the day I usually defrost it, only I've been that busy—"

Jennifer considered. These were questions that had never come into her life before, but now she must do the best she could with them.

"Is there much in the refrigerator that will spoil?" she asked, trying to look wise.

"Well, there's a good bit. There's the big part of a roast. You folks scarcely ate a bite yesterday. And there'll be some chicken left the night, perhaps. I cooked a-plenty. There's eggs, too, and quite a lot of butter. The week's order just came this morning. If I had known we was all going away for a time I wouldn't have let him leave it. And there's three bottles of milk—"

"Well, I guess you'd better defrost the refrigerator," Jennifer decided, realizing that she wouldn't know how to do it herself after Maggie was gone. "You can put anything that will spoil out on the kitchen table and I'll have the gardener come in and take some things to his cottage. I guess he'll be glad to use them up."

"You're right there! He certainly will be glad to get anything, with all his flock of kids. All right, Miss Jennifer. I'll see to it all. And I'll leave the keys out on the sideboard for you to attend to. The silver and that like'll be all right in its regular place, like your father used to fix it when we went to the shore."

"Thank you, Maggie. But when are you going to do your packing?"

"Oh, I'll manage that easy," said the woman. "I went up while the chicken was cooking and got most of my things folded. It won't take long. Miss Jennifer, do you mind if I take a couple of those big pasteboard suit boxes in the box closet? There's a-plenty of them up there. And if ye don't mind, I'd like to take a pound of that nice fresh butter to my sister as a present."

"Yes, do take it," said Jennifer. "Perhaps Letty would like a pound too. She said she was going to board herself while she was away."

"I'll tell her, Miss Jennifer, and thank you kindly. Ye're gettin' more like yer blessed mamma every day."

"Thank you, Maggie," and Jennifer choked back a sob that suddenly swelled into her throat, and sped away up the stairs. How hard it was going to be to break even this humble link to their old life. Maggie had endeared herself to them in many ways, and she had a sudden appalling feeling of her own inadequacy. How was she ever going to be able to take the place not only of father and mother, but of all the servants as well, to her dear young family? She who knew so little about the routine of daily living?

Heather put out a cautious head from her door and called softly:

"Sister! Come here and tell us. Are these dresses too fancy?" She held up a brief gingham outfit of dark blue with scarlet rickrack edging on thin white ruffles. It was just a cheap little dress, but evidently one that Heather admired greatly.

"No, that's all right! Now, let's see how much you have done!"

The girls had really done good work, and little piles of socks and underwear, a row of shoes to be selected from, and piles of neatly ironed cotton dresses were duly displayed to her. She made a few changes, suggesting an addition or two, and eliminating one or two items.

"Now," said the older sister, "that's fine. You might run in my room and get those two suitcases under my bed. I had Jerry put them there. I think they will about hold your things, and then we can hide them in the closet for the present." Quietly the two girls tiptoed into their sister's room and brought back the suitcases, looking furtively behind them as if they expected to see an enemy-aunt lurking in every corner.

With awe they brought their piles of clothing and handed them to Jennifer as she knelt by the open suitcases, and laid things carefully in.

"What about our brushes and combs and things?" asked Hazel practically.

"We'll have to take a couple of little old overnight bags," said Jennifer. "One for us and one for the boys. They have all the fittings in, and then everything will be easy to get at. Get your necessities together. Now, are you sure you've saved out all you'll need for the journey?"

They hurried around and got a few other things, hats,

coats, and then stealthily shoved the suitcases into their closets.

"Now," they said, "what shall we do next?"

"Come in and help me get Robin's and Karen's things packed. I got some of them together a little while ago, but I think perhaps you will know better whether I have forgotten anything. You have been around with them more every day, and know what they need."

Another hasty session followed, getting Robin and Karen packed, and into the midst of it came the soft notes of the dinner gong.

"Now, I wonder where Jerry is," said Jennifer. "And the children. Hazel, you run out and bring them in. Wash their hands and faces in the hall lavatory. No, don't bother to comb their hair now. Or, here's my little pocket comb, just smooth them up a bit. You never can be sure that some relative won't drop in while we're eating, and everything must look perfectly all right or they will think I can't take care of you children. Smooth your own hair, Hazel, before you go down, and try to act as ladylike as if you were all dressed up. Don't let Maggie see any excitement about you. Now, hurry and get the children! Heather, you see if you can find Jerry. He's in his room, perhaps."

Heather paused on the top step of the stairs.

"Jerry is just coming in the front door," she said. "Jerry, dinner is ready!"

"Okay!" said Jerry. "I thought I heard the gong."

They came quietly into the dining room and took their seats. Even Robin and Karen were not far behind the rest. They were tired and restless in spite of their naps, and filled with excitement besides. The curtain of shock and sudden death was always hovering just behind whatever occupied their minds, reminding them that there was such a thing as death, though it had never entered their consciousness before. It made a sombre background to everything.

"I fink," said Robin gravely, speaking out of an uncomfortable silence that had seemed to envelope them as they sat down, "I fink my nuss must av died. I—hope—her has!"

"Why, *Robin!* What an awful thing to say!" reproved Hazel with a grown-up air. "That's *wicked,* isn't it, Jennifer? You mustn't ever wish anybody to be dead."

"Oh, no, Robin," said Jennifer quickly, "your nurse isn't dead. She's merely gone away. She's not going to be your nurse any more."

"Well, then I is glad," said the baby, still gravely. "I don't wike her! 'Sides, I'se a big boy now. I don't need a nurse."

"That's it, Robin," smiled Jennifer, with a warning look at the others who were inclined to laugh at Robin. "You know, Robin, it's sort of up to you now, whether you have to have another nurse or not. If you keep on being as good as you were this afternoon, perhaps we won't have to hunt up another nurse for you."

"Awight!" said Robin thoughtfully, "I will be good. It's up to me!" and then he bowed his golden curls into his chubby hands and laughed. "It's—upta—*me!* See?"

They all grinned at that, and then Jennifer cleverly changed the subject.

"Did you succeed in getting all your work done, Jerry?" she asked, in quite a commonplace tone, as if she were talking about some college arrangements.

"Well, yes, pretty much," said Jerry, as if the affairs of the universe were upon his shoulders. "I arranged about the stable boy and the farm, you know."

"Yes, that's good," said the sister.

"Any more aunts telephone?"

"No, I think that is finished, for tonight anyway."

"Here's hoping," said the boy. "I just met Jim Delaney down town. He was running for his train, and he waved at me and called out that we'd be hearing from him soon, but he had something important on tonight. He said Uncle Blake would be round soon too, but he had to run up to New York this afternoon and might not get back till tomorrow. He tried to see some of us when the morning affair was over, but he couldn't find any of us around and he didn't have much time."

"Well, that's nice!" said Jennifer with satisfaction. "That helps a lot. And those two always were good scouts. When I ask advice it will be of them, but not when the aunts are within hearing."

"Here too!" said Jerry with emphasis. "There goes that telephone again! I'll bet that's Aunt Petra! No, you sit still! I'll answer it."

Jerry came back after a brief interval, grinning.

"It was Aunt Petunia all right. She was in high feather. She said she was bringing over the cousins from up state this evening for a little while to cheer us up. But I told her nothing doing. I told her you were just worn to a frazzle and I was crosser than two bears with a sore head, and we didn't feel like talking to anybody, and we didn't care to be cheered up tonight. I said that after we ate our supper we'd more than likely sign off, and if they came here they'd find we had faded out of the picture for the night."

"Jerry! Really? What did she say?"

"She said 'sign off? What do you mean? Don't think of *signing* anything, either of you, till you get some uncle's advice. But of course, I forgot, neither of you are of age, so it really wouldn't matter. But that's what you always have to be careful about, *signing* things, to be sure you thoroughly understand them. Any man would tell you that. What is it they want you to sign? Who wants you to sign it? Don't *do* it, Jeremy! I'd better come right over and see it. I'll come at once!' My word but I had a hard time explaining. I told her I wasn't going to sign anything and nobody wanted us to sign it anyway, and it was just a slang phrase for hitting the hay. Then she began on that, and pranced out a whole farmyard to discourse on, till I headed her off by saying in plain English I meant we were going to get rested, and then she just said *'Oh!'* very coldly. I thought she was going to quit then, but after a pause she began to discourse on slang. She said she shouldn't think I would dishonor the memory of my father and mother by using slang so soon after they were gone, and she guessed she had better come over and talk to me anyway. But I told her if she did I wouldn't be here, that I didn't want to talk to anybody tonight. So at last she hung up, after saying she'd be over the first thing in the morning, and I was to be sure to tell you to wait here till she comes."

The brother and sister had a good laugh over that.

"I scarcely think she'll find me here," said Jennifer with a grimace. "I wish there was some way we could keep her from coming for another day at least."

"Well, I hope I did," said Jeremy, dropping into his seat and attacking his chicken and mashed potato and gravy with a vigor. He had worked hard and was hungry. "I told her to make it the next day instead, if she didn't mind. I knew you had a lot of letters to write and you wouldn't have time to talk to her yet. So she said perhaps she would. She wanted to go over to Aunt Majesty's tomorrow, and since you had your day planned and didn't need her, she guessed she would go there. So! That's that!"

"Nobly done, brother dear!" said Jennifer. "You certainly are clever. I'll always send you to the phone and the door when people call that I want to get rid of."

"Okay with me, Jen. Does that hold for Pete too? I certainly would like to give him the go-by sometime. He's patronized me insufferably for the last two years and I'd like to get it back on him. But I suppose you'll draw the line at him."

"Hop to it, brother, so long as you are polite and don't get into a fight. But I hope Pete understands he's not to come tonight. I told him I couldn't see him."

"Oh, yeah?" said Jerry. "Well, if I know my Pete that won't discourage him the least little bit. But you say the word and I'll just be ready to hand him something that will clear him out of the running for the night. Say, Jen, how about you going up to your room and lying down with your light out, for half an hour, *after* you are ready? Couldn't you manage that? He couldn't do anything about it if I told him you had retired, could he? It wouldn't be a bad idea for all the rest either. It's not going to be so good having anybody come and find no servant to open the door, you know. That will start people wondering too soon."

"Of course," said Jennifer thoughtfully, "I see what you mean."

But Robin's lip began to pucker.

"I don't vanta take anozzer nap! I did take a nap—!"

"Look out, Robin, I'll have to send Jerry to hunt up your nurse again, if that's the way you're going to talk!"

Robin stopped weeping aghast, and straightened his face out in short order, and Jennifer smiled.

"That's the talk. Robin is growing up, Jerry. See?"

Jerry grinned at him, and he trembled out a weak little smile.

Then there occurred an interruption. Letty's young man had come for her. She came apologetically. It was the only time he could get a car. And could she go now?

They bade her good-bye and drew a breath of relief. Another anxiety out of the way.

Soon dinner was finished, and Maggie whisked the last dishes out of the way, and came down with her hat on.

"Seems as if I hadn't oughtta leave you this way."

"Oh, that's all right, Maggie. We'll be fine."

"Well, I guess you'll find everything in order, Miss Jennifer. The things for the gardener are out on the table. And I disconnected the refrigerator. I put a note out in the bottle for the milkman, and one for the bread man. I guess there's nothing else. And here's the address where you can reach me if you need me. I put down a telephone number too, in case you want me in a hurry. But I'm glad to get this little rest, and thank you kindly. You're like your blessed mamma, Miss Jennifer."

Maggie wiped a furtive tear away, kissed the children, and was gone at last, Jerry taking her away in his little car.

Then Jennifer flew into action. She took one glimpse of the kitchen table full of food that Maggie designed for the gardener, and then was back among the children.

"Tryon, will you go up to the trunk room and get the outfit for camping? The basket with dishes and knives and forks and spoons, you know, that we used to take on picnics in the car? Get the little alcohol stove, too, and the coffee pot and saucepan."

"Sure," said Tryon, and went at a bound.

"Oh, are we going to have a picnic?" asked Karen with eyes alight."

"I shouldn't wonder, if you're all good," said Jennifer. "Now, Hazel and Heather, can you spread some bread for sandwiches? When Tryon comes down get him to cut nice thin slices of meat. There is a roast, and an end of ham. And there is quite a lot of chicken left, too. Get wax paper and wrap them neatly. Can I trust you with that?"

"Of course!" said the young sisters, "we know how."

"And Karen, here are two paper bags. You fill one of them with oranges from the storeroom shelf, and the other with apples. And when you have that done you come up stairs with Robin and me to get the baggage ready for Jerry to put in the car."

By the time Jerry was back the packing was finished, the suitcases counted and stacked at the head of the stairs, and the lunch was well under way. The material for the gardener was reduced to a basket of vegetables and what was left of the fruit after Karen had filled the bags.

"Well, Maggie's off and that rids us of all encumbrances at last. Now, what's next?" asked Jeremy standing in the doorway and looking at the eager youngsters who were enjoying their unusual privilege of working in the kitchen.

"What on earth are you kids doing?" He glared down at the children just as Jennifer arrived.

And then suddenly the doorbell pealed through the quiet house. They stopped and looked at each other aghast. What had come now?

"Scram!" said Jeremy in a low tone, and with one accord the little company flew silently up the back stairs, turned out their lights and crept to their beds, lying motionless while the big brother went to the door!

7

And then after all it was only a great box of flowers, lavender and white orchids, for Jennifer from Peter Willis!

"How un*speakable!*" said Jennifer, when Jeremy brought them up to her dark room, turned on her light, and showed them to her. She rose up from her bed where she had been only too glad to lay her weary self for even that brief rest, and scowled at them.

Poor Peter Willis? Only he wasn't in the least poor. He was very rich. And the orchids were really lovely.

"What can I possibly do with them?" she asked in perplexity.

"Put 'em down the drain!" said Jeremy in disgust.

"But we can't do that!" said Jennifer. "Beautiful flowers like that!"

"Well, wear 'em then!" said Jeremy vexedly, slamming down the cover in a rage. "Wear 'em pinned all over you, and be a marked woman! Let old Peter come running to marry you when they've traced you by his flowers!"

"Jerry, don't be a fool!"

"Well, but what *can* you do with them? We can't carry along the right kind of vases to hold them. I tell you you'll have to chop them up and make cold slaw out of them and send it to the gardener."

"Jerry, be sensible. I can't leave them here. *Some*body would be sure to find it out and tell Peter!"

"What's the difference? But of course if *you* care so much about Peter's feelings!"

"Jerry, don't you remember what mother used to say? Even if a person has what you feel are bad manners, you mustn't do the same thing yourself, or you prove yourself just as bad as he is. It's not that I care about Peter, but I care about my own rudeness if I let him know that I do not prize his flowers. He meant to honor me, of course, by sending them. I've got to manage this somehow so he will never know that the flowers came at an inconvenient time for me."

"Okay! Take 'em along if you must, but some of us will have to ride on the running board if you do, for everything's absolutely full!"

"If we could only send them to some poor sick person who never gets flowers and would enjoy them," said Jennifer troubled.

"I know!" said Tryon. "Drive by the charity hospital and leave them at the door. Tell them to give them to the poorest sickest one there!"

"That's a good idea, Try," said his big sister. "We'll do that, and you can take them to the door."

"Somebody'll be sure to recognize us," grumbled Jeremy. "I knew somebody would throw a monkey wrench into this trip somehow."

"Don't worry, Jerry. We won't run any risks, even if we have to throw them in the river as we cross the bridge. Now our first concern is to get out of here quickly, before some pestilential relative catches us and spoils the whole scheme. The baggage is all out there in the hall at the head of the stairs, counted and numbered, and there's a list of the bags, so we can't forget any. You and Tryon carry it out and stow it in the car. Heather, you and Hazel get those sandwiches in the box I gave you in short order! Everybody skitter, quick! Robin, come here and I'll wash that jam off your face. It's well to *start* clean anyway."

They were all packed into the car at last, and just about to start, when Jennifer remembered the blankets she had left on a chair in the back hall.

"Yes, and there's someone coming up the drive on a

bike!" announced Tryon. "Better lie low! Besides, you've left a light going in the front hall, Jerry."

"Okay!" sighed Jerry wearily. "You scout around, Try, and see who it is. I'll go get the blankets and turn out the light."

"Be sure you lock the cellar door," warned Jennifer.

Tryon came back with a telegram. It was from Abigail Storm, addressed to Jennifer.

"Am coming to you at once. Starting first train in the morning. Please have Stanton meet my train tomorrow night.
Cousin Abby."

"Holy Mackerel!" said Jeremy as he returned with the blankets. "Now what shall we do? She'll stir up all the relatives. We've *got* to stop her coming! You can't tell but she'll manage to get the house sold or something, and appropriate all the furniture, if we don't stop her. Wait! I'll go back to the telephone and telegraph in your name, Jen. I'll say: 'Your suggestion very kind but not convenient at present. We shall all be away for a little while. Just starting. Will write you later when we get back.' How's that, Jen?"

"Fine!" said Jennifer. "I couldn't have done it better if I had thought all day!"

They waited in a quiver while he went into the house again to telephone the message, and when at last they saw him snap the house light out, and heard the door close, they drew a breath of relief.

"Get in quick, Jerry! Let's get off before anything else happens," said Jennifer. "I feel it in my bones that Aunt Petra will be coming around with a hot water bottle or something to coddle us."

Amid suppressed laughter Jerry climbed in and started the car. Stealthily it rolled down the incline of the back drive and out the gate by the garage. Then Jerry got out and fastened the gate, and they slid silently down the little back street that skirted the hedge.

Three blocks down they sailed around a corner, and

slipped into what Jeremy called "a backer street," and so on threading a way he had carefully worked out that morning, a way that the Graeme cars did not usually travel and people would not be likely to recognize them. As they went they spoke no word, for Jennifer warned them that they might spoil the whole thing if their voices were heard. So even Robin, with his head snuggled against Jennifer's arm in the front seat was absolutely speechless, though his eyes were bright and alert and he kept watch of everything they passed. The naps during the day had done their work, and Robin was having the time of his life.

They had traveled thus in silence for perhaps an hour when Jeremy drew up in the shadow of a group of trees by the roadside and pointed up to a big rambling building on the top of a slope. "There's your hospital, Try. Hop to it! Slide up to the door on the grass, and keep in the shadow. Don't make a sound. Lay those darned flowers on the floor in the vestibule in front of the big door, then ring the bell and scoot! Sure you took the card out, Jen?"

"Oh, yes!" gasped Jennifer.

"Okay, then, Tryon, get around in the shadow of the building so they won't see you even if they come out. Then you meet us down the road. We'll stop again by that big silo, and mind you don't get caught, or we'll all be in the soup!"

This was a job after Tryon's own heart, and he got out gravely and disappeared into the shadows, while Jeremy released the brake and the car began slowly to go down grade.

Silently the children twisted their necks to see when the bell was answered, and try to find Tryon in the darkness. This was the most exciting thing they had ever done. But they didn't see Tryon again after he slid off that top step until they came out to an empty place in the road just beyond the big silo, and there was Tryon nonchalantly waiting in the road.

He climbed quietly in as if he did these things every day, and the younger brother and sisters regarded him with awe. But the silence was upon them deeply, and nobody spoke for a long, long time. There was the night to look at, and the moonlight in and out of the clouds, and the strange little back roads that Jeremy had studied out, and the queer lonely houses gone dark, and the closed filling stations with their pumps like a row of weird old men and women reaching out appealing hands.

At last Jeremy said: "We've come a hundred and seven miles since we left home." He said it with satisfaction in his tone.

Then spoke Heather from the back seat.

"That means we're safe, doesn't it, Jerry? They wouldn't come this far to find us, would they?" There was a tone of anxiety in the little girl's voice that made the older ones realize that they were not the only ones who had been feeling the strain.

Jerry turned with a sorry little grin and glanced at Jennifer, and then said:

"Don't you worry, kid. We'll be all right."

"But Jerry, they couldn't find us now, could they?"

"Well, of course if they broadcasted us, and sent the cops out, that would be something else again. But I don't think they are going to find out we are gone till sometime tomorrow. Uncle Blake won't get Jen's letter till he gets home from New York tomorrow, and the others may not get around to go up to the house till afternoon. Of course they might call up if they had some shceme on hand. And if we didn't answer they'd think the servants were not doing their duty, and they'd get ready to give them a good bawling out. Boy! I'd like to be present when they find out. I'm glad I'm not in Uncle Blake's shoes. Still, maybe he won't tell he's had a letter."

"I wish we knew whether they've found it out and are broadcasting it," said Jennifer. "We'd better keep to the back roads. Have we plenty of gasoline?"

"Now *you* worry, will you?" growled Jeremy. "What do you think I am? Of course I've got plenty of gasoline, full up, besides some in a couple of bottles in the tool chest, and an oil can strapped among the luggage."

"Say, you're great, brother!"

"Yes, I am not! But I brought the radio from my car. Got it attached. Turn that button and see what you can get. Fixed it so we could get police reports."

In wonder they turned on the radio quite softly and listened to the mysterious night calls, warnings of fights in various places, a man asleep on a back porch to be investigated, a shooting affair, a hold-up! They listened a long time, but there was no suggestion that seven Graeme children had stolen forth from their ancestral home and were lost out in the world in the night. No uncles and aunts as yet on the warpath! And Robin, at least, was sound asleep, with Karen running a close second to his regular breathing.

The night went on and the moon waned, and Jeremy fairly fell over with sleep.

Suddenly Jennifer came to herself.

"Jerry," she whispered, with a quick look behind, "stop the car and you slip out and come around this side. Take Robin in your lap and I'll slide over and drive. You are fairly dead with sleep."

Jeremy slowed down and stopped, but no one woke up. He came around and gathered Robin in awkward strong arms, and Jennifer slipped into his place and took the wheel. Then they were on again, into an unknown night.

"Keep on this same road," murmured Jeremy sleepily. "If anything comes along wake me up."

Then his head and Robin's snuggled together and he dozed off.

And now Jennifer, for the first time really alone since the tragic death of her parents, had a chance to think clearly. As her brain cleared from sleep and she drove on in the darkness, heaven and earth seemed to get together and make her stand in awe. She had never thought so much about living before.

She had to go all through that awful experience of getting the word about the disaster, and the tragedy that followed, and then on through each day till she sat again in the library and was roused from her sorrow by Aunt

Petra's voice and the inexorable words of them all. Well, she had frustrated them! At least she hoped she had, for the time anyway. They might keep on hunting, and eventually might find them, but the days would be going by and her majority would be almost at hand. Then surely, *surely* she would have a right to say what should become of her darling brothers and sisters! It seemed to her that she had never realized before how she loved them.

How those outrageous aunts had been disposing of them all so calmly. *Had* they any right? Well, anyway, if she found out that they did have rights she would take the children and run to the ends of the earth with them before she would let them come under any auntly power. It couldn't be that daddy had realized any danger like that. He would surely have done something to prevent it!

Then it came over her what the aunts had said about herself. How they had so easily settled her fate to marry Peter! Peter! She almost seemed to hate him now, just because the whole thing had been so definitely arranged for her.

And of course Aunt Petra, or Aunt Majesta must have talked to Peter, or he never would have come around at such a time as this and made those propositions about getting married right away and going away to Europe where she wouldn't have to be bothered with her family at all. What did he think she was anyway, that she would consent to do a thing like that!

Then she thought of her father and mother and lifted her eyes to the blackness of the sky. Her heart cried out, as if those two who were gone from her forever could hear her thoughts.

"Oh, daddy! Oh, mother! You know I wouldn't do a thing like that to your dear babies!" Over and over she said it to herself, and more and more she felt she despised Peter.

She had never thought much about Peter, except that he was good fun to go about with. It hadn't entered her head to think of loving him. She wasn't thinking of love yet, she had merely been having a good time. And now the good times were all over, and grave living had begun. If she could only get away with this act, and keep the children safely away from those cormorants who were so determined to get their hands upon everything and everyone! If she could only hold out until the time was up and she was of age, what did it matter whether she ever got married or not? She certainly wouldn't want to marry Peter. If she ever did marry it must be somebody like her father. But probably there weren't any more men in the world like daddy. And if there weren't, she wouldn't ever marry at all.

Having settled that she laid aside the thought of Peter as an unpleasant topic, and began to consider where and what they should do in the immediate future.

Jerry of course must go back to college in the fall. It wouldn't do to have him fall behind; there would be a terrible family row. But of course by that time they would be at home again, and she could manage all right as soon as her majority was once established and she had made them all understand that she was mistress of the family. She wouldn't stand for having them interfere, even with advice. She might make some mistakes of course, but that was up to her.

In the back seat Hazel was asleep with her head back on the cushions, and with Karen's head in her lap. Karen's knees were curled up. And in the middle seats Heather and Tryon, backs hunched against the locked doors, heads against the windows, were asleep. By Jennifer's side Jeremy with Robin soundly sleeping in his arms, had his head back, his eyes closed as if he were dead to the world. But Jeremy wasn't asleep now. The change to another seat had only sharpened his senses.

This was Jeremy's hour to think.

All the afternoon, ever since Jennifer had told him what the relatives were planning, he had done a lot of practical thinking about ways and means for their immediate safety and exit, and if his dead father could have been there and talked with him he would have been sure to commend him for his sensible plans. But now, the family was well on its way, and, the immediate hurry over, Jeremy had opportunity to do some thinking for himself. How was all this going to affect him personally?

When the accident had first happened he had been aware only of horror and loss. Now as he looked through the night at his own future and saw it emerge dimly from a fog of uncertainty, a number of things stood out plainly that he had not even visioned dimly at first.

There was the fact that he was the oldest son. Jennifer was older, of course, and her majority would set them free probably, from the interference of the relatives, to make their own plans. But he was the oldest son. And while he might not so soon be counted as a legal dependence for the rest, still there were things a son could do, should do, for his orphaned brothers and sisters, that a girl, no matter how wise and willing she might be, couldn't be expected to do, things a girl would not even realize were necessary. Therefore it was up to him to stick around and do them. He had done quite a number of them that afternoon, though he did not realize that they had been unusual. He had thought of things that a man would think of, and a girl might not. He had looked after things his father always did. As a little boy he had often been with him and questioned him about what he was doing and why. These things had naturally come to his mind with the sudden pressure for maturity on his part. It was as if a vacancy had been there, his father's vacancy, and there wasn't even a servant to step in and take it, so he had taken it. The functions were, most of them, obvious. He had somehow known what he ought to pack for himself and Tryon, just how to arrange for extra baggage, how to proceed stealthily about filling and preparing the car, how to prepare for contingencies, how to study the map and hunt out back roads, little traveled; where to plan to stop for necessities.

But now that they were away, and the route was all planned out, he began to see vistas opening ahead. They would go on now, and somehow get through the three months before Jennifer was of age, and they would finally emerge from oblivion and come back to their home and begin life again, of course. But Jeremy saw that even then his work would not be done. He was the man of the family, even if Jennifer was the one who would come of age first, and he must take his part, and protect her as well as the younger children. He couldn't go back to his college! So that was the thing he had been feeling, unidentified, in the back of his mind all day, was it?

Well, it was all right. That was to be expected. He couldn't go off to a distant college and leave them all by themselves, even if he wasn't legally equipped with years enough to make him a real protector.

Of course, too, he couldn't stop college. No one would stand for that. The horde of relatives would rise up in a mob-rage and down him. He couldn't get away with stopping college. And of course he knew it wouldn't be the right thing either. Since there was money enough to finance it, and since it had been his father's wish, his father's son must have the right education. But he didn't have to get it nearly a thousand miles away from the rest of the family, now that they were orphaned. There was a university in their own city to which he could go. The college he had planned for had been his own choice, but there was no reason whatever why he couldn't change it all and stick around home. The university in the city had just as high a reputation as the one in the far west.

So Jeremy thrashed that out all by himself. Definitely he decided in the dark hours of that night that he would arrange for that change before any meddlesome uncles and aunts could butt in and say what he ought to do. He would show them that he was a man to make his own decisions, even though he wasn't of age yet.

Then too there was another thing to think about, and that was Jennifer. She was through college, and that was a help. Good for Jennifer! She certainly was smart, finishing so young! But there was another thought that was disquieting, and that was Peter Willis!

Did Jennifer care for that poor fish? His heart sank. If she did, there wasn't a thing he could do, was there?

And just then Jennifer's thoughts were on the same

subject again. Why was it that the memory of Peter made her uncomfortable? Was it Peter himself, or was it just the foregone conclusions that her aunts had uttered? She must get that straightened out in her mind and understand it. She couldn't have it hanging around tormenting her like something she had evaded, something she hadn't been fair with.

Of course Peter had been dictatorial, annoying, possessive, as if he owned her, and she realized that that had a great deal to do with her resentment at him. But *did* he own her in any way? Had his companionship become anything definite to her, so that he had a right to presume to think for her?

But even as the question presented itself to her mind memory brought back sharply Peter's utter disregard of her young brothers and sisters, showing that he had no conception whatever of her own feeling of loyalty to them. That might be explainable by the fact that he had no brothers and sisters of his own, and might not understand what family ties were. It might be that when these things were explained to him his attitude would be different, but she found herself gravely doubting it. Peter was essentially selfish. A quick glance backward through the years of her acquaintance with him showed that plainly. When a person was born selfish did he ever get over it? Did she want to pin her faith to a young man who thought for *himself*, first, and foremost, and *always?*

To be honest, she realized that he was selfish even in his professed love for her. He hadn't asked what she would like to do. He had suggested that they get married at once so that they could run away from all responsibilities and have a good time. He hadn't suggested that he would like to share her responsibilities, and help her to love and care for the orphaned sisters and brothers. He had only looked bored, and talked about schools, even for a mere baby like Robin. No, she couldn't think of Peter as ever taking an interest in, and growing to really love, her family. If he knew what she was doing now he would laugh at her for a fool. If he should meet her now out on this dark unlit way, he would merely try to block her path, and even telegraph at once for some of those domineering relatives to put a stop to her foolishness. He would never feel that he must help her, and try to make the way easy for her to take care of the children.

So, if he was like that, was it conceivable that she could ever possibly love him? And it she didn't love him of course she couldn't endure it to marry him.

Money? Yes, he had slews of money. But then she probably had enough of that herself to get along on, and even if she didn't, what was money? One couldn't love a man for his money. And money wouldn't ever make a happy home.

Thoughtfully, as she gazed out into the night, she remembered the thrill that had come to her, tired though she was, with the little sleeping brother, dear and warm in her arms, his sweet young breath like clover blossoms wafting now and then against her cheek. She tried to consider the young man who earlier that evening had urged her to come to his home and forget her dear ones. Urged her to consider going away with him, and leaving behind all the burdens that disaster had brought upon her life.

Peter was extremely good-looking, it is true. She had at times been intrigued by that. It had amused her to realize that her escort was one of the handsomest young men in town. Oh, the way he could look at one with those great melting eyes of his, under the long silky lashes, eyes full of deep admiration, eyes full of adoring love! At least that was what she used to think it was in the days when she was proud to go with him. But was it real love for her? Or was it just admiration of something he thought would bring pleasure and honor to himself? Was there something hard and selfish even in his love?

The smile on his full well-shaped lips! How it used often to stir her! Yet that smile today somehow had not stirred. Those lips had looked too full and petted, like the lips of a spoiled boy. Had the vision she had had of him this afternoon been one of disillusioning?

Well, the future might possibly bring some better view again, but somehow she felt pretty sure of herself that so far she was not in love with Peter Willis.

If only the brother and sister sitting there so silently in the dark could have looked into one another's thoughts, what relief it might have been, and perhaps what an enlightenment for both of them.

But Jeremy went on worrying about "that chump, Peter," and wondering if there was anything he could possibly do about it, and Jennifer went on trying to be honest with herself and not too hard on Peter.

8

Suddenly as she drove along through the night Jennifer was weeping, the tears pouring down and dropping on her dress, on her hands, on the wheel. It was the first time she had wept since that awful hour in the library when she had heard the aunts discussing their affairs, and the whole overwhelming change in their lives came over her. How terrible it all was! Suppose they shouldn't succeed in evading the aunts after all. Suppose they should find them and bring them back, and fix things so that they could bend them to their will!

Suppose they should take little Robin and send him off to a school all by himself! Just a baby! Oh, what was the use of living?

Firmly she set her lips, and caught the bitter salt tears. The taste of them was awful in her mouth, like the bitterness that had come to all their lives. Daddy and mother gone and only herself and Jerry to stand between the others and the world! She caught her breath in a little quick sob, and then Jerry turned and looked at her through the darkness.

They were traveling through woods, and there was no visible sky, even overhead, so it was thick darkness on all sides.

But Jerry put out his hand and touched her face and startled her.

"Kid, you're bawling!" he said gently, almost tenderly. She had never heard Jerry speak that way before. It was as if he were older, were almost like an elder brother, and wanted to comfort her. And suddenly the thought of comfort from him overwhelmed her, and she almost broke down.

But that must not be! Besides, she couldn't drive if she broke down. She must conquer this.

"I'm—all—right—Buddie!" she gasped out with a choking little voice. And then she lifted a brave young hand and reached over to pat his hand.

"Say, Jerry, where are we supposed to be going?" she asked suddenly. "Where does this road lead? Or—are we just—*going?*" She tried to summon a little laugh, and he grinned in the darkness.

"We're going to the boat!" he said, and tried to watch her face by the fitful light of the dashboard. There was something dogged about his tone of voice, as if it carried a challenge for her objection. He hadn't asked her advice about this. He wasn't at all sure she would approve, but it was the best thing he could think of for a goal.

"To—the—*boat?*" she breathed in amazement. "I—didn't—remember—we *had* a boat! I thought daddy sold it! But—Oh-h! Won't they come right to it? Won't that be one of the first places they will look?"

"No," said Jeremy gravely. "They don't know we have it. Dad did sell the other boat, but that last day when he and I went down to get out the personal things we wanted to keep, dad bought another one. He heard of it through a friend, and we went down that day and bought it. It's away down a hundred and fifty miles farther, even, than the old place, but that's all the better for us I guess. Nobody knows anything about it. Dad bought it from the owner. It's a peach. Jen, you'll like it. I was with dad when he tried it out, and it handles remarkably easy for a boat its size. It's a forty-five footer, twin cabin. It sleeps six, besides crew's quarters, and the extra upholstered seat on the bridge is big enough for one of the kids. Dad figured Try and I could use the crew's bunks. It's fully equipped and of course has quite a load of stuff from the other boat. Bathing suits, and coats and things, besides some games we had the last time we were down, and some blankets mother wanted to keep. You see, dad was figuring on us all going down for six weeks or more this summer."

Jennifer caught her breath again. That was bringing memories near again. If dad could have known *how* they were going down! She hastened to say something, anything so she wouldn't cry again.

"Are you sure it will be safe? Nobody will recognize us?"

"Well, I thought it would be as safe as anything. It's a hideout for a couple of days anyway, till we get our bearings. And of course if we see anyone who might tell where we are we can always run down the bay and land somewhere in a hurry."

"Oh, Jerry, it will be wonderful!" said Jennifer with deep relief in her voice. "We can really get rested. And we can make some plans. I don't know what, but *some!*"

"That's what I thought," said Jerry, "only I wasn't sure how you'd take it. But it was the best thing I could think of on such short notice."

"Oh, yes, and it will be wonderful for the children not to be cooped up in the car all the time. But you said you could run down the bay. Are you sure you can run it?"

"Oh, sure! Dad made me take the wheel part of the time, and learn all the gadgets. It's a pip and no mistake. Dad got this particular boat so we could run it ourselves. He said he didn't want a crew along when we went on a cruise. It's something like the old boat only much larger, to take in the whole family at once. Say, we ought to be getting near there in a little while now."

He snapped on the light and looked at the clock.

"Yes, it's almost morning! Say, Jen, you slip over here and take this kid now and get a little more sleep yourself. You must be all in."

"No," said Jennifer, "I don't feel like sleeping now. If this boat really materializes I can sleep when we get there. You sleep some more yourself. You had a hard day yesterday. Besides, we don't want Robin to wake up yet, and he might if I tried to take him. Jerry, are you sure there won't be people from home down there on their boats? They would be sure to write to somebody they had seen us."

"I think not. Dad left the boat here because he thought it would be more secluded," said the boy. "He asked Captain Andy, the man in charge of the harbor, whose boats were here, and there wasn't a soul he knew. Of course someone might drift in any day, but it isn't likely. It's farther away, and most people don't want to be bothered going so far from home when they run down just for a day or so. Captain Andy is a swell person. Dad took a notion to him right off the bat. And I thought perhaps we'd just tell him about the accident, and say we'd brought the children down here for a few days to get them away from people, and help them not to grieve. I thought I'd tell him that my sister was pretty well broken up and wanted to get away from seeing people who came to call all the time, and ask him not to tell we were here. I think I could work that."

"Oh, that would be good!" sighed Jennifer wistfully. "If you only could work it! But Jerry, you know it may come out in the paper, or on the radio, that we are missing, and if it does we'd have to explain somehow."

"No," said Jerry, "we'd just beat it and they would think we had gone home. There's a nice little radio on the boat and we can keep in touch with things."

"That's wonderful!" said the girl drawing a deep breath of relief. "If people that have died can look back to this earth ours must be glad they left this boat for us."

"Sure thing!" said Jeremy.

"Do you believe they can?" she asked after a minute.

Jeremy was still a minute, and then he answered speculatively:

"Why, I don't know. I never thought anything about it. Sure, I guess they must, or else perhaps they're just asleep. That is, if there is anything afterwards. You see, Jen, I don't think I ever believed anything one way or the other till this happened. I never thought about things. I just took life as it came, the way other fellows do, I 'spose. Had a good time, and that was all I cared. But now this is different. You've *got* to believe something, or you can't stand it."

"I know," said Jennifer thoughtfully. "It's awful if you can't. I remember when I was a very little girl and first found out about death, I used to wonder why people stood for it. I wondered why they didn't do something about it and stop it, drive it out of the world so people would live forever. But of course I soon forgot about it. Not many people I knew died. But—now, well, I don't know what I think. It's startling."

"It sure is! I wonder what dad and mother think now, if they are so they can think at all. It's queer dad didn't ever say something to us about it. He knew death was in the world, and everybody was coming to it sometime or other. He always tried to prepare us for things he thought were ahead for us, but I don't remember that he ever said anything about death."

"Mother taught us to pray, when we were little. At least she taught me to," said Jennifer. "She had more time when I was little, not so many engagements evenings and things. But I remember saying 'Now I lay me' when I could just talk a little."

"Yeah, I remember that, too. She used to come in at night even when she was going somewhere for the evening, and sit by my crib and make me say my prayer, and when I was bad and wouldn't, she'd tell me God wouldn't bless me if I didn't pray to Him. Not that I cared just then whether He blessed me or not of course, but I did care when mother got that hurt look in her eyes, and then for a long time afterwards I used to think of God with that hurt look in His eyes, too, and somehow I thought better of God, I guess, than I would if mother hadn't heard me say my prayers."

"Yes," said Jennifer, "I guess mother believed in God all right. And dad too. I'm sure they did!"

"I 'spose they did. Only they were busy, and they didn't really think things were going to end this way. But Jen, I guess you and I've got to get at it and give these kids something more to go on than we had. Something solid, I mean, that they can bank on if there *is* anything. It's awful desolate when things happen if you don't have anything."

"It certainly is," said Jennifer sorrowfully. "Only I don't just know what we'll tell them. I used to go to church sometimes, but I don't remember that I ever heard anything there that would help. Perhaps I didn't listen. I haven't been much since I went to college. They didn't think so much of church in my college. They seemed to think it was sort of mid-victorian to go to church. But I don't know that it was so bad to be victorian. I think they must have been pretty nice people back in those days when Queen Victoria was living. They didn't seem to drink so much, nor get mushy and silly."

"You've said it! But say, I suppose we could teach the kids whatever it was that dad and mother taught us, even if we don't know much about it. And maybe we'll come on something else to help if we keep our eyes open. But, Jen, there's one thing that bothers me. Maybe I oughtn't to say anything. Maybe it's none of my business. Maybe you'll get mad at me, but I don't mean any harm. Only, if we're in this thing together, and we're going to do right by these kids, we've got to keep straight ourselves, haven't we? We can't just go on and do as we please, and expect them to keep straight without any help, and with us doing as other people do, can we? We've got to watch our step, and not get into any mess we don't want them to get into, haven't we?"

"Why, of course," said Jennifer looking over at him wonderingly, though she could see but the merest outline of his face against the darkness. "Why did you think that would make me cross? What's on your mind, Jerry?"

"Well, if you insist, I'll tell you," said the boy hesitantly. "It's that chump Peter Willis! He's no fit playmate for you, Jen, and I'm telling ya! He's rotten and that's all there is about it. He may be rich and lousy-handsome and all that, but he's not fit for you to wipe your oldest shoes on, not *my sister!* He's drunk half the time, and he goes with the lowest kind of company. Girls too, girls worse than he is, even. I've seen him, and I know what I'm talking about!"

Jennifer turned toward her brother seriously.

"But why the warning, brother? I don't see Peter anywhere around, do you? And I don't seem to have been breaking my neck to run after him, do I?"

"That's all right, Jen, but I came in by the back stairs last night and went up to get my wallet I'd left in my room when I changed my coat, and I couldn't help seeing that chump standing up there on the stairs, daring to follow you up into our private home apartments, and saying things to you about how to manage *our children,* and about *marrying you,* and taking you out of it all to play around in Europe, and let somebody else take the penalty, and I got plenty mad. Talking to my sister that way! And I almost came out of my room and kicked that poor fish downstairs. I did! Daring to talk that way to my sister! If it hadn't been that we were running away, and I didn't want to get into any scrapes that would hinder us, I certainly would have given him plenty! And I would, too, anyhow, if you hadn't been there. You ought to hear the way he talks about some of the girls he takes out! The big fat rotten old fish!"

Suddenly Jennifer put her face down on the wheel and laughed! She wanted to cry too, but she laughed. This was her young brother talking this way about defending her! This was the brother so much younger than herself that she had felt she must care for him! and here he was trying to care for her, warning her against one of the most admired and sought-after young men in the whole city! It gave her a thrill to have Jeremy care. It seemed almost as if it might be the spirit of her dead father come alive in Jerry to protect her, and it was very precious and sweet to her. It brought those unbidden, undesired tears to her eyes. But she laughed, there in the dark, and brushed the tears aside.

"Jerry," she said, laying one hand across the sleeping

Robin to her brother's hand, "you needn't ever worry about me and Peter. I told Peter last night just where to get off. I told him I had no idea of running off and leaving my family to shift for themselves, and that if I were going to get married I certainly would never marry him! But I do appreciate your warning, and of course I didn't know these things you've told me about him, or I never would even have played around with him. I don't like men of that sort, not even boys of that sort who are too young to know better. And of course I wouldn't be angry at you warning me. I think I can pretty well promise you I'm not going to lie down on my job and get married to *any*body, at least not unless you approve. And I think it will be a long time before I ask you to approve anybody. Besides, if you only knew in whose class you've just put yourself!"

She laughed again.

"Aunt Majesta! Can you beat it! *You* arranging for my marriage! You don't know that that was the thing that made me the maddest in their talk yesterday, when I heard those two old hawks marrying me off to Peter! They seemed to think that would be a lot off their hands when they accomplished that. They didn't know that even if I had been particularly crazy about him, which I wasn't, their ideas would have made me actually hate him."

"Great Scott! Jen, I withdraw all my remarks, at least while you continue of that mind, though I will own that if you ever changed and got to favoring Pete, he'd have *me* to deal with, and I don't mean maybe!"

"Well, you can just put that thought out of your head, brother. If that man comes around I'll call you in to protect me. But really, Jerry, I'm not wanting to marry anyone, at least not for years and years. And not then unless I find a man as fine as daddy."

"Righto! When you find one let me know, and I'll withdraw my objections. You will look a long time before you find a man as fine as dad!"

"Yes," said Jennifer with a sad little sigh, "though I hope *you*'ll be like him some day."

"Couldn't have a better model," said Jeremy gravely.

"Here's hoping. But honestly, Jen, I don't know any boys myself that are even started that way. They don't come that way nowadays, I guess."

"I've only met one I thought might be like that some day," said Jennifer with a serious voice.

"One?" said Jeremy with a quick look toward her.

"Oh, it was long ago," said Jennifer in a dreamy voice. "I was just a little girl, and he never thought anything of me of course. He was a great deal older than I was, five years perhaps. But I remember thinking at the time that daddy must have been a boy like that, and I've often thought about him since and wondered why the boys I knew afterwards were not like him."

"Say, this is some revelation, sister. Who was this paragon? I'd like to give him the once-over, and see if my conclusions match up with yours."

"You don't know him, Jerry. He doesn't live around here. I'm not sure where he is any more. I haven't seen him in years."

"What's his name?" asked the boy, still scowling in the dark. "Where did you meet him?"

"His name is Jack Valiant," said Jennifer, her voice still dreamy. "I met him when I was nine, that time I went away up in New England to stay with my old nurse, Kirsty Mac Carne, that time just after Heather was born when mother was so ill. You wouldn't remember that, you were only a little kid then."

"I wasn't so small," said Jerry with dignity. "I remember when you got back. You seemed like a strange person. But get on with your story. What's that got to do with this Jack Valiant?"

"Oh," laughed Jennifer, "he was just a boy who lived next door to Kirsty, up on an old stony farm on the mountain. He brought milk down to Kirsty's every night. But he was as polite and nice to me as if I had been quite grown up. I remember thinking daddy must have been like that when he was a boy. Daddy was always polite, even to children. Even to servants."

"And have you never seen him since then?"

"No," said Jennifer, "but I'd be sure he'd be just the same."

"Well, I guess I don't need to worry about him," said her brother, "just a farmer's boy. He's probably a great lout by this time that you wouldn't look at twice."

"He was very nice-looking," said Jennifer.

"That's what you thought at nine," advised the wise brother. "If you were to see him now he wouldn't be the same."

Jennifer was thoughtful at that.

"Maybe," she said slowly, "but—he was going to college. He was planning for it even then. I heard him talking about it. He had to earn the money himself."

"Well, I shan't begin to get het up about him yet," said Jerry easily. "Time enough if he ever comes into the picture again. I'll concentrate on Pete. He's all I can handle at once."

"Well, I don't suppose you need worry about him. I was just a little girl. He never was anything to me. He took me fishing once to the brook, and he brought me a gray kitten to play with, but that was all. I was just thinking that perhaps there were a few boys like daddy. I don't believe there are many."

They were silent for a few thoughtful moments, and then Jennifer spoke.

"You don't really remember Kirsty, do you, Jerry? Kirsty was wonderful!"

"Sure, I remember Kirsty!" said the young man. "She used to make strings of paper dolls, and soldiers, out of the edges of the newspaper, and stand them up on the table and blow them away."

Jennifer smiled.

"Yes, I remember," she said, "and how we used to laugh when they went whirling down on the floor! Mother used to say she was the best nurse we ever had. She could trust her perfectly. I wish we could get someone like that for Robin and Karen!"

"Robin's too old for a nurse!" said the brother. "But it would be great if we could hunt up Kirsty sometime and get her for a housekeeper or something. A person like that would sort of keep a house together and look after things when we get started again."

"Yes," said Jennifer, "but we don't even know if she's alive yet."

"Well, we'll see when this business is over and we can get back home. Now, Jen, if you still insist on driving awhile longer, I'm going to sign off for a few minutes, for I'm just groggy with sleep!"

So the night went on, and Jennifer partly dreaming of the past, and grieving over the days that were gone forever, drove on through the dark woods, and past occasional little detached dark dwellings, driving into a new life and a new world, leaving all that had made the former life glad. What would the new life bring, she wondered?

9

Aunt Petra had gone to the telephone around ten o'clock that evening and called up the Graeme house. When they didn't answer she gave the operator a fine line of argument that would have done credit to a high pressure business executive.

"Operator! Operator! Why don't you ring that number? I certainly shall have to report you if this goes on many more minutes. I've been standing here for fifteen minutes holding this receiver, and I've had no service at all. What in the world is the matter? They don't answer? You've been ringing them all this time? Well, I didn't hear you ring, but I suppose I've got to take your word for it. Please ring them again, *now*. Yes, I said ring them again! They *must* be there. Of course they are there! I *know* they are there! They've just had a death in the family! Two in fact. They wouldn't be out the first night after a funeral, would they? Well, I *know* they are *there!* Is it possible that the much boasted telephone service has failed? Have I got to get someone to take the car and go *after* them? What? Twenty minutes? No, I don't want you to call them in twenty minutes, I want them *now*, and it's your business to rouse them. If you were ringing that bell in the right way I *know* they would hear it! Asleep? Not they. They are the kind that sit up till all hours. What? Who? The chief operator? Well, I suppose I can talk to her if you won't do anything more about this, but if I do I certainly will make it plain just how inadequate *you* have been!"

Aunt Petra had it out with the chief operator, gave her several pieces of her mind, and at last hung up and came back into the living room indignantly.

Her sister Majesta Best and her brother-in-law Pemberton Best were sitting there in large comfortable chairs. They had been taking dinner with her and discussing the turn of affairs that day in the Graeme situation. It had been to settle some trivial point about what had happened last week just before the Graemes met their tragic death that Aunt Petra had gone to the telephone to call up Jennifer and ask a few questions.

She arrived back in the living room with her eyes flashing fire and her chin up. It wasn't going to be very pleasant for the telephone company the next morning, that was plain to be seen, nor for the young Graemes when Aunt Petra got into touch with them.

"Well, I declare, things are coming to a pretty pass when you can't even depend on the telephone company! And I own some stock in the company too. I certainly shall take steps to get rid of it tomorrow unless they dismiss that operator. Yes, and the chief operator too. Did you hear what I said to them, Majesta?"

"Yes, we heard. We couldn't well help it!" said Majesta, nodding her head sleepily. She had eaten heavily of the duck dinner with accessories, and was beginning to be drowsy, and to feel that all her garments were too tight. Her answer was almost in the tone of a purr.

"We *heard!*" echoed Pemberton Best, touching his long fingertips together as he rested his elbows on the arms of the chair he was enjoying. "It's outrageous of course, Petra, but you can't do anything about it. Those large companies are so thoroughly entrenched in their own wealth that the mere individual is helpless, at their mercy. However, Petra, had you reflected that it may be quite true that nobody answered? If the children were out—say, to some of their young friends' houses, you wouldn't find the servants staying home to answer the phone. They were probably off, out of the house, as soon as the children.

You can't expect servants to stay at home and mind the stuff when the master and mistress are dead!"

"Of course not!" said Petra indignantly. "And those servants always were horribly spoiled. I've often told Miriam that she wasn't half strict enough with them. Though I think it was mainly John Graeme's fault. He overpaid them, and servants when they are overpaid always get insolent and lazy. If I had my way I'd get rid of every one of them, and shut up most of the house. But of course since the law seems to have the upper hand just now I'll have to wait till we can get things settled and be really in command. But as for the telephone company, I certainly intend to do something about that immediately, tomorrow morning! And as for the servants, I shall make it my business to interview every one of them tomorrow morning also, and let them understand just what they should do, law or no law! I got in some good work on the cook yesterday, before I knew anything about that ridiculous will, and the guardianship. I told the cook not to have expensive things like roast chicken when it was just the children, and no company. Those children eat too much. But the servants eat more. You ought to have seen how many chickens that cook was getting ready for their dinner! But of course I suppose the servants were going to get the biggest part of them."

"Well, Petra, I shouldn't advise you to do much meddling with affairs until Blakefield gets home!" said Pemberton Best. "You know he is the only one who really has a right to say what shall be done, and what shall not. You don't want to get into a snarl with the law, you know. It would be better for you to work whatever you want corrected in the household through quiet casual suggestions to Blakefield. He's a reasonable soul, and I'm sure he'll be glad of help. He'll probably be utterly confused and confounded by such heavy responsibility."

"Not he!" said Petra sharply. "Didn't you hear the way he spoke several times today? Asserting so importantly that the children ought not to be separated? Speaking right out against Abigail Storm, calling her a hard woman! I declare I couldn't believe my senses when I heard the lawyer read right out that *he* was to be guardian. John Graeme must have taken leave of his senses to appoint a man like that to take entire charge of all those children! Especially when it involves such a large fortune! I think John Graeme was crazy, and I shan't hesitate to say so in court if it becomes necessary. But I don't anticipate it will go that far. I'm going down to see my own lawyer in the morning of course before I proceed in any way, but after that I intend to go and have a session with Blakefield as soon as he returns from New York, and if I can't bring him to reason then I shall see what the law can do. We can't let those poor innocent children be neglected, and their fortune devastated. We'll have to take it in our own hands, and break that will! The fact is that both Majesta and I can bring plenty of proof that John Graeme was not of sound mind, if we care to go that far. You know he was always odd, always did the opposite from what any other sensible person would have done. Too easy-going, too sentimental you might almost call it, too filled with irrational ideas for the betterment of the world. Too fanatical sometimes. Oh, there are plenty of things Majesta and I know."

"I wouldn't get into it, Petra!" said Uncle Pemberton, patting the tips of his delicate fingers together serenely, "and I sincerely hope Majesta will have the good sense not to meddle with the matter. It is never wise to get into lawsuits."

"Now, look here, Pemberton," said Majesta Best, lifting her chin and looking her husband in the eye with such a glint in her own that his mouth should have been utterly closed for the time being on any wisdom he might be disposed to offer, "I shall certainly do what I think is right in this matter, no matter *what* you think or say! I know my duty where it concerns my relatives, and I certainly do not call it meddling when it concerns the affairs of my dear niece's children. I shall do my duty!"

"Your duty is to keep out of things that are not your

business," persisted the old man sadly. "I think I have often told you that before, Majesta, and I hope you will not let Petra's over-zealous nature drive you into something that will make trouble for us all. Blakefield is a good man, and a man of common sense, and if I know anything at all about him I feel sure he will resent any interference on the part of any women, whether in the family or out of it."

Then Majesta Best arose in her might and turned toward her sister.

"Petra, let us go into the other room and discuss this matter. Pemberton does not understand our position, and it is not wise to discuss it before him. I know my duty and I intend to do it, whatever Pemberton may say!" and she swept from the room with a royal air, followed by her brisker sister. Pemberton was left, as he had been left many times, to beat off time on his finger tips and wait until Majesta was ready to go home, knowing that his unwanted advice would bring him but the punishment of coldness and utter silence on the part of his wife for the next few hours. He sighed deeply, and wondered why women were so anxious to take on responsibilities that were not even remotely theirs and could not possibly bring them any rewards. And gradually as he meditated to the accompaniment of the subdued vigor of the conversation of the sisters in the other room, his eyes closed, and he slept.

But Majesta and Petra were not sleeping. They were evolving a plan by which to intimidate Blakefield Graeme, and set the Graeme children free from his care, so that they two could manage the entire flock, and also the estate, and get a goodly share out of it for themselves.

"Well, there is one thing certain," finished Majesta as they rose by common consent to go back to Pemberton, "Blakefield is no kind of a guardian for those children, and we must act quickly before he gets to perpetrating anything peculiar. Now, Petra, I think you ought to call up the house again, or I shan't sleep all night thinking of those poor little orphans."

"Yes, of course I'll call again. If they all went out, certainly some of them ought to be at home by this time. That Stanton takes such airs upon himself! But I'll see that he understands that his rating as a butler is low if I find out he has stayed out all the evening and left the house without a soul to answer the telephone."

Majesta lingered while her sister tried the telephone again, with as little result as before.

At last nonplused, she turned from the telephone and looked thoughtfully at her sister.

"You don't suppose, Madge, that they could have gone to the Willises, do you? You know I had a talk with Peter this afternoon and he told me that he was planning to ask Jennifer to come over to the house tonight and stay for a few days. He was going to suggest they get married right away and run off to Europe somewhere. In fact *I* practically suggested that and he seemed quite willing. Maybe Jennifer went off to Willises and left the children with the servants, and the servants have either gone off for the evening, or gone to bed. But you'd think Stanton would expect to stay up to a reasonable hour to answer the door and the telephone. You would think he'd know that without telling. But perhaps he listened around and found out that Blakefield was the children's guardian, and he wouldn't be afraid of Blake. He'd know he could get up a good alibi with Blake. Miriam always seemed to think she could trust that Stanton, but I always said she'd find out some day he wasn't so wonderful as she thought. I certainly shall give that man a piece of my mind in the morning."

"Well, why don't you call Willises, Petra? If Jennifer is staying there it will ease your mind, and sort of open the way for you to go over everything with the servants in her absence."

"That's an idea! I will."

So Petra called the Willis house, and Majesta stood and waited. It was some time to wait, for the Willis servants seemed to have retired also. And even when the butler finally answered the result was not helpful. The household had retired, he said, all but Mr. Peter, and he didn't know where he was, nor when he would come in. No, he didn't think Miss Graeme had been there, and he had heard nothing of her being expected. So at last the dominant aunt hung up and gazed at her sister again.

"I should think there might be other servants besides the Graeme's that needed disciplining?" she remarked vexedly.

"Oh, well, I wouldn't worry," said Majesta Best yawning. "Peter likely has taken Jennifer out somewhere, and he'll bring her safely back. Just let the whole matter rest till morning. It's not your lookout anyway. If anything happens it will be just a good lesson to Blakefield, and perhaps he'll be ready to ask for a little advice now and then."

"Yes, well, believe me I'm going to make it hot for him as soon as he gets home from New York," said Petra.

"Oh, New York. He went to New York, didn't he? How do you know that he didn't take his group of orphans with him?" This from Majesta, lifting her chin and snuffing the battle from afar again. "Perhaps that's the explanation."

Petra eyed her startled. Then her brow cleared again.

"No," she said quite decidedly, "he didn't take them with him! I talked with Jennifer myself after he left, and so did you. She said, you know, they were going to bed early and get a good rest. It might have been true of course. Only somehow I never did trust that Jennifer. She always seemed to have some ulterior motive well masked in righteousness, so good you had to suspect it."

"Well, maybe it is true this time for a change," said Majesta, yawning again. "Maybe they all went to bed, and let the servants go out. But in the morning if I were you I would advise that girl that she should never let *all* the servants go out at once. There should always be one there to answer the door and the telephone. Just let her understand what inconvenience she has caused us. Well, now I think Pem and I had better go home. It's really been quite an exciting day, and I feel the need of rest. Good night,

Petra, and don't worry too much. It will all come out right. I really think you'll have no trouble with Blakefield if you can only go at him in a gentle manner and flatter him a little. He is one who has to be managed. It's humiliating, I know, when our family was really so much higher in the social order than his, but if you want an easy victory it's certainly best to use a little finesse."

But after they were gone Petra Holbrook tried the telephone again. At least she would have plenty of gesture recorded to report in the morning.

And then, not satisfied with that, she lay awake for some time fiercely contending in her heart with Uncle Blakefield who had taken his guardianship so much as a matter of course, and gone off so inconsequentially, after it was announced, refusing to contend with them about it, just quietly excusing himself from their company and taking his way to New York, professing a business appointment. As if any mere business appointment were of importance just now when the guardianship of a princely fortune was at stake. He took it so calmly that it couldn't be possible that he realized how great the fortune was. Strange, she thought in passing, that mere John Graeme had been able to amass a fortune like that! Miriam really had done well for herself, in spite of all their warning to the contrary! What a pity she couldn't have lived to enjoy the fortune now, instead of leaving it all for a stupid old man like Blakefield to administer, and no telling what he would do!

And then suddenly it occurred to her that Lutie might have come and got the children and taken them home. But that of course wouldn't account for the servants not being there.

Petra Holbrook got herself upon her well preserved limbs and pranced over to the telephone. She would never humor herself enough to have the telephone moved to her bedside as that fool of a Lutie did, but she remembered with satisfaction that Lutie had her telephone close beside her bed so it wouldn't matter if it was late. She wouldn't have to get out of bed to answer it, even if she had gone to bed early for once in her life. So Petra called Lutie's number, and demanded to know if the Graeme children were with her.

"With me? My goodness, no, Petra! You must be crazy! As if I would have that whole hoard of children! Even if they would come I wouldn't have them. You know what I think of those young turks! My goodness, no! What's got into you, Petra? Do you know what time of night it is? After all we've been through today! And you calling up in the middle of the night to know where they are! Why do you think they're not at home and in their beds? The very idea! Even such wild young things as they are must get tired sometimes, and especially when they've been through the shock of death. Even they must feel that, tough little nuts as they are! For heaven's sake, Petra, go to bed and forget it. What's the matter with you?"

"Well, Lutie, Majesta and I have been calling up several times this evening to talk with Jennifer, and we haven't been able to get an answer. I just thought that maybe she was with you."

"No, she's not with me! And isn't likely to be. And if she was couldn't it wait till morning? I really don't see the point, Petra. I thought you were practical. You can't do anything about it tonight, anyway, can you? I don't see why you don't think those children need some sleep. They can't sit up all night to answer telephones."

"Well, Lutie, I was thinking about the servants. Surely some of them ought to be able to answer the telephone. I thought I'd just make sure whether you knew anything about them, because I think we ought to be able to check up on what's going on. You know Jerry and Jennie can't really be counted on to take any responsibility."

"Yes? Well, what's that got to do with tonight? Were you trying to imply that I ought to wake up Adrian and send him out in the car to hunt those wild Graemes? Because I *won't*. Adrian has one of his frightful sick headaches, and if I wake him up he'll have it all day tomorrow, and that's the only time when he is unreasonable, when he has one of those frightful sick headaches. I wish you'd hang up, Petra. I'm afraid he'll hear me talking, and wake up, and then the damage will be done."

"Oh, certainly, Lutie! And thank you for being so helpful!" said Petra in a sour voice, as she hung up and pattered back to her bed. But she told herself as she climbed in and settled herself for sleep, that she was thankful she wasn't as unpleasant as Lutie. Selfish thing! And she further ruminated as she drifted into oblivion that Lutie needn't think if there was any division of the Graeme treasures when things were sold that *she* would get any. That she, Petra, would see that she didn't have a chance at anything.

Then she fell into the sound sleep of one who has done her duty.

Off in the blackness of the night the Graeme children were traveling on into their own life, and all those servants who ought to have been answering the Graeme telephone that night were far and away out of the ken of any of those interfering relatives. And the dim faraway stars looked wisely down upon a tempestuous sleeping world that would presently wake and go at their chosen activities again when morning began to dawn.

10

Gray dawn was beginning to steal over the earth when Jennifer, driving, came at last to the edge of the wooded road, and swept out into a wider way. There was a vacant empty stretch of dim high grass on each side, and now and then a clump of bushes.

There were no lights anywhere except those faraway stars that seemed so dim. But over toward the east a band of dim light seemed to be breaking the darkness. It was impossible to forecast where she was or what might be ahead. There might be a body of water not far off, but there was nothing to show it yet, no luminous stretch, no glimmer of brightness, nor even any stretch of darkness that might be water.

She drove on because there was no turning anywhere. Jerry had given no directions. If she came to a turning she would have to stop, or else wake Jerry, and she hated to do that. She knew how tired he must be.

His head was back, his face turned slightly from her, and she could dimly see that his whole body was slumping wearily. His arms must be very tired. She was so tired herself that she could hardly keep her eyes open. Oh, would there be a way to sleep pretty soon, or would they find when they came near the boat that someone had started a search for them, and they would have to go on, tired as they were?

Occasionally now they passed a little house by the side of the road, still dark, for it was so early no one would be up yet. And now the sky was showing a decided streak of light, which gradually grew rosy as they went on. A new day was coming. What would it bring to them? Would those awful relatives pursue them, and drag them back to be parceled out among themselves or to schools, or worse still, sent up to the farm under Abigail Storm? Oh, that couldn't be! It *shouldn't* be! *She* wouldn't stand for it! She would hunt up some of daddy's friends and make such a protest that somebody would have to do something. But of course the best thing would be not to be caught until she was of age, and had a right to say what should be done. She wondered just how much power guardians had, and wished she had stayed in the library long enough to find that out. But then she couldn't of course, for if Aunt Petra and Aunt Majesta had found her there, and known that she had heard all they had said, the matter would have come to a head, and she would not have been able to do a thing. They would have taken the children right away from her influence and made it appear that she was bad for them. They would undoubtedly have had their way, and it would have done no good whatever to protest. She knew those aunts.

She began to wonder if there was a guardian. They had spoken as if they expected there was. And if there was one who could it be? Did they always appoint relatives as guardians, or were guardians usually lawyers, or business men? She was quite ignorant of the custom in cases like theirs. If she could only get to a dictionary or better, an encyclopedia in a public library she might be able to look up the subject and find out something. But what would she look up? How would she start? Would the word guardian bring her any light? Well, she couldn't go to a library at present to find out, and anyway, what difference did it make? They were off, and they just must not get caught, that was the whole thing. When she was of age she would see what the law was, but meantime she would hide those children where the aunts couldn't get their hands on them, if she had to lose everything else she cared for. And that did not include Peter Willis, because she had definitely decided now that she did not want Peter Willis in her life any more!

The sky was growing lighter now, and the far dim stars were paling more and more. The morning star which had been bright and cheery when she swept out of the woods, was now so dim she could scarcely make it out. The dawn was coming up beautifully. Jennifer didn't remember ever to have watched the dawn come up alone before. Now and again coming home from occasional parties there had been a dawn, but there had been a lot of noisy companions along, and nobody looked at the sky. Besides it was usually in a city where there wasn't any sky to speak of. Here it was high and wide. The rose of dawn was creeping higher every minute, and it thrilled her.

There were more houses now along the roadside. There was a filling station, but it didn't seem to be open yet. She glanced at the gauge. There was still some gas. Was it far to the boat, she wondered? Would there be gas there? And where would they park the car? Of course the aunts—even the uncles—wouldn't be likely to know the number of the car license, not that car anyway, because none of them likely knew it existed, unless it was Aunt Petra. Aunt Petra never missed anything.

There! There was a house with a light in the kitchen! Now people were beginning to get up. There seemed to be a side street on ahead a little way. Would she have to wake up Jerry? Poor Jerry. She glanced at him, and a moment later he stirred. Then he spoke and his eyes were wide open, alert.

"Turn left here! Cross the bridge, and on about a couple of miles farther," he said.

Then he shifted Robin and setting him down in the seat between them, pushed his hair back from his forehead.

"Wake up, old man!" he said gently. "Going to cross a bridge and see some boats. Going over a river, old man. Better get your eyes open. You'll miss something."

Tryon stirred in the middle seat and sat up alertly, stretching his stiff limbs and blinking around in the dawning.

"Yeah?" he said. "What bridge, Jerry? Is it a draw bridge?"

"Why, I believe it is," said Jeremy.

"Fwat's a dwaw bwidge?" said Robin, speaking out of the depths of a deep sleep, and squinting one eye open to gaze about him.

"It's a bridge they can draw up in the air out of the way, to let a tall sailboat, or a steamer, go under."

"Ship?" said Heather, suddenly sitting bolt upright and staring straight ahead. "We aren't going to Europe are we, Jennifer?"

"Well, no, not this morning," laughed Jennifer, so weary that she had either to laugh or cry.

Jeremy gave her a quick keen look.

"Stop the car, Jen, and give me the wheel," he ordered. "You're all in. I ought not to have slept so long."

"Oh yes, you ought," said Jennifer. "I'm absolutely all right, and if it's only two or three miles farther why not let me finish?"

"Well, it's a little farther than that," said the boy. "Besides I know where I want to park the car, and you don't. I've got it all thought out."

So Jennifer stopped the car and took the other seat, and Jeremy took the wheel.

The river lay still like a ribbon of silver in the dawning with flecks of rose color shimmering on its surface. Little boats here and there, masts penciled against a sky of promise, a soft melody of wood-thrushes at matins on shore, gulls stirring against the beauty of the morning. The children, still drowsy with sleep, stared in wonder at it all, gazing in silence, as if it might still be a rosy dream. Even little Karen roused and sat up to look.

Then they swept on down the road, through a little town, past more fields of tall grasses, and out into the open road again, stopping at a filling station that was just opening, because there was less risk now than later in the day. A station that had been closed all night wouldn't be on the lookout for their license number. "Don't make any noise!" Jerry warned them as the service boy came out to them, and they all shrank down in their seats again until they were out and away. Then Tryon spoke.

"Why not?" he asked his brother.

"Can't you figure that out, kid?" said Jerry. "We don't want to attract attention to us so that they will remember we have been here, and report which way we were going, in case some of the aunts get busy and try to find us."

"I see," said Tryon, and looked wisely at his sisters.

"Yes," said Jeremy at second thought, "and that reminds me. If at any time on this journey you hear me say: 'Scram!' it means you are to pipe down and shut up, and be as out of sight as possible. Get me?"

They all nodded solemnly at him, and looked a bit like a squad of young soldiers about to enter battle.

"You know," explained Jennifer, "that'll probably be when Jerry sees somebody he thinks might know us and go home and tell Aunt Petra where we are."

"Oh! Yes!" they chorused with a relieved smile, and then added one by one, "Okay!"

In ten minutes more Jerry came within sight of another bridge, and suddenly turned right, sweeping into a short road which led behind several tall white buildings with glimpses of a river beyond.

"Here we are!" he announced in a tone that carried relief mingled with a bit of excitement.

"Was that anuvver dwaw bwidge?" questioned Robin, quietly alert now.

"No, that was just a plain bridge. Don't you see there aren't any towers or weights to haul it up with?"

"Wes," said Robin turning to study the bridge. "Why isn't it a dwaw bwidge?"

"Oh, because this river isn't important enough to have big ships on it, and the bridge doesn't have to rise up to let them through."

"Oh," said Robin solemnly, and then added with a sigh, "Well, I'm hungwy!"

"Of course you are!" said Jennifer with a smile, "and we're going to have a nice breakfast pretty soon. Just you be patient."

"Do theys have bweakfast in that big white house there?" he asked after a moment of reflection.

"No, we have it with us in the car, but we have to wait till Jerry gets ready to unpack things. We're going to eat it in a boat."

"Ummmm!" said Robin round-eyed.

"Really, sister, are we?" whispered Hazel leaning across.

"Pipe down all of you till I find out how the land lies," said Jerry, swinging out of the car and disappearing between the two houses out onto the slip in front.

They sat very still waiting. They could hear a strange gruffly pleasant voice talking, and then Jerry's, and presently Jerry came toward them again, and they caught a glimpse of a big stranger with a kindly smile looking toward them.

"Okay!" said Jerry as he came back and began to unbuckle the straps that held the baggage to the running board. "Captain Andy says our boat is here, and ready for service. He had heard about the accident and was waiting for instructions. I told him you kids were all in, and we'd run down here to rest for a few days and get away from people. He said that was okay. He wouldn't let on to anyone we were here. He recognized me right away. He said he'd do all he could for us, and it was all right for us to go right out. He'll take us in his service boat. So Jen, you get the kids together and we'll get off before the people on other boats wake up and look us over. You know of course there may be somebody down here we know, and we'll have to lie low till we find out. So keep your mouths shut, and don't make a fuss at *any*thing."

He glared around on his brothers and sisters and they regarded him with awe, and shut their firm little mouths tight.

So, ignoring stiff joints, the game little party climbed out of the car into the clear morning air, and walked down the board walk to the slip where the boat was tied that was to take them over to their own cruiser, moored at a little distance. They followed their brother solemnly and filed across the slip and into the boat, Robin coming last with Jennifer and trying to act as old as the rest of them. It wasn't an entirely new experience to them of course, for they had been with their father and mother, two at a time, on the old boat, but coming as it did on the steps of all the injunctions they had received they felt that they were living out a kind of mystery-story of their own, and their dignity was astonishing.

Jeremy saw them safely aboard their own boat and went back with Captain Andy to get the rest of the things from the car, and park the car in a safe place where its license wouldn't be under the public gaze. Jennifer gathered her little flock in an orderly group on the sheltered part of the deck, and provided them with sandwiches and a glass of milk apiece. They were charmed with the whole performance, and hungry as so many young bears. But if one of them ventured a word aloud Jennifer put her finger on her lips and shook her head. They looked fearsomely toward the other boats anchored at little distances about them, and subsided.

Jeremy came back and brought more milk and a big chunk of ice for the refrigerator, and then ate his share of sandwiches and milk.

A family of young ducks came quacking up to the boat and the children were delighted to throw them a few crusts and watch them gobble them up, but Jennifer quickly put a stop to that lest they would waken someone on the other boats. She was full of fear lest it would be reported at home that they had been seen.

Then she marshaled them all into the cabin and made them help put their things away. They had difficulty stifling their squeals of delight over the various cosy nooks and clever gadgets on this new boat that none of them had seen. But one by one they were lured into their bunks, just to see how comfortable they were.

"Because you didn't get your full night's rest, you know," she explained, when they were about to protest.

Jennifer found a lump rising in her throat as she realized what this trip might have been with daddy and mother. Again and again little comforts reminded of her father's care for them all.

The children were surprised to find how good it felt to take off their shoes and stretch out full length on the nice soft mattresses. There had been no suggestion that they were to go to sleep, only to lie still for awhile and rest, but before many minutes everyone was asleep, and Jennifer and Jeremy were only too glad to follow suit. And so the first morning, and early afternoon passed, for the whole group were utterly worn out.

It was Jennifer who woke first and stealthily went to the complete little galley to look over her larder and prepare another meal. More sandwiches and a big pot of cocoa. That was enough for a hasty lunch. Pretty soon the fish would come and they would have that for dinner. Both she and Jerry had been to camp enough to know how to cook fish. She was thankful for that. Besides, she had spied a cook book on the shelf. She felt sure they were going to be able to get along all right, and it was going to be grand, if only nobody turned up hunting them, who would run home and tell. They couldn't expect to keep the children quiet indefinitely though. Well, they would just have to go a day at a time and see what developed.

Jerry woke up when the smell of the cocoa began to make itself keen. He unfolded a delightful leaf-table from a concealment within a panel, then he brought forth dishes, plates and cups and spoons. It was really fun. If only mother and daddy could be there with them!

And presently Karen voiced the thought which was more or less in all their minds.

"Sister, do you suppose mother and daddy can see us now? Do they know we are down here?"

"Why, I don't know," said Jennifer sadly, wondering just what was right to say. "I shouldn't wonder. Perhaps!"

"Of course they can!" snapped Jerry unexpectedly, and quite crossly.

"Does they know I'se being dood, Jerry?" questioned

Robin, pausing with his sandwich half way to his mouth.

"Oh, *sure!*" said Jerry almost hoarsely, and got out his handkerchief and blew his nose vigorously.

Then he arose and looked at the three little girls.

"Why don't you three girls clear off this table and wash the dishes. And don't make a racket doing it, either. There are a lot of people over on that next boat, and I haven't had a chance to look 'em over yet. So pipe down, and remember, if I say scram, you're every one to slide into your bunks in short order and don't open your lips. You don't want to have to leave here in a hurry and have a policeman or somebody chase us half over the United States to take us back to our relatives, do you? Well then, let's see you do it! SCRAM!"

With round excited eyes the five children disappeared into their bunks and lay like mummies until Jerry said "Okay!" and then they all flew up and began to clear off the table.

In a very short time the boat was in immaculate order, and Tryon who had been set to hunt bathing suits discovered a lot of other things, among them several boxes of picture puzzles, some of them simple enough for even Karen and Robin. The children quite willingly settled down to work at them, the older ones at the table, the two youngest on the floor. Jennifer looked at them in wonder, and couldn't believe that this would last. They had not always been model children at home. But then they had never all been together this way without a nurse before. They seemed to enter into the occasion in a rather wonderful way. They would surely feel the confinement of the boat if it lasted too long, but it was great to have this first day going so well.

About the middle of the afternoon the fish arrived, and after disposing of them safely in the refrigerator, and getting the oilstove filled and ready for cooking them later, Jerry started up the engine. To the great delight of them all they started down the river. They were a silent little company, and when they met another boat they ducked into the cabin and peered out the portholes, studying the faces of those on board. But though Jerry and Jennifer had glasses and were watching carefully, they saw no familiar faces. They went on their way to a pleasant anchorage Jerry remembered from his last trip, and there they cooked their supper of fish and ate their bread and butter and drank their milk with a relish. Then they weighed anchor and started back to the harbor.

The sun was dropping down like a great ball of fire when they reached their haven, and Tryon, following his brother's instruction, stood on the bow with his boat hook and picked up the mooring. Then there was a quick rush to get out pajamas and brushes and combs, and have everything in order for retiring before it got dark, for Jerry had ordered that there were to be no lights on board that night. He didn't want to have curious eyes upon their hiding. After everything was in readiness so they could undress in the dark, they came back and crept silently out on deck, nestling down together on the big couch among the cushions, and in the wicker chairs, to watch the sunset. It was a lovely picture, the crimson from the slowly dropping sun streaking up into the sky and making every tree and house and object stand out clearly, and rippling the water with a thousand tints. A little company of wild ducks came by quacking their pleasantries of the day to one another, and hastening to their resting place for the night. A sea gull floated over, flapping its wings, and came to rest on a tall piling of the dock. A tiny light gleamed on the tallest mast of a nearby sloop. It was all as if the stage had been planned and set for the twilight performance.

One by one, as darkness dropped down, the children grew drowsy and were ordered off to bed.

But Robin hung back as he was led away to bed and pointed to where the evening glow still lingered in the west.

"Jennifer, is dat vere heaven is? Out vere the pwetty is?"

And when he was gone the rest were left looking off into the dying red of the west, thinking of the father and mother who had left them alone in a world that wanted to separate them.

When they were all settled at last in their bunks, Jennifer slipped softly back and sat down beside Jeremy. He moved to make room for her beside him, and said in an anxious questioning tone of wistfulness:

"I guess there's a God, don't you think so, Jen? It seems as if there ought to be, with all that out there."

"Why, I guess so, Jerry," said Jennifer. "I never really thought much about it before. Not many people in college believed that, of course, but I used to think sometimes they just said that because they thought it sounded smart. I always had a kind of feeling that mother and daddy really believed there was, so I didn't pay much attention to what the others said."

"Dad and mother always gave me that impression, too," said Jerry. "Gee! I wish those days were back! I never thought our mother and father would go and leave us, did you, Jen?"

"Well, they didn't exactly *go* of themselves, you know," said Jennifer thoughtfully. "They must have been taken. They never would have chosen to go and leave us here."

"I know," said the boy sadly. "I was thinking about that too, and wondering, if they can look back, what it was they would be wishing they'd told us before they left. Because of course if there is any place *after* this, things must look different over there from what they do down here. I don't believe this world will ever look quite the same to me after this."

"No," said Jennifer, "it can't! I know that! Why, suppose it was set somehow that you and I had to go out and meet death the way daddy and mother did, I wouldn't feel ready, would you?"

"I should say not!" said Jerry huskily.

"Well, what we've got to do is get ready," said Jennifer earnestly.

"We could stay out of airplanes, and dangerous things like that," suggested Jerry.

"Yes, but airplanes aren't the only places people die. You couldn't even cross a street lest a car would run over you, if you went on that plan. Sooner or later everybody has to die, and even if it weren't a tragic death like airplanes, it would be tragic enough just the same."

"I know," said Jerry drearily. "I guess there isn't anything to do but grin and bear it, or forget it," said the boy with a sigh. "I suppose the fellows at college would think I was a sis to talk like that, but honestly, I can't see life, what it's all about. Even if you do right as best you know how, what does that rate you? You might get rewarded for it in Heaven, if there is a Heaven, I don't know."

"Of course there's a Heaven!" said Jennifer. "Everybody knows there is, only they haven't the nerve to own they believe it. Kirsty used to tell me all about Heaven when I was going to sleep nights. She used to say there was a lot of glory there. I always thought she meant the kind of golden glory that comes just before sunset. I thought of that tonight when Robin said that about sunset being Heaven."

"Well, but how did Kirsty know?" asked Jeremy. "Kirsty never went to college. She wasn't educated, was she? How would she know?"

"I don't believe you have to be educated to know about Heaven," said Jennifer dreamily. "I think it's something you know with your spirit. It's something God tells you. Of course Kirsty used to read the Bible a lot. Maybe she got her ideas out of that."

"Did you ever read it, Jen?"

"Oh, I took a course in it the first year in college, but they didn't make much sense out of it there. Just beautiful language. I remember they said there were some very fine literary passages in it. But I don't really remember much about it. It was an easy course and came at a convenient hour, and dad seemed to think it was a good thing to take, so I took it. I don't believe I got much out of it. But we both went to Sunday School for a long time. Didn't you learn any more than I did?"

"I guess not," said Jeremy, "just the story of Jonah and

the whale, and the feeding of five thousand on some little loaves and fishes. The way they taught there I decided it was all a lot of bologny. I asked a couple of questions, and the teacher just floundered around vaguely, so after that I didn't pay much attention. I don't suppose the Bible amounts to much or somebody would know the answers."

"Well," said Jennifer, "they have their answers, but not the way you mean. The people who taught Bible in our college thought it was clever writing, but just a book, like a novel, you know. But I know Kirsty used to get a lot of comfort out of it. I believe *she* would know the answers, some of them anyway! She used to sit and read and read it with a lovely smile on her face. She had her Bible all worn ragged on the edges she read it so much. I always meant to get her a new one sometime, but of course I forgot it. Maybe I'll get her one yet. My! How I'd like to see Kirsty!"

"Why don't we hunt her up?" said Jeremy. "I'd like to see her myself. Though I suppose she's pretty old by now."

"I can't think of her as being old," said Jennifer dreamily.

"Well, do you know where she lives?"

"It's away up in New England somewhere. I can't just remember the name of the place. If I thought real hard it might come back to me. It was some little dinky country place, and she didn't even live in it. She had a tiny little house up on the side of a hill, about a mile from the village. A neighbor's boy plowed her farm for her; she had a sick sister who had to come home and live with her. That's why she left us. And that's why they sent me up there to stay when mother was sick, because it was in the country and would be good for me, and because Kirsty couldn't leave her sister to come back to us."

"Was that boy that plowed the farm the one you said was such a gentleman?"

"Yes," said Jennifer. "I suppose you'll laugh, but he was. Even if he plowed other people's farms he was the most courteous boy I ever met."

"I wonder if you would think so now?"

Jennifer's eyes got their faraway look.

"I wonder!" she said softly. "I'd like to meet him sometime and find out."

"Well, he's probably big and fat now, with a red face and rough hands, and wears blue jeans or overalls most of the time."

"He might be big," said Jennifer, "but he wouldn't be fat. He wasn't that build. He was tall and lean, with big eyes and nice eyelahses. And even when he had muddy boots on he walked as well as if they were expensive shoes. He never was hobbledehoy like some of the farm boys. And he had a kind voice. His horses loved him."

"Yes? Well, you were only a kid, remember. I used to think Danny O'Riley was handsome, and I wanted to be a policeman the worst way just because he was one."

"Yes, I remember," said Jennifer. "But that's not like this. Sometime I'd like you to meet that boy. You'd see what I mean. Why, Ted, he lived by his Bible. He used to carry his Testament with him everywhere he went. Even when he was working he had it in a little pocket in his blouse, and I've seen him sit down at the end of a furrow and stop to read for a minute or two before he went on. He seemed always to have something on his mind that he wanted to look up, or make sure of."

"But I don't understand. He wasn't getting ready to be a minister or a missionary or anything, was he?"

"Not that I know of. He never said anything about it. I asked him once what he was doing and he just grinned, and said 'I'm getting it into my mind, kid, so I can use it when I need it.' I wanted to ask him more about it, but Kirsty called me in just then, and I didn't have another chance. But he called after me as I went away. He said, 'You know it's a pretty good book to have at your tongue's end.' I wondered about it several times, till I forgot about it. Daddy came after me the next day and I never had another chance to talk to him, just said good-bye as we were leaving."

"Well," said Jeremy, "maybe we can hunt him up some

day and see what he's turned out to be. You say he was only about thirteen or fourteen then? You can't tell anything about what he is now. You're liable to find a big disappointment if you ever see him. If he's stayed the same after all these years he must be some man!"

"I don't think he'd change," insisted Jennifer. "It seemed as if he had something that was firm like a foundation under him. Like a house built on rocks."

"Well, maybe we'll find out some day," said Jeremy. "I'd like to see him, anyway. Say, hadn't we better turn in? Those young fiends are liable to wake us up at almost any hour in the morning, and remember, tomorrow's another day. We don't know what we've got to face tomorrow."

11

Quite early in the morning Petra Holbrook arose and girded on her armor for battle. Those Graeme children were going to learn a thing or two right away, and so was Blakefield.

She tried the telephone first, and fairly snorted when there was no reply. Of course it was entirely thinkable that the children were not up yet. They never did have very good habits about early rising. At least she didn't think they had. She didn't really know anything about it, for she had never frequented the Graeme home at that hour in the morning. But it was scandalous that the servants were not around yet to answer the telephone.

She stabbed the hairpins into her stringy gray hair, omitting her usual attentions to it; so it took occasion to slink, and gave her sharp face a more severe expression than usual. She made short work of her breakfast, which usually she took as a ceremony, and then she started out, ordering the chauffeur to drive first to the Graeme place. If those servants were still in bed she would make it hot for them. She would dismiss every one of them, without characters. It was an outrage for servants, trusted servants, to play a trick like that. Of course they would excuse themselves by saying they were all tired out with extra work, and company and all that. But that was absurd. There hadn't been but one meal at which there had been relatives from out of town. Such servants were not worth their salt!

But as she drove up to the house she was struck by the aloofness of its appearance. At first she didn't analyze just what it was that gave it that appearance, but as she looked again she saw that the shades were all down, and on the east wing where there were inside blinds they were all closed. Now what on earth did that mean? The house had its regular summer appearance of being closed while the family were all away at the mountains or seashore! And it wasn't twenty-four hours since she was in there herself, with all the other relatives, and the children running around out in the yard. Had some terrible catastrophe occurred? She tried to think what it could possibly be, her mind growing more and more upset. Then it occurred to her that of course Blakefield must be responsible for this. Petra Holbrook was one of those who always had to find somebody to blame for everything she didn't like or understand.

What in the world could Blakefield have done? Closed up the house and taken the children somewhere? Without saying a word to any of them? The idea! It certainly was time that they all took action! But first, perhaps she ought to go right to Blakefield's house and find out if it was all true. When was it they said he would be back from New York? Oh, probably that was all a blind, and he hadn't gone to New York at all; he had taken the children off to some camp or resort, just to get them away, so she and the rest couldn't influence them. Well, it was awful to think a thing like this could happen! But they shouldn't catch her napping. She would turn heaven and earth to get those poor little orphans away from that visionary man. What John Graeme could have been thinking of to leave them under Blakefield's guardianship was more than anyone could fathom!

All the time she was being driven as fast as possible to Blakefield's house, hoping perhaps to find the children there.

But Blakefield's housekeeper knew nothing about them. She hadn't seen the Graeme young people at all. No, Mr. Graeme never told her of his plans, except to say when he would be back for meals. Yes, he had gone to New York. He left yesterday noon, telephoned her from the station that he would not be home to lunch. He had an appointment with a man in New York. He got his lunch on the train. He said he would likely be home for dinner that night, unless he telephoned her, and no message had come as yet, so he would be coming of course. Yes, she would tell him as soon as he got in that Mrs. Holbrook wanted him to call her up at once.

Petra Holbrook, baffled again, hurried to Majesta's house. She had it in mind to report the whole matter to the police, but she wanted to make sure that Majesta would approve. Of course, reporting a thing to the police *was* going a little far. Perhaps she had better talk it over with Pemberton, though Pemberton Best was such a temperate man. But of course men knew a good deal about law and things, and it wouldn't do any harm to hear what Pemberton might suggest, and then she could do as she pleased afterward. But Pemberton was always so afraid someone was going to overstep some right!

But before she turned into the street where Pemberton and Majesta lived she saw Jim Delaney driving along a cross street. He bowed to her and she waved frantically, so he stopped and drew up near where she had ordered her car to stop.

"I'm so glad you came along, Jim," she said, though she didn't usually care much for Jim Delaney. "I'm so excited and nervous I'm nearly out of my mind!" she stated with bated breath. "Jim, do *you* know what has become of the Graeme children?"

Jim looked at her astonished.

"*Become* of them?" he echoed, with lifted brows. "Why, no, I don't. What could have become of them? What do you mean Petra?"

"Why, they're *gone,* Jim! Absolutely gone! I called up last evening at a very reasonable hour, soon after dinner, and nobody answered! Not even a servant! What do you think of that? Those servants that Miriam boasted so about, and thought she had so well trained! Not a one on the job in the early evening! All the evening at intervals I tried. I even telephoned the Willises to know if any of them had gone over there. Peter, you know, is so fond of Jennifer. I thought he might have coaxed them over for the evening. But they were not there, and I've been fairly frantic! I telephoned everywhere I could think of, but no trace of anybody, and I finally settled down to think they might have gone to bed. But this morning I phoned again, and still the telephone didn't answer. So I drove right over there. And what do you think! I found the house closed! Yes, *actually!* The curtains drawn and even the inside blinds shut! I tried every door, and the house was as much closed up as ever it is in the summer when the family are all away at the shore. Now isn't that the limit? Can you imagine what's happened?"

"Why, no," said Jim Delaney, "but if I were you I wouldn't get excited. Everything's likely all right. Probably Blake knows all about it. It's his business after all, not ours."

"Oh, *his* business!" sniffed Aunt Petra. "Well, if it is, he isn't attending to it very well. And he couldn't have known all about it, because I understand he's gone to New York. At least they *say* he has! But dear knows, that may all be a bluff. Perhaps he took the children with him."

"Oh, no!" said Jim. "I saw him just before he left and he didn't have anybody with him at all. What would he do with a lot of children in New York?"

"Well, that's what I thought. But perhaps he didn't go to New York at all. Perhaps he's just taken them all off somewhere to annoy the rest of us. He has no more sense than a pussy cat about looking after children."

"Oh, I wouldn't say that," said Jim with a grin. "I think you'll find he has rather good sense. You know John Graeme evidently thought so or he wouldn't have left the children under his guardianship. If I were you I wouldn't worry."

"Well, I certainly *shall* worry," said Petra Holbrook firmly. "I'm not one to sit and fold my hands and let my dear niece's children go to destruction, even if you are! I shall go straight to the police and have this broadcasted! I intend to find those children before night, or I'll have the law on Blakefield. He is no fit guardian for them, or their money either."

"Well, that's not for you to say, Petra," said Jim. "If I were you I wouldn't get this matter in the public eye right away. You'll be sorry if you do. You'll have a big laugh on you when the children turn up in some perfectly reasonable place. You would make yourself appear to be a fool, to say nothing of letting the world know that there is dissension in the family. Just simmer down, Petra. Go see some of your friends, or get up a bridge game, or take lunch at your club, and forget it for a little while. Wait till Blake gets home and see what he says. After all, if anything is to be reported to the police Blake is the one to do it. It's really none of our business, you know."

"And you think that Blake has a right to spirit those children away out of our sight without telling us a thing about it?"

"Blake didn't spirit them away. I'm sure of that," said Jim Delaney grinning. "He didn't have time. He just caught his train. But I'm mighty certain if they are away somewhere he'll know something about it, so don't you fret."

"Look here, Jim Delaney, don't tell me Blakefield is so smart as all that. If he didn't spirit them away, it's some prank of that impish Jennifer, and she ought to be curbed. It would serve her right to get her pranks broadcasted all over this country and shame her. She's capable of doing almost anything, that girl is, and getting us all disgraced. I don't understand why Miriam and John had such wild children. They were well brought up themselves."

"Now, Petra, you're too excited. You just wait till Blake gets back and you'll find everything will be all right."

"You're no help, Jim Delaney! I thought perhaps you would get to work and help find those children. Wait? Why should I wait? And just give some gangster time to get away with them if they've been kidnaped."

"Oh, now, Petra. You know you don't think they've been kidnaped."

"Well, what *am* I to think? What *could* I think?"

"Well, I don't see why you should think anything at all. It isn't your responsibility, you know."

"But how do I know but they've all been murdered in their beds and we're sitting down folding our hands and letting them lie there slain!"

"Oh, bologny! Petra, I thought you had better sense than to get all wrought up like this over nothing. It's time enough to get excited when Blake asks you to do something. Look here, Petra, Blake gets back from New York some time this morning. He told me so himself. Now you just go quietly home and compose yourself. I'll make it my business to see him as soon as he gets back, and if there's anything that needs doing I'll telephone you. In fact I'll promise to telephone you even if there *isn't* anything you can do. Come, can't you be reasonable and do that?"

"But I really think, Jim, that I should tell the police, and let them use their judgment, don't you?"

"No, I *don't!*" roared Jim. "And I'll just tell you now for your own good, Petra, if you don't keep your hands off this you're going to be good and sorry. That's all!" and with a grim set of his jaws Jim Delaney put his foot on the starter, and bowed a crisp farewell.

"Why, the very idea!" said Petra Holbrook snapping her eyes angrily. "I knew Jim Delaney was opinionated, but I didn't think he'd be actually *rude*. Well, now, I shall do exactly what I *please!* I am firmly convinced that the police should know about this matter at once. But perhaps I'll go and see Adrian first. Or, would it be better to go and consult with Peter Willis?"

In the end she told the chauffeur to drive to Adrian Graeme's, because she reflected that people of the social position of the Willises might be offended to have the police brought into the matter. One never could tell. Perhaps she had better go slowly as Jim Delaney said. But she would see Adrian. Or would Pemberton be better? But no, Pemberton had advised her last night to keep out of it. Adrian would be better. He wouldn't of course take the responsibility off her hands and offer to go to police headquarters and attend to it for her. Adrian never did things like that. Adrian was really lazy. But Adrian of course was always respectable.

But it turned out that neither Adrian nor Pemberton were at home, and both Lutie and Majesta had gone out on errands.

On her way back to her own apartment Petra stopped again at the Graeme mansion, reflecting that the children might have got home by this time, and before she did anything really definite about the matter she had better be perfectly certain that they were still gone.

But though she tried every door, and went from window to window investigating, she could find no opening, nor get any response from bell or knocking. The house was closed as thoroughly as ever John Graeme had closed it when he went afar.

Back at her home, baffled in every attempt, she ate her lunch and then lay down for a brief nap before starting out again, determined to find Blakefield Graeme and make him suffer for all she had gone through.

But she had been asleep but a few brief moments when the telephone rang sharply at her side and wakened her into keen remembrance of her grievances.

It was Blakefield.

"Is that you, Petra? I find a message here that you wanted me to call you?"

"I *certainly did!*" said Petra. "What kind of a guardian are you, anyway? Do you know what has happened to your orphan charges, Blake, while you go running around the country to New York?"

"Happened?" said Blakefield genially. "Just what happening do you refer to, Petra?"

"I refer to their all having disappeared, Blake! Did you know they were gone? Absolutely vanished in the night!

Even the *servants* have apparently dropped out of existence! What do you think of that?"

"Why, yes, Petra," said Blakefield, still genially, "I knew they were gone."

Blakefield had but just read Jennifer's letter, but from his tone it would appear that Blakefield had helped to plan the whole thing.

"You *know* it!" screamed Petra into the telephone. "Who *told* you? Have you seen Jim Delaney?"

"No, I haven't seen Jim Delaney since I came back, Petra. What's he got to do with it? Is he excited about it, too?"

"Oh, no, he's cool as a cucumber of course, but I told him about it, and he seemed to think it wasn't worth worrying about. Said it wasn't any of my business, and that you would look out for everything when you got back. So, naturally I supposed he had told you. But if he didn't, I couldn't think how you would find it out, unless perhaps Pemberton had told you; and I was sure he hadn't because he was very indifferent about the matter too. Pemberton, you know, never does favor taking any responsibility about anything. But, of course, if you know all about it, Blakefield, *what* are you going to *do* about it? That's what I want to know. It seems to me that something ought to be done *at once*. I suppose you went around to the house after you got home, to see them, and found they were gone, didn't you, the way I found it out?"

"Oh, no," said Blakefield. "I didn't need to do that. I knew all about it."

"You speak as if you approved of it!" charged Petra angrily.

"Why, yes, I think it's a very good idea," said Blakefield.

There was a distinct pause in the conversation while Petra, aghast, took this in. She was speechless for the space of several seconds.

"You—think—it—is—*a good idea!*" she gasped at last.

"Yes," said Blakefield, "don't you?"

"I certainly do *not!*" flashed the woman furiously. "A good idea for those harum-scarum children to float off alone to the ends of the earth! You must be crazy!"

"Oh! Do you think so? Well, you know I thought it would really be a good thing for them."

"Where have they gone, Blakefield?" demanded the furious aunt. "Do you know where they have gone?"

"Why, they are quite safe, Petra. I assure you they will not come to any harm."

"Safe in *your* opinion, of course. The rest of us might not agree with you. I *demand* to know where they are!"

"Well, I'm sorry, Petra, not to be able to tell you that. You see, it was their special request that no one, not even their relatives, should be told where they are."

"Out*rage*ous!" said Petra. "And you agreed to a heathenish arrangement like that! You didn't see how inhuman that was! And you *allowed* them to dishonor us all by declining to let us know their whereabouts! Well, I should say you are just as much to blame as they are, if not more so. Because *you* really *know* better! Such disrespect is as*tound*ing!"

"Well, you see, Petra, when you reflect on what you and the other relatives *did*, it doesn't seem so astounding."

"Did?" fairly screamed Petra. "What did *we* do?"

"You came to their father's house and coolly sat down and plotted to take those children in hand and work your will among them. You talked openly of their behavior and said they were spoiled. You called them brats and imps, and arranged to put your own curbs on them, and then you all but made arrangements to separate them from one another, or worse still to send them up to the dismal old farm and put Abigail Storm over them, a woman whom they all dislike with all their hearts! And all this was discussed while Jennifer sat in the next room weeping her heart out over her own loss. Jennifer heard every word you and Majesta and Agatha Lane said, even the sharp criticism of their dead parents. I am sure you will understand that it is no wonder that the children wanted to get away from this vicinity for a time, and I heartily agree with them in their desire. That is the reason why I am upholding them in their wish to be away, and to run no risk of anyone interrupting their seclusion."

Petra Holbrook's voice was hoarse with fury as she answered:

"Blakefield, I feel that I can *never* forgive you for this inhuman stand you have taken against us. I am quite sure that all the connection will be *out*raged at you, and will feel that what you have done is *un*forg*iv*able."

"Petra, it was because I knew that the children would all feel that way toward *you,* who have desired to separate them, that I felt it would be a good thing for them to be away for a time till this could be forgotten, and their lives arranged in a normal and happy manner. They were deeply outraged at your suggestions, and the younger ones were very much frightened at the idea of being separated from each other. Remember, Petra, this is not anything that *I* have gotten up. It was what you said yourself, most of it in *my* hearing, and *all* of it in *Jennifer's* hearing, that has precipitated this exodus. And I have felt that it was as well for them to carry out their plans, until you all realized that you are not responsible for them in any way, and that you can have no voice whatever in the decisions that have to be made. I am sorry to have to say these things, but is quite necessary for you to understand that you cannot interfere."

"Interfere!" snorted Petra Holbrook. "As if it would be interference to give suggestions about the care of those precious children. What right did Jennifer have anyway to be sitting there eavesdropping where she could hear us? She always was a little *sneak!* She's a young *devil,* that girl is!"

"You forget, Petra, that it was *you* who entered *her* home, her father's house, and began to plan what should be done with her. If someone had been doing that to you when you were her age wouldn't you have resented it?"

"Of course you *would* take her part! But you know she

should have left the room, or else come out in the open and let us see she was there. I tell you that girl is not to be trusted! She shouldn't have stayed there and listened."

"And *I* say that *you* shouldn't have gone to her home and talked as you did."

"Well, I didn't expect the children to be lurking around eavesdropping. But that's neither here nor there. What I said was the *truth,* and I'll say it again, too! Those children are not well brought up, and they are going to be a handful to handle. And the only way it can ever be done is to *separate* them. It will be like handling a mob of gangsters if you leave them all together."

"Petra, excuse me, but you really haven't anything to do with the matter. That is all in my hands. And I do *not* intend to have those children separated! Now, don't you think we have talked about enough? We are not getting anywhere."

"Blakefield, you are pre*pos*terous! As if *you* could bring up those children! Why, they will ride all over you, and will be a scandal in the town! John was *crazy* to name you their guardian."

"I'm not going to discuss that, Petra. The fact remains that John not only made me the guardian of his children, but he talked over with me just what he wanted done in case of his death. Remember these were *his* children, not yours, and he has left very careful directions both oral and written regarding their welfare."

"Well, of course," said Petra haughtily, "of course John Graeme wasn't the *only* parent the children had, and it happens the *we* are *closely* related to their dear mother. I'm quite sure that Miriam would never have wanted us to sit quietly by and leave her darling children to the maudlin management of a bungling man! Of course if you will not listen to reason, we shall have to have recourse to the law. We shall regret very deeply to have to do that on account of the scandal that will arise, but we shall do it if necessary. We shall not sit by and let you do your worst. We shall contest the will!"

"Yes?" said Uncle Blake calmly. "Well, if that is what

you want to do I shall not attempt to stop you. You will have to take the consequences. And you will find in the end that the law is a pretty hard and fast matter to deal with."

"Oh!" said Petra furiously. "I suppose you will try to fight us. It won't be an easy matter to get you to relinquish charge of that immense fortune, of course; you who have always been in such moderate circumstances! But you will find that you can't just walk in and take over a family and a fortune so easily, even if you *were* related to their dead father."

Blakefield Graeme's voice sounded tired as he made reply.

"Well, Petra, I guess that's about all I have to say. If you think that of me I don't care to dicuss it any further."

"No, I suppose not," said Petra with biting sarcasm in her voice. "Well, you'll answer me a few questions before you stop, anyway. Are those children in your house?"

"No, they are not in my house."

"Well, who are they with? Who is taking care of them? And what has become of the servants? You're not keeping up a big house somewhere with all those servants for them, are you? Because that's a foolish waste."

"The children are safe, Petra, and living quite modestly and quietly. As for the servants, they have been dismissed, some to other positions, and others to rest until such time as they shall be needed again."

"Do you mean that you dared to take it upon yourself to do *that,* Blakefield Graeme?"

"Oh, no, Petra, I didn't do that. Jennifer did it. She felt that there was no need to keep the house open while they were away, and she arranged all those matters before they went away."

"Well, *really!*" said Petra. "I'd like to know what right anybody had to do that. I was expecting to take over a couple of those servants myself. I should have been consulted."

"Well, of course that is Jennifer's affair, not mine. She is the natural head of the house."

"Blakefield, is it possible that you have no more foresight than that, that you will allow Jennifer to have her own way, take over all that responsibility and spoil all her brilliant prospects?"

"Brilliant prospects? What brilliant prospects am I spoiling?"

"Why, you certainly must be aware that Peter Willis is expecting to marry her, and here you are allowing her to go away with that horde of children. And you are letting her take over the household as if she were an old woman."

"It was her father's and mother's wish, Petra, in case anything happened to them both."

"Well, that's ridiculous! Of course they didn't expect anything to happen to them when they said that, and they would be the last ones to wish to spoil Jennifer's prospects."

"If you call Peter Willis a brilliant prospect, I personally don't care how soon it is spoiled, and I don't believe her parents would call him a prospect either."

"There you go!" said Petra. "That shows just what you are! There isn't a wealthier, handsomer, better appearing young man in town than Peter, and he stands ready to marry her at once and take her over to Europe and show her a good time. He told me so himself."

"You don't say so!" said Uncle Blake dryly. "Then I must say I am glad that the children have gone away. I certainly wouldn't care to have Peter Willis take over Jennifer. He's not fit to fasten her shoe latchet."

"Well, I don't think you could find another person in the whole city that would agree with you. However, this is immaterial. There is just one thing I want to know. *When* are those children *coming home?"*

"Not for a while," said Blakefield blandly. "Jennifer doesn't wish to come back until she is of age, and none of you can question her right to run her family the way she thinks she ought to!"

"Blakefield! You don't mean that you are going to countenance their staying away all that time? Why, that is simply sui*ci*dal! Jennifer won't be of age for several months, will she?"

"Oh, it won't be so long," said Uncle Blake with more assurance than he really felt.

"But—Blakefield—*Jerry* has to go to *college!* And the other children ought to be entered in good schools. I've been looking over advertisements of schools, and have selected several that I think look hopeful."

"All those things will be arranged, Petra!"

"Oh, you mean that you will arrange them, I suppose, but you know *you're* not in the least fitted to attend to things of that sort."

"Too bad, Petra, but I guess I'll have to rub along. Besides the children have their minds pretty much made up about what they want to do anyway. And now, would you excuse me? I have a very important appointment with a business man and must go to it at once."

"But Blake! I *must* have the keys to the house! I shall need to go over there and take care of things. Shall I call at your house for them, or will you send a messenger boy down to my apartment with them? There are things that should be looked after *at once.*"

"Sorry, Petra, I can't let you have the keys. But you needn't worry. All those things have been looked after by Jennifer. Good-bye!"

"But Blake—*Blake*—Jennifer wouldn't *know* what they were. She's never had any ex*peri*ence. She wouldn't know what to do—"

But Uncle Blake had hung up and gone!

12

Almost four lovely long weeks the children stayed down at the boat and vegetated, enjoying every minute of the time, as much as it was possible for them to enjoy anything after the shock and loss they had been through.

Getting acquainted with each other, they were, all over again, and because of that, feeling nearer to the dear parents who had been so swiftly taken away from them.

"Daddy wouldn't want you to do that, Robin!" Jennifer would say when Robin started out to tour around the narrow ledge outside the window frames.

"Oh! Vouldn't he?" Robin would say in a disappointed tone, and then slowly step back and down into safety.

There were difficulties, it is true, when it seemed as if all the children were especially trying. But Jennifer found that if she just suggested that mother or daddy would like them to do a certain thing, they generally succumbed promptly. She found, too, that even with Jeremy and herself, this thought was uppermost most of the time: what would mother or daddy have said, or thought, or wanted them to do? It seemed somehow to salve the wounded affections to feel that they were pleasing their parents in little ways.

It was perhaps the best thing those children could have done, to go to that boat. It not only was a refuge from the things they most feared, but it became a little home where they were necessarily bound together within circumscribed limits, and it gave them a chance to study one another and grow into a love that they had never before had opportunity for, in the rushing life at home. Naturally the children turned to their older brother and sister, as next to their parents, and became delightfully devoted to them.

"I wuv you, Jennifer!" Robin would say, climbing up in her lap in the early evening as they sat on deck and watched the dying glow in the west. "Jerry's a nice bruvver, too," he would add with an approving glance Jeremy's way. And Karen would slide along behind Jeremy's chair and run her fingers through his hair, and say nonchalantly, "Course he is."

So for the most part it was willing obedience that the younger ones gave to all directions.

The older ones found themselves spending much thought on amusement for the younger ones.

Every day they took a trip to the bay, or explored some new little river, learning the nautical language, the older ones becoming more familiar with the routine of handling the boat.

Often Jerry would take them, one or two at a time, in the little dinghy and teach them the technique of rowing, until Tryon and Hazel were at last allowed to take the little boat themselves, with one of the others for passengers, though Robin and Karen of course always donned their life jackets for such excursions, and they were warned to keep within watching radius of the big boat. Sometimes they went swimming, quietly, at an hour when most other boats were off on a cruise. Jerry was very careful that they should not run any risks of being discovered and reported. He did not allow the children to forget that they were in hiding, knowing only too well how easily a false move or a telltale voice might betray them to a world they wanted to avoid. And to that end he had daily what he called "scram" practice, though not at a stated time. When they were least expecting it, he would suddenly appear among them and utter the magic word "Scram!" and the whole little huddle of them would disappear like frightened mice, and in a trice be lying flat and quiet upon their bunks. They had practised this so much that they would practically do it without sound of going, and apparently in but one motion. They were like soldiers, always alert and ready.

Early in the first week on the boat they subscribed for the *New York Times* in Captain Andy's name. They told him they wanted to see it every day, but didn't care to give their friends this much clue to their whereabouts. So, they studied the personals carefully every day. Uncle Blakefield's first reply to Jennifer's note was brief and characteristic:

"J.J.
I heartily approve your attitude. Will do as suggested. Let me know of your welfare often through these columns or otherwise, as convenient. B.G."

It gave Jennifer quite a thrill to read that first message. Uncle Blake was true to form. She had known he would take it that way. Yet she was half aware that through the calmness of his brief words there might still be an uneasiness that he would not own. But he would be loyal and true. He would never betray the trust she had put in him. He would not let the others start a search if he could possibly help it. Somehow he would manage to warn them if danger were seeking them through overzealous relatives. Yet little as was this small link to their old life, it warmed all their hearts and cheered them through the days that to the two older Graemes at least were more or less filled with continued anxiety.

But each day as it went by peacefully, with no invasions, and continued kindliness from Captain Andy, reassured them, and made them feel more secure in their lovely hiding place.

"If we could only just stay here until it is time to go home!" sighed Jennifer one afternoon as she and the little girls finished clearing up after lunch, and she settled down on the big couch to rest awhile.

"Well, perhaps we can! Who knows?" said Jeremy.

And then that very day it had to happen! Right out of the blue as it were!

They had been fishing all the morning without very great success, and Jerry had gone over with Tryon to the shore in the dinghy to get enough fish for their dinner that night, promising when he came back to take them a little ride down to the bay where they could eat their supper. Then they would come back and tie up for the night to watch the sunset. This had come to be the regular program for the lovely lazy days that went by almost like a dream, from which they all dreaded to wake up and come once more to the realization of the tragic situation.

Hazel was reading an old book for the third time.

Heather and Karen and Robin were playing paper dolls on deck, sitting on the floor near the companionway that led to the cabin. It was sleepily quiet and Jennifer had fallen almost asleep. She was just conscious of the voices of the two little girls, naming the paper dolls they had been cutting so laboriously.

"Now, Robin, don't you step there! That is the house where our dolls live. Why can't you play with your automobile and not bother us? Play you are a truck driver delivering our packages."

"Awwight!" said Robin, racketing around on all fours, shoving his battered red toy automobile before him.

But somehow he seemed to feel detached from his young sisters, and not really in the game. Presently he wandered over near to Jennifer's couch, and stood gazing out across the water dreamily.

It was very still. There was only the soft ripple of the water lapping at the boats, the distant hum of a saw at the boatyard on shore, the cadence of wings from a little grayblue gull that settled down on the water nearby.

Robin was watching the shore where Jerry had disappeared, studying the people that came out on the wharf over at the harbor, trying to identify the boat that was slowly coming nearer. He had grown very keen on the ways of this new simple world that had replaced the old grave sophisticated one he had known.

It was a rowboat that was coming across the water toward him. He watched the bright dip of oars, fascinated. There were three people in it. He caught the flash of color in the bright garments of a lady in the stern.

He was very still as he stood there watching, one hand lying on the rail, the other clutching his little red toy automobile, his golden hair blowing back in the breeze, his white young brow puckered in perplexity.

He was identifying that oncoming boat. It wasn't just any boat, it was one he was sure he had seen before. Yet it wasn't the boat that Captain Andy's son used, to bring people out to their boats. That one was bigger and went chug-chug and had a motor hidden in a box in the middle. This went by oars. The man rowing it was one of Captain Andy's sons, the one who always smiled at Robin, and said "Hi! Rob!" Robin liked him. Maybe he would smile at him now as he rowed by. But no, he wasn't going by, he was drawing alongside that big boat right next to theirs. Robin's eyes got very large. Why, that was the dinghy that belonged to that next boat. That's where he had seen it before, swinging about at the stern of its cruiser like a puppy on leash following its mother. And now he saw the man and lady. He didn't know the lady. She had hair like Karen's doll, and her lips were very red; her eyelashes seemed to be thick with some kind of shiny black dust. But he wasn't much interested in the lady. It was the man beside her that held his attention. Was that someone he knew? His small heart almost stood still for an instant. The man beside the lady turned almost his full face toward him, glancing at their boat for an instant. Then he looked sharply back to the man who was rowing them, and Robin heard him say clearly:

"Is that the boat you said was for sale when I was down last fall?" he asked.

Robin tried to think where he had heard that voice.

"Yes," said the oarsman, "but someone bought it this spring."

"Who?" asked the man, and now Robin knew who he was and his little heart quaked within him. Filled with consternation, like a flash his young lips set in determination.

"Skwam!" he said in a sharp little imitation of Jerry's tone, as he dropped to all fours and cast a frightened look at Jennifer.

"Skwam!" he said again guardedly, and there was grave warning in his voice and face as he slithered toward the companionway, from which his sisters had already vanished.

Jennifer, alert at once, opened her eyes, heard the splash of oars and although the rail hid the couch almost completely, she rolled to the deck stealthily, getting herself down into that cabin.

"What was it, Robin?" she whispered, as she saw him watching her with wild eyes, from his own bunk.

"That vas Petah Villis out theah in that boat!" whispered Robin back hoarsely.

"Oh, Robin! Are you *sure?*" she said, as she reached her hand and stealthily pulled the sheltering curtain across the entrance.

"Wes!" said Robin firmly. "I is shooah!" and he closed his eyes tightly as if that would help to make them safe.

Jennifer put one eye to a porthole.

Yes, there was Peter Willis! The girl didn't matter. She was no one Jennifer knew, a tough looking creature showily dressed. Peter was helping her into the other boat and Jennifer as she watched did some rapid thinking. They would have to get away from here at once of course. But how could they manage it in broad daylight? Of course they could stay hidden and quiet till evening but it would be a long anxious time to keep the children still, and suppose Peter should take a notion to come over and look at the boat? What could they do to prevent it?

He was turning now to look toward it again, and she distinctly saw his cool calculating eyes taking in all its comely parts. Her hand trembled as she held the curtain. He evidently was interested in their boat. Was it just as a boat, or did he have some inkling whose it was, and was he trying to search for them? Not very likely with that girl along, and yet they must take no chances. How was Jerry going to get across to them without being seen?

The two new comers on the boat nearby were standing on their deck now, taking in the scene, but Peter's eyes were distinctly on the Graeme boat.

"I'd like to have that boat over there," she heard Peter say to the young man who was preparing to leave. "Be sure you ask your father about it, and tell me when you come back. Are there people on it now? I thought I saw a child by the rail there when we came up. I'd like to go on board and look around before dark. Ask your father to see if it's all right."

Jennifer could see it was Captain Andy's son Bert who was spoken to, and he had a conscious look about him as he answered indifferently, with averted eyes. "Okay! But I think there's some people on board. Some of the family I guess."

"Well, you find out for me," said Peter.

"Okay." And then the little boat dipped its oars and began to glide away. Oh, what could she do?

The two on the other boat had turned their attention now and were examining everything. Surely that wasn't Peter's boat. She didn't know of his owning a boat. Perhaps it belonged to someone he knew who had let him take it for awhile. Ah, they were stepping inside the cabin, perhaps to look around there, or to change to yachting clothes. If they stayed some time why couldn't she get those outer curtains closed and make it look as if the owner had departed while they were inside? But she must not go out herself. She turned quickly toward Heather's bunk.

"Get up quick, dear," she whispered. "Put on these old knickers of Tryon's. Where's his old cap? Here it is. I want you to slip outside and pull all the curtains down tight. Don't stop to fasten them till you have them all down. Don't look at that other boat over there, and don't turn your face so they can see it. Wait now, I'll peek out and see if the coast is clear."

"Shall I leave a curtain open for Jerry and Try?" asked the little girl softly.

"No, we'll keep watch for them. Now, quick! They've gone inside! Do the ones on their side first. Be quick!"

Heather, lithe and agile, arrayed in her brother's garments, slid out like a wraith and whisked down the curtains in a jiffy, feeling very important that she was trusted to do it.

"Now," she said as she crept back, "that old Peter can't see inside at all. Old nosy thing! What does he havta come around and spoil our nice time for, I'd likta know?" Suddenly Heather ducked her head down into her pillow and wept with all her might, softly, her little shoulders shaking violently under Tryon's torn sweater, and her spindly legs quivering forlornly out from the mammoth knickers that almost hid them.

"There! There!" said the big sister, coming close, "don't cry, Heather darling. You've just done a great big brave thing getting those curtains all closed quickly and not getting caught, and now you mustn't be a softy and cry! Come, we've got lots to do, and you must get up and help. Keep that rig on awhile. We may need to send you on deck for something when Jerry gets here; and nobody, not even Jerry would know you in those togs. You don't know how dear and funny you look, Kittykins."

The comforting was all done in whispers, for that other boat was perilously near, but bright eyes looked down on Heather from the other bunks, and presently the tears were dried, and she smiled at them all.

"Now," said Jennifer, "you get all the hair brushes and tooth brushes and combs together, and put them in the two overnight bags. You know which they belong in. Karen, you know where the suitcases are. Bring them out and put them by our different bunks. Hazel, you fold the clothes. Heather can help when she gets the overnight bags ready."

"Are we going away?" asked Hazel in dismay.

"I don't know yet," said Jennifer, "but we'll have to be

ready. We may have to go in a hurry, and it's better to have things ready. Then we won't be in danger of leaving something important behind. Don't make a noise. Robin, you lay these handkerchiefs smoothly in that nice box, and don't talk. When you get that done you can sit out there on deck and keep a watch out for Jerry. But don't you call, or make a noise! Just watch, and if anything happens, or you see Peter and the girl come out, you slip softly in and whisper to me."

"Awwight!" said Robin solemnly, and in no time at all he handed over the handkerchief box and took his place gravely by a curtain where he could peek out.

It was amazing how quickly that packing was done, compared to the time it had taken them to gather things together at home.

"What about food?" asked Hazel as she snapped her suitcase shut and looked around on the other laborers. "There's quite a lot of bread, and there's some of the beefsteak left over from last night. I could make some sandwiches."

"Yes," said Jennifer, "get something ready. If we have to go away we may have to eat in the car. There are two or three apples, aren't there? Slice them and put them between bread and butter. They'll be good if we get thirsty."

One by one the suitcases were packed. Jennifer even began on Jerry's, for there was no telling if they might not have to rush as soon as he came. Why didn't he come?

She looked at the ship's clock, and knew he had been longer than ever before when he went shopping. Every two or three minutes she came to the lookout and swept the water with an anxious glance. Jerry had meant to come right back and start toward the bay. What was keeping him? She feared to have him come, lest he should be seen, yet she feared because he was so late.

"Haven't you seen anything of Jerry, Robin?" she whispered.

Robin shook his head.

"No, but—but—there vas a boat—looked like ours—started—started—fum—fum—over zere!—But it vented avay up zat ozzer side of the wivver, toward the bayvay!" said Robin with a troubled look. "Jerry vouldn't go zat vay, vould he?"

"Oh, no, of course not," said Jennifer, but she gave another troubled glance out and wondered. Was it conceivable that Jerry had found out that Peter was in these parts? Had he perhaps seen him? No, that wasn't in the least likely, for Jerry would surely have come at once to the rescue. Or was it possible he was waiting till dark?

The anxiety made the work all the harder.

It was growing quite late in the afternoon. Could anything have happened to Jerry? Ought she perhaps to sound the horn that called the Captain? Find out what was the matter with Jerry? But no, that would be but to call attention to themselves. It was better to remain utterly silent as long as possible. And nothing could have happened to Jerry and Tryon of course. There must be some reason for this delay.

Investigation showed that the two occupants of the next boat were out swimming. But Peter seemed to be coming over toward their boat! Jennifer's heart was in her mouth as she watched him anxiously. Then she went searching for a scarf in her suitcase, which she tied about her head and face so it would be somewhat of a disguise in case he really did venture to board the boat. Of course it wouldn't be at all a gentlemanly thing to do but Peter was always taking chances, and getting away with them too, and she knew just how gaily and handsomely he would laugh it off in case he decided to try it.

The voices of the two were really coming nearer now. As they lazily floated along they were discussing the size of the boat, its lines, admiring it. With the curtains all down they would surely think nobody was aboard.

Hastily she remanded the children to their bunks by uttering the magic word "Scram!" and she herself sat tensely waiting, enveloped in a large apron, her face bound around with one of Jerry's handkerchiefs, as if she had the toothache. A pair of black goggles covered her eyes, and the scarf was over her head. She found herself trembling from head to foot.

Of course there was nothing awful to be afraid of, except that their whole plan would be utterly spoiled. If Peter found them out he would take strenuous measures at once to report to all the aunts, especially Aunt Petra, and there would be orders from home at once before they could possibly get word to Uncle Blake for help. And even so, Uncle Blake didn't bulk very impressively with the rest of them. There probably wasn't much that Uncle Blake could do about it if the relatives took things in their own hands.

Why did they want to anyway? Did they want to manage the property? Of course that was a possibility. But Jennifer had but a vague idea of what advantages there might be in managing her father's fortune, or whether, indeed, it was a fortune.

But now she could hear those swimmers coming steadily on, making their way entirely around the boat, discussing its every advantage.

Had Jerry taken in the extension ladder they used for swimming? Jennifer couldn't remember. If he had not they could walk right up and board the boat. If he had, still the boarding ladder was out, she knew, though it was almost impossible to pull one's self up to that from the water.

She cowered, waiting. But at last the voices suddenly diminished, and then she could see the two heads making their way rapidly toward their own boat. A little later there was no sign of the swimmers. They had probably gone inside to dress.

"And there comes Jerry!" breathed Jennifer with quick relief.

"Wes!" said a soft little voice beside her. "They—they—they—*seed* Jerry's boat tumin', and they—they—they—just ducked wite down in the vater, and svimmed avay!"

Jennifer glanced down beside her, and there stood Robin, his grave little earnest face all puckered with responsibility. She stooped and kissed his forehead softly.

"You blessed baby!" she whispered with her lips against his soft gold hair. "And I thought you were in bed!"

"I couldn't stay zere, Jen'fer," he said earnestly, "I vas the only man! I'm *not* a baby, Jen'fer!"

"No, you're not a baby, darling. You're our brave protector! We'll have to tell Jerry about that. See! He's almost here at last!" She glanced out of the galley window and saw their own little dinghy put-putting along.

"But he's not coming from the direction of the wharf! He's coming from away down toward the bay!" said Hazel, who had sprung down from her bunk and come to look out. "What do you suppose that means?"

"Don't bother about what it means," said Jennifer hurriedly, "get ready for anything. Go and put your shoes and stockings on, and the clothes you wore on your way down here. If Jerry wants to go away from here we'll have to be ready to start at a moment's notice."

The children gave her a frightened look and skittered around to find shoes and stockings, and do little last things, while Jennifer sliced some onions and slipped them into some more sandwiches. She was learning that even a few slices of raw onions must be conserved on this expedition. Then she hastily washed up about the neat little sink, and made everything shipshape to leave, in case they had to do it in a hurry.

But she did not remove her disguise yet, for there was no telling what would happen next.

So she stole to a curtain where she could peer out without being seen, to reconnoiter once more.

The swimmers were not in the picture. Probably dressing. That might take some time. Casting an anxious eye out another cranny she saw that Jerry's boat was stealing cautiously up on the opposite side from the other boat. Jerry must know! She hurried quickly over to unfasten the curtain on that side, and let Tryon come aboard. In a moment more Jerry stepped on board and all three hastened down the companionway into the galley to talk. Jerry's face was weary and anxious.

As he appeared in sight Robin stuck his head out from his bunk and said solemnly; "Skwam, Jerry! Skwam your-se'f!" and suddenly the whole little company bubbled into suppressed giggles.

13

Even Jerry's careworn face broke into a momentary grin.

"Okay with me, old man!" he said, and whirled himself into his bunk for an instant, and then was up, casting a quick keen glance around at the piles of baggage, and the children standing in a prim row. Then his eyes rested on Jennifer in her extraordinary outfit and he studied her in amazement.

"What the heck is the matter with you, Jen? You haven't scalded your face, have you?"

"No," laughed Jennifer almost silently, "this is just a disguise. Would you know me, brother, on a dark night?"

"No, I'm afraid not. But Jen, what kind of goings on have you been having? Bert gave me to understand there was some nosy person around wanting to find out about our boat, and as near as I could understand he answered to the description of Pete Willis, all but the painted lady whom I couldn't identify, though I've always presumed there were some. So I hiked me over and looked at the car, and it was his all right. I could see you were onto him, for I sighted the curtains down. So Try and I took our car several miles down the river and hid it, just in case, in a good safe place Captain Andy told me about. Bert went down in his car so we could come back from down that way. He's staying down there in case we need him tonight or sooner. And he'll call his father later for orders. Now, Jen, what's the story? What's been going on here? I've been near crazy lest I ought to have come back first, but I knew if I did I might be seen and recognized and give the whole thing away too soon, and I trusted to luck you folks would know enough to protect yourselves for a few minutes at least. I didn't think it was going to take me as long as it did."

"Well, it's Pete, all right," said Jennifer with a wry smile. "But he hasn't seen us yet, not to recognize us, thanks to Robin."

"Robin?" said Jerry, casting an eye up at the solemn baby in his berth. "What did Robin do?"

"He saw him coming over in the dinghy and he dropped to the deck and said 'Scram' and we all scrammed from force of habit, I guess, and then he told us it was Peter Willis and we pulled the inner curtain shut. Then Heather dressed up in Try's knickers and sweater and put on your old cap and went out and pulled down all the curtains and fastened them while the neighbors were indoors, and here we've stayed ever since. But we haven't been idle. We're all packed, even your things. I didn't know what you'd think we ought to do when you came, but we thought we'd better get ready. Did you bring any fish, or do we eat what we have?"

"No, I didn't stop for fish or anything. I thought we'd better get the car out of sight where we could beat it without being followed if necessary."

"Well, we've got some potatoes we can roast, and there is plenty of butter, and lots of milk. I guess we can make out a meal without touching the sandwiches the girls made up to take along. But how much time have we? Would the potatoes get done?"

"Well, I figured we'd pull out of here as soon as it was dark. It'll take us six good hours of running to get down by water to where we left the car. There's a full moon due at nine so it won't be too dark to run down the river safely. Tryon, you scout around without showing yourself and see how the land lies."

"They've just got done swimming," said Jennifer. "They came over here and were about to come aboard, we think by the sound. Then according to Robin who was watching out a crack between the curtains, they spied your boat coming, and beat it."

"Pretty good for Robin! We'll have to put him on the detective force. Well, that being the case I guess there's no reason why we couldn't pull out immediately. If the enemy is still out of sight so much the better."

"Okay!" said Tryon, swinging back from his mission. "Not a soul in sight!"

"All right! We're starting! Put in your potatoes, Jen, and let them bake while we go. I could eat a house afire. We'll anchor somewhere near shore, after awhile, where we're sheltered, and can watch for enemies till after dark. Then we can go on and pick up our car. We'll just dock the boat and lock it up. Then Bert and his father will go down the first thing in the morning and take it back. I arranged it all with him."

"Smart man!" said Jennifer.

"No other way to work it!" Jerry shrugged as if his sister's commendation meant less to him than it did.

"Now, Tryon, let's go! Wait till I start the motor and give you the high sign—from below this time. Then do you think you can reach up out the forward hatch and throw the mooring can clear without being seen?"

"Sure thing!" answered Tryon importantly.

Jerry swung open the engine hatch, tinkered a moment with his engine, shut it down carefully and swung up into the pilot's seat. In a moment more the engine was heard from in a soft throb. Tryon's hands only were seen unfastening the mooring line, then came a soft splash, and the Graeme boat moved slowly away from its neighbor.

But it was only an instant before the two little scouts Jerry had placed on watch were at his side.

"Petah Villis is comed out on deck!" announced Robin, his eyes saucer-wide.

"That funny girl is out there too, with a kimono all flowers and her hair all frowsy," reported Karen.

"Okay," smiled Jerry calmly. "Go back and watch. Don't both of you come away at once."

But Robin was back almost immediately.

"He—he—he's *call*ing you, Jerry!" he said excitedly, and then he dashed back to his post.

Then Karen was there in a second more with the same tale.

"Did he call my name, Karen?" asked Jerry.

Karen shook her head.

"No, he just said, 'Hi, there, mister! I want to speak to you a minute. Come alongside, can't ya!' "

Jerry smiled. Then perhaps Peter didn't know who he was!

The boat was well under way now, and the breathless little company of voyagers went silently about getting together a supper. They mustn't leave anything to spoil here if they were going away. Five more breathless minutes, and then they were around the curve and could no longer see the Willis boat. Would it try to follow them? Perhaps, but at least they had the start.

The sun was drooping lower and lower and the river was lovely. Jennifer was standing by Jerry now and they were discussing the possibilities.

"They may not have an idea who we are, of course, or they may think we are servants in charge," said Jerry, "but Captain Andy said the man was very determined to find out the price of the boat, and quite set on buying it. He may chase us to find out."

The sun was just slipping down behind the trees, a bright red ball against a luminous sky, when at last the potatoes were done and Jennifer called them to supper. Jerry put Tryon at the wheel after the boy had finished his own supper, so they need not lose any time. Jennifer had fixed a plate all ready for Jerry, with a steaming fluffy potato, a great lump of butter powdered with pepper and salt in the middle. Plenty of milk there was, too, rich and creamy. It seemed a supper fit for a king in spite of the fact that there was no meat nor bread.

"Gee! I didn't know just potatoes were so good," gasped Jerry handing back his plate for another.

"I guess we always had so many other things along with

'em that we never took time to taste the potatoes," said Tryon.

The lookout at the stern, who happened for the time being to be Hazel, reported a boat coming after them, and Jerry, armed with binoculars, sprang to attention.

"That's not the Willis boat," said he after a moment. "Don't you see it has a lot more freeboard than his? I guess I haven't sat and stared at that boat for almost a month without knowing its lines by heart."

"Oh," said Hazel, "I guess it has!"

Darkness slipped around them slowly until there was only the gorgeous sunset to light them. Suddenly, looking back, Jerry said sharply:

"There's the Willis boat. If he's really chasing us there's no hope of escape, for he has more speed than we can make."

Jerry moved up his throttle to the limit, and the whole little company sat tensely watching the other boat slowly gaining on them. Then suddenly he noticed it was turning. It was taking a decidedly different course, bearing directly toward the lights of a shore resort farther down the bay.

"Well, that's that!" said Jerry with relief. "Ten to one Pete's going down to dance with that girl!"

He cast a sidelong glance at Jennifer, as she sat looking thoughtfully toward the sunset. That was a view of Peter that had never occurred to her before. Always the Peter she knew had been going somewhere with her. But now it occurred to her that he seemed equally at home with this very common looking person he had with him. But there wasn't even the least bit of a twinge of jealousy on her part, nor any evidence of it in her face as her brother had feared there might be. She just sat there looking at the gorgeous sky and answered quite indifferently:

"Perhaps. Here's hoping, for that would really give us some time to get away calmly. But you can't trust to that. If he's been wished on us by Aunt Pet you can't tell what he'll do. Jerry, do you think any of the aunts or uncles knew about this boat and where it was?"

"I don't believe so. Dad wasn't one to go around telling his private affairs, and this boat was a comparatively new acquisition, you know. No, I don't believe even Jim Delaney knew anything about it yet. You see it was only a week or so before—" he paused with a quick look at the children.

"Yes," said Jennifer. "Well, that's good. Oh, Jerry! That sunset looks like the gate of Heaven! I wish it were, and we could go right out there and get in, where it is all safe and sure. Look, Jerry! See that dash of crimson the sun just flung down in the midst of that clear lovely yellow. It looks like a tattered flag! And see the tree branches etched against it off there to the right. Oh, if I were a painter I'd like to paint that! See the ripples of fire on the water. I don't think I shall ever forget this sunset. It's the most beautiful one we've had since we've been down here. It's a picture. Before this we've seen them all up by the harbor, perhaps that is why this one is so much lovelier. It's a wider view."

As soon as the last glory in the sky had faded, Jennifer hustled Robin and Karen off to their bunks to get a little sleep before they docked.

"We've still two hours to go," said Jerry anxiously. "Let the kids get some rest. But you, Jennifer, and Tryon had better stay up and keep checking up on the chart. We don't know these waters, remember! The tide is with us though, and if we can keep the right course and not run aground we ought to make it all right."

Intently the other two pored over the chart announcing the buoys that must be passed. Once Jennifer took the wheel and Jerry studied the chart carefully to be perfectly sure what he would meet in the little inlet where he had arranged to leave the boat. At last he sighted its lights.

"Here we are, Tryon, have your bow line ready. Jen, can you handle the stern? I told the man what time to expect us, so there will likely be someone on the slip to take your lines."

"Okay," said Tryon briefly.

In a few minutes more they were tied up safely at the dock.

Silently they worked, taking off their stuff, Jerry and Tryon and Jennifer. Then they woke the children. Robin was still tired and sleepy after all the excitement.

"Sun all gone!" he remarked at last sadly. "Other boat all gone! Pete all gone! Jennifer, vy can't ve go back to the harbor? I *wike* my boat! I don't vanta go vay and leave it!"

"Oh, we'll come again to it sometime, boy!" said Jennifer cheerfully. "It's our boat, you know!"

"Wes," he said with a heavy sigh.

Then the boys were back for the last load.

"Better let Heather and Hazel come with us now," said Jerry, as he was ready to start. "You and the kids sit here till we get everything ready. It won't be but a minute or two now."

So Jennifer sat in the darkness and marveled at the quiet of the little out-of-the-way place. The children at her side were also quiet, listening to the tree toads, and the frogs kerchugging and the soft sleepy twitter of a bird overhead. The silence of the woods stole over them. A sense of quiet security and peace.

The darkness was dense now all about them, except where the water made a luminous path, but the sky showed a lot of deep purple clouds that seemed to have been dragged into the picture hastily.

"There's going to be a storm tomorrow," said Karen meditatively as she looked. "Captain Andy said dark ragged purple clouds meant a storm."

"Well we won't be there to see it," said Jennifer with a little shiver of thankfulness. The day had been a trying one, and she was glad they were getting away from Peter Willis. At least it seemed as if they were. Of course one could never tell but he might turn up somewhere else. But at least they had escaped tonight. And tomorrow, what was before them? Would there perhaps be something worse coming? Oh, had it been all wrong, this running away? But no, Uncle Blake hadn't seemed to think so. And they couldn't be separated, that was all there was about it. No, they must go on and be brave. She must not fail nor falter. Almost a month was over now, and the other two would soon pass. Then they could go back home again, and somehow settle down. Although that was going to be rather awful, too, to go on through all the days without mother and daddy!

But she mustn't think of that. She must be brave!

Then they could hear Tryon dashing back through the woods, coming after them, and Jennifer brushed all sad thoughts out of the way. She had to forget, and get ready for the next stage of their exile.

"Jen, Jerry says he can't find the little picnic alcohol stove. He says for you to look and see if it's in any of the lockers. And he left his sneakers behind. I'll find them. He says for you to look all around and see if we've forgotten anything we'll need. And he says for you three to come on back with me."

So they cast a quick look about the little home that had been such a pleasant refuge these weeks.

Robin, as he climbed over the rail on to the wharf turned and looked back at the boat.

"Good-bye, nice boat!" he said, waving a wistful hand. "We'll come back some day and see you!"

And then they stumbled onward through the darkness, by the light of Tryon's small flash.

It was quite a little walk, but Tryon went ahead with his light to guide them, and finally they were stowed away in the car and ready to start. Jennifer settled back with a deep breath of relief and closed her eyes. She was tired, and so glad to be settled for awhile.

Then Jerry tramped off again to the boat, to be sure everything was safely snugged down for the night. Captain Andy had a key, and he and his son would be down the first thing in the morning to take it back to its mooring. Meanwhile Captain Andy's friend here at the wharf had promised to watch it.

At last Jerry came back and took his place at the wheel

and they started off again, not knowing whither they were going.

"Seems as if we ought to have at least God to take care of us and show us the way!" said Heather, suddenly, out of a long silence, as the old car carried them steadily over the rough woods road.

Nobody answered her at first. Hazel tried to giggle, but choked all up instead, and everybody felt tears near the surface, though they couldn't have explained just why, because they felt they really ought to be laughing that they had escaped Peter Willis so easily. Peter had come to typify to them the whole army of relatives who wanted to separate them.

Then Jerry spoke.

"Well, I guess you're right, Heather. Suppose you all shut your eyes and ask God to look after us."

Then there was a long reverent silence as the car sped onward through the night.

14

Aunt Petra had not given up, even though nearly four weeks had gone by since the exodus of the Graemes, and nothing, *simply nothing* had been done about it. She had subsided for a brief space, because she confidently expected them to turn up very soon. Blakefield Graeme was still at home, going to his office every day, coming home every evening and sitting quietly in his room with his newspaper and his books, always going downtown to his office again at the regular time every morning. He wasn't acting as if anything out of the way was happening at all. Aunt Petra knew for she had lain in ambush and come upon him most unexpectedly morning, noon and night. Never once had he failed to appear at the regular time.

Aunt Petra had fairly haunted his office for the first few days, demanding attention, no matter what important personage he was busy with at the time. She would declaim in a loud tone concerning the ridiculousness of *his* attempting to be a guardian to such a set of crazy children as the Graemes, and then demanding anew in some unique way, to be told where those children were.

But Blakefield had reached the point where he no longer attempted to argue with her. He just smiled and said they were quite well and all right, and then went on with whatever business he had in hand. Aunt Petra would talk herself out and threaten and browbeat, and finally take herself away till she could think up some new form of attack.

But at last one morning Aunt Petra arrived in the office before Uncle Blake got there, planted herself in front of his desk and said, as he arrived:

"Now Blakefield, I think the time has come to do something strenuous. Those children have been away almost a month, and not one word have any of us heard from them. We have decided that it is high time to bring the law into the matter. I have just come to warn you that if you do not divulge the hiding place of those children we shall not only inform the police, and claim their protection for the children, but we shall also publish this thing far and wide in the newspapers, so that you will no longer be able to live in a decent town, or to maintain your position of guardian to them. We think that we have already shown more patience and forbearance in this matter than could possibly be called for, and now we are going to *act.*"

"Yes?" said Blakefield. "And who is 'we,' Petra?"

"We? Why, *all* of us. All their relatives."

"Yes?" said Blakefield. "Well, have you got that in writing with all their names signed to it, Petra?"

"Well, no, but I can easily get it, if that is what you want."

"Oh, no, I was not particularly wanting it. I was just wondering," said Blakefield. "I always supposed that most of the Graeme relatives had good sense, and I didn't quite believe that they would sign their names to any such fandango as that. However, go ahead and get it if that's what you want, and just take it to my lawyer when you get it. See what he says about it. Now, you'll have to excuse me, Petra, this is a busy morning. I haven't any more time to spare."

"Look here, Blakefield, aren't you going to be sensible and tell me where those children are?"

"No, not as long as they wish me to keep silence."

"Well," said Aunt Petra, rising angrily, "then I shall certainly visit several of the prominent newspapers of the city and give them information at once about what you are doing."

"Go ahead, Petra! Suit yourself. If that's the kind of publicity you want for the family, it's all right with me. I'll simply put the matter in the hands of my lawyer, and he will inform you what you are laying yourself open to, and that you'll only succeed in delaying the return of the children. You'll probably have a lawsuit on your hands into the bargain if you keep on. But I suppose you wouldn't mind that. However, I would suggest it might be well for you to consult my lawyer before you start on this campaign. It might save you some trouble and expense."

"Lawyer!" said Aunt Petra sharply. "I didn't know you had a lawyer. What's his name and address?"

For answer Blakefield handed her a lawyer's card, and then she said contemptuously:

"Well, we have lawyers too. My lawyer is one of the best in the city."

"So?" said Blakefield. "Just ask him what he thinks of mine."

So Petra went to her own lawyer, and found that Blakefield's lawyer, Robert MacKenzie, ranked even as the despised Blakefield had said. Moreover she was advised by her own lawyer to keep out of the affair entirely.

"There is no better lawyer in this part of the country," he said, "and there is no man more respected in the whole of this city than Blakefield Graeme. He is quiet but he is solid and absolutely square in everything. If he is guardian you cannot do a thing, and if he warns you to keep out of anything he certainly must have the authority to do it, and you had better be warned."

Crestfallen, Aunt Petra went home to consider how she might stir some of the men on her side of the case to do further battle.

That was the morning of the day after Jerry and Jennifer piloted their small family down the bay and off the boat into an unknown way.

The ragged clouds of purple had developed into thunderheads of high voltage, and the world was drenched and dark and forbidding, as, sometime after midnight, they emerged at last from the woods road to a highway that was under a violent state of repair.

The little woods road that was scarcely defined enough for even the searchlights of a powerful car to discern, had a fork in it that Jerry had not noticed the day before when he had driven down with Bert. After a moment's hesitation he decided to bear left. Right would take him to the highway that led back to Captain Andy's place. Left must surely open on the same highway, only farther down, which would be even better, for he must go in the opposite direction from where Peter Willis would be. But the left fork opened in a section where the way had been thickly strewn with sharp-cut boulders of granite, pointed and forbidding, set close and deep, awaiting a filling of asphalt or the like, and set about with little red lanterns smoking menacingly.

Coming out of the darkness of the woods, his eyes heavy with sleep, Jerry lurched the car into the midst of this terrifying display of road-mending before he realized what he was doing. Having had to mount up to the highway over a steep and treacherous gully of sand he found he was unable to get back again, for turning on those stones was impossible.

The road at either side went down suddenly into deep mushy sand. "Soft shoulder!" a sign announced, and even if the car had been willing on that uncertain bed to veer to the side, it wouldn't have been safe. Backing was quite as impossible. So Jerry bumped on ahead, uncertainly and fearfully.

He was thoroughly aroused by this time and began to realize his predicament, even before Jennifer waked to the lurching of the car and cried out:

"Why, where are we? Oh *Jerry!* Why did you come up here?"

"Yes, *why?*" said Jerry solemnly, and drove on because there was nothing else to do, yet it seemed that each revolution of the wheels spelled disaster. His lights showed that the rough section lasted but a short distance farther, yet the ten feet ahead seemed miles in perspective, and

Jerry felt that every inch he progressed was agony not only to the fine old car he was driving, but to his own body as well.

"Oh, don't, *don't, don't!*" cried out Robin from his uneasy sleep. "I vanta go back! Back to my dear boat. I vanta go ho-oOO-ome!"

Jennifer sat and held her breath until Robin's wails made it impossible to hold it any longer, and then she tried to soothe him. The rest of the children woke up and clung to the seats, clutching each other's hands, maintaining a frightened silence.

Jerry, as the car lurched forward like slow sure doom, looked ahead to where the deadly work had apparently been begun on the road. He saw the smooth road roll out like a ribbon down below their level at an awful descent. Was he going to make it? Could he ever get down that incline without tearing the heart from his car? The stones seemed sharper the farther he went, and he would fain have bowed his head on the wheel and groaned aloud, giving up the fight. But he set his firm young lips and went on.

There was the dim shadow of a car ahead, parked on the smooth road, its tail lights showing. It must have come up from the other end, met the impassable barrier, and turned to go back. Yet it had not turned all the way, for it stood there as if watching Jerry.

Someone stepped out of the shadow, came slowly forward to the end of the stone bed, and stood.

Jerry sat up and nerved himself for the last effort. He was being watched. He must somehow acquit himself with dignity, if not with success. And then slowly, cautiously, like an old frightened man, the car lurched down with an awful bump, paused a moment with its fore wheels on the smooth road, and then dragged the rear wheels down, with a tearing, rending sound.

Jerry paused an instant to take breath and be sure he was over the hard going, and then cautiously threw in his clutch again, just as the figure at the side of the road stepped nearer and waved a hand.

"Tough going!" called the man. "You did well to get through!"

"Thanks!" said Jerry perfunctorily, and then gave attention to his car. He wasn't just sure yet whether all this was well or not, and he was going cautiously, listening to the engine and the rear. But the children, looking back, noticed that the stranger stood still watching them, then he stooped and looked down at the road, walking along as if he were studying something on the asphalt.

Little by little Jerry increased his speed, watching, listening.

Then suddenly, just at his left a horn sounded sharply, several times, and he jumped, startled! That must be the car that had been standing by the roadside. There had been no other car in sight. Was this a hold-up? His first impulse was to step on the gas and leave the man behind. But the horn sounded again imperatively, and then the man's voice called, and his voice was pleasant, friendly, not gruff.

"There's something the matter with your car, brother," he called. "Better get out and investigate. You're losing oil badly!"

Jerry didn't get all the man said, but something in his tone made him involuntarily slow down, and the man called again.

"Something must have happened to your crankcase, friend!" said the stranger. "You are leaving a trail of oil behind you!"

Jerry put on his brakes then, and Jennifer looked up in horror. What did this mean? What was the crankcase, and how important was it to their car? She didn't know the least little thing about machinery, but it sounded ominous.

Then suddenly she remembered that this might just possibly be someone trailing them. She must not be recognized. So she drew her silk scarf over one side of her face, and snuggled down still farther in the corner of the car, to make it appear that she was asleep.

Jerry was studying the pleasant kindly face of the young man now standing in the road, and was at once convinced that he was not a tough character, nor yet someone hired to trace them.

He sprang out of the car and stopped to look down.

The stranger pointed back, along the few rods he had already come, and there, sure enough, was a distinct line of oil, driveling along in the whiteness of the road.

The stranger stepped ahead of the car and stooped down.

"Here, come here!" said the stranger. "Already there is quite a puddle of drippings under the engine."

Jerry stooped to see, and then looked anxiously into the face of the other young man.

"Great Scott!" he ejaculated. "I wonder what's happened. I thought I heard a queer sound those last few inches before I got into the road."

"Yes," said the other, "so did I. So I thought I'd better catch you and let you know, because that oil is coming out pretty fast. After it's gone you'll burn your bearings out if you try to drive, you know!"

"Gosh!" said Jerry appalled. "Of course I will! I wonder if there's a garage, or even a filling station near? Did you come from that way?" He pointed down the good road.

"Yes," said the other young man. "I hoped there was a way through in spite of the detour sign down there at the edge of the town. I have an appointment that I want to keep in the early morning if possible, and I didn't know about this detour till I got here. But when I looked up and saw you turn into the road I thought if you could get by I'd make a stab at it too. So I came on till I saw what you were up against and then I stopped. Yes, there's a garage down about half a mile. I didn't notice whether it was open all night or not, but it's getting pretty light. It would likely be open pretty soon now anyway."

"Do you think I could make it before the oil is all gone? I wouldn't like to injure the car."

"Oh, yes, I think it will be all right. Unless you'd like to stay here and trust me to send a repair man back. I'll be glad to do that for you."

Jerry considered what that would mean.

"No," he said, "I'd better try to get there before all the oil is gone. It can't leak out all at once of course. But thanks awfully just the same. You're very kind."

"All right. I'll trail along behind in case you need any further assistance."

Jerry got back into the car and drove cautiously down the road, reflecting on the kindness of the stranger, and the predicament he had got his family into now. There had been one minute before he landed on those awful stones that he had almost dropped back. He could have done it then, why hadn't he? Just because he was too sleepy to know what he was doing. And now the poor children would have to wait a long time for the repair to be made. What would they do? And what might not happen? This was ordinarily a fairly well traveled highway. He had hoped to get beyond it into a back road before daylight. Well, the detour would stop at least part of the traffic.

They hurried on and found the garage was open. All but Jerry got out and went into a little restaurant that served midnight and early morning breakfasts for railroad men. It was hot and sticky. They had cereal and weak cream and Robin fell asleep again before he finished his.

The stranger soon drove up and followed Jerry into the workshop. Jennifer saw him from the window of the restaurant. He seemed very kind and pleasant, but she warned the children not to say anything about themselves or where they came from, if he should speak to them.

There were two holes in the crankcase, torn by the stones they had crossed. Jerry came in and told her about it while he swallowed a cup of the bitter muddy coffee. He said the stranger had been very kind and helped with the mending. He seemed to know how to do everything.

When at last the car was finished and they might start on again, Jennifer and the children were waiting at one side of the road, sitting under some inhospitable poplar trees with their backs turned to the road. Jennifer was taking no risks about being recognized even in the dark of this unlikely hour in the morning.

They got into the car, pausing a moment to thank the stranger.

Jennifer had instructed the children what seats to take, and had hidden herself in the corner of the back seat, but as the stranger stood there for that minute talking to Jerry she could see his face clearly, and she was haunted with the feeling that she had seen him before, or else he reminded her of someone she had known a long time ago. Then he bowed and smiled, tipped his hat in a general gesture to the whole carload, got into his car and sped away, while they followed more slowly behind him.

"Who was he? What's his name?" asked Jennifer.

"Why, do you know, I never asked him! I was so afraid he would ask me who I was that I kept off topics like that as well as I could. But he's all right! He's a real white man. Why, he lost a whole hour and a half on our account, just because he thought we might possibly need him. And as it turned out, we did. That fellow in the garage was only an apprentice, and he was afraid to tackle our car. He said it was 'too ritzy' for him. He said his boss wouldn't be here until eight o'clock, and he guessed he'd 'leave it rest' till he came. And then this other fellow spoke up and said 'Oh, that's not such a hard job. Here, I'll help you. Get your solder ready,' and he just kidded him along till he got to work, and they did it together. Gosh! I was ashamed! Nice clean fellow like that getting down under our car on his back in all that dirt, getting his hands and face all grease! And he's on his way to speak at a conference or something in the mountains! I got that much information from him about himself. Good night! He'll be a mess when he gets there! And he thinks he's going to be late to his meeting, too. I tried to make him let me pay him something, but he wouldn't hear to it. Just smiled, and said I could return the favor some day if he got into trouble. I think he was great! I'd like to get to know a fellow like that."

"Where was it he was going?" asked Jennifer.

"Why, I don't remember the name. Maybe it'll come back to me. He spoke as if we would know where it was.

Said it was up in the mountains. I think I'd know the name if I saw it. I'll get a map and try to look it up when we get somewhere. But say, Jen, where are we going?"

"Yes, that's just what I was going to ask. Have you any thoughts, Jerry?"

"No, I was only thinking of getting away from that chump Pete Willis. But we might as well go on for a while on this road till we come to a good place to turn off and study the map awhile, don't you think so?"

"Well, I guess so, only I know you're all in. Why don't you let me drive awhile?"

"Well, after a bit. Wait till we find a nice quiet place and then we'll all rest awhile. What's the matter with Robin? He hasn't spoken a word since it happened."

"Oh, I guess he's just sleepy. Come over here, Robin, and sit beside me, and put your head in my lap."

Robin came willingly enough and was soon asleep again, and they traveled on silently. As morning dawned clearer there was more and more traffic.

Presently Jerry veered off into a side road, and soon they were in a wood, where they could be free from staring eyes. There they rested awhile and ate the lunch they had hurriedly packed on the boat before they left.

The children had a chance to run around and exercise, and Jerry and Jennifer retired behind a map to try to see where they were and what they should do next. But they found it exceedingly difficult to decide anything.

It was almost five o'clock when, reluctant to leave this quiet place, they at last called the children together and piled into the car again. They had decided to drive as far as they could, until they got too tired to keep on, and then to take the first likely resting place, be it hotel, or cottage, or tourist camp.

15

As they went on their journey grew more and more upward.

"We are getting into the mountains," said Jennifer looking about her, somewhat troubled. "I wonder if that is wise?"

"Why not?" asked Jerry. "It looks good to me here. It'll be good for the children to have some mountain air."

"Yes, but you forget. The mountains are where a lot of our family acquaintances go in the summer. We're liable to come right into a nest of them, and of course they have heard we are away, and they'll rush right at us to know where we went and why, and they'll call up Aunt Majesta, or Agatha Lane and tell them we are here, and that will be the end of us."

"Well, but it's getting toward night, and they'll not be likely to spot us on the highway at night. And by morning we can find a pleasant byway, and keep out of their haunts. Besides, if we steer clear of the well known resorts we are practically safe, don't you think? And after all we haven't got the money to go to the hotels where they go."

"I don't know," sighed Jennifer. "I don't know as we are safe anywhere. Even if we went to the north pole there would be somebody we know, I'm sure."

"I do' vanta go to the norf pole," said Robin wearily. "I vant my nice little home beddie or my bunk."

Jennifer cast a look of despair at Jerry.

"And that's that!" she said in a low tone as she gathered

the little boy into her arms comfortably. "He hasn't seemed like himself all day."

"Well, let him take another nap and perhaps he'll feel better. I don't know where else to go, not at this stage of the game."

So they settled down for the night, and Jerry, weary already and sick at heart, drove on, while Jennifer in the back seat held the heavy limp little boy, who tossed about in her arms and moaned every little while.

She tried to get to sleep herself, but her mind went to and fro, worrying about Robin. Oh, nothing must happen to Robin! He was her mother's baby! She decided that the shock of watching Peter, together with the shock of seeing him upstairs frowning the day they left home had been too much for his small mind. He really had been rather wonderful yesterday on the boat, using discretion that even a more mature mind might not have had. But finally she fell asleep.

Sometime in the night she awoke with a start to realize that the car was not moving. She opened her eyes and peered out of the window, seeing nothing but darkness at first. Rubbing her eyes and continuing to gaze out, the darkness resolved itself into dim, darker tree trunks everywhere, dense and black. The road beneath the car was black also. They seemed to be parked in the midst of a dense forest. As far as she could see, ahead, behind, at either side, it was all alike!

Startled, she looked where Jerry had been at the wheel and there she saw him slumped comfortably down, his head against the window frame, his arms relaxed, his breath coming steadily as if he were in a deep sleep. Poor Jerry! She blamed herself that she had not waked sooner and relieved him at the wheel.

But perhaps it would be as well not to disturb him just now. They were here, and certainly in no immediate danger of being discovered. Why not just stay till at least a little daylight would show them the way out. Jerry had evidently turned out all lights and settled here deliberately. Perhaps that was the best thing he could have done.

So she relaxed once more and dropped into oblivion again.

Morning found them all stiff and sore and cold, for there on the mountain summer seemed not to have penetrated. The children awoke miserable and cross and hungry and shivering. Robin awoke sneezing.

"We'll have to get out into the sunshine somewhere quickly," said Jennifer anxiously. She had a sudden realization of what it would be if one of them got sick, or even caught a heavy cold. Robin had been a croupy baby, she recalled, and what if he should get one of those fearful attacks! She hadn't much experience with them. Mother and the nurse always looked after him then. What would she do? Or was he too old for croup now? She didn't know. How many things there were that she did not know.

Jerry roused, heavy-eyed from sleep, and manipulated the car out of the darkness of the woods into a sunny spot.

"I just couldn't go on another rod," he apologized, "and I saw you were all in. I was afraid if I tried to drive any longer that I would fall asleep at the wheel and run you all into a tree, or into a river somewhere."

"Poor soul!" said Jennifer. "I know. We shouldn't try to drive late at night. Not unless a regiment of police are after us, and we have to to save our lives. Though in that case I guess we would be so excited that we wouldn't be in danger of going to sleep."

Jennifer herded her flock out of the car and made them run in the sunshine until they were warm and glowing again, and then they sat down on the running board, or stood around, and cleaned up everything eatable that they had brought along.

"Now," said Jennifer when they were back in the car and had started on their way again, "for pity's sake let's find a habitation before night, even if it's only a tourist camp. I don't see having these children sleep in a close little heap another night, let alone ourselves. You and I have got to keep fit, Jerry, or we never can take care of the children!"

"I know," said Jerry wearily, "I feel all crumpled up!" and he stretched and yawned wearily.

So when they came to the next little town they drove about its outskirts hunting a place to stay. They didn't want to be in a town. Too many acquaintances might be going through. But they wanted to be near enough to one to get what provisions they would need.

But it was two days later before they came on a forlorn little shanty that seemed a possible answer to their need.

They had spent the two nights between, one in a tourist camp, the other in the car again, drawn up in the woods. They hadn't dared try the better looking camps lest they might meet someone they knew. For even a servant who had been acquainted with some of their servants, might inform on them by chance, or in case by this time Aunt Petra had got under way, and offered a reward for their return. But it was nervous work, those nights, with that feeling of heavy responsibility resting on the young brother and sister who had never had any responsibility in their lives before.

So when they saw this uninviting little cottage with a big sign "FOR RENT" on its ugly front door, they stopped and Jerry got out and went to investigate.

The house was back from the road among the trees, and on a little private road, just a homemade road marked by the wheels of an old-time car that stood in the unkempt yard.

The door was opened by a forlorn woman with untidy hair, and a soiled cotton dress. Jerry stepped in and looked around. He went upstairs and then came down briskly.

"It's fifty dollars for the month of August. Twenty-five more if we want it in September," he said. "She says she'll throw in the rest of this month, it's only three days more anyway, and we can come in right away if we want to. There's a parlor and dining room and kitchen if you can call a thing like that bare place in there a parlor, and there are three bedrooms and a bathroom. The bedrooms each have a double bed, and there is a cot, so I guess we could make out. We have to pay the fifty down, because she wants to get away. Her daughter's sick, and she needs the money to go to her. What do you say? Shall we take it?"

"Oh I guess so," sighed Jennifer. "It doesn't look very inviting, but I shouldn't think any of our friends would look for us in a place like this. How far is it from a village?"

"About three miles either way, a village each way."

"Well, let's take it."

The woman, it appeared, was about to go to her daughter anyway, money or no money, for an ancient car drove in behind them just then, and a man yelled out: "Ready, Auntie?" So the old woman accepted the fifty dollars Jerry hastily handed out, took her bags and cardboard boxes, and departed. Jennifer got out to take her first lesson in renting houses, and finding out what to do with them after they were rented.

She entered the house and looked around in despair.

"Why, it's *dirty*, Jerry!" she said in dismay.

"It certainly looks so," said the boy. "Well, shall I get in the car and chase her back and tell her we'll take our money and go on?"

"Oh, no!" she said sadly. "I suppose we can clean it. Soap and water make things clean, of course, though I don't really know how, but I guess I can learn. Somebody had to learn how to clean the first time it was done."

"Oh sure!" said Jerry cheerfully. "What one person can do another can!"

There was a wood stove, and only three sticks of wood in sight, so Jerry brought in the alcohol stove from the car and set some water to heat in one of their own clean kettles. Then he set about trying to make a wood fire in that impossible stove with no kindling, and no newspaper, only matches to start it with. But he lacked skill, and knowledge of dampers, and it required time to learn all those things.

Jennifer went upstairs and looked around and came down with her nose in the air and a firm look around her pretty mouth.

"Jerry, it's *awful!*" she said. "Dirt everywhere! And there aren't but four sheets in the place, and they have been used! As for the mattresses they are made of corn husks, I think, and have been used by generations, to judge by their looks. They're just impossible. We'll have to get quite a lot of things."

"Okay!" said Jerry. "What'll I get? It's either get things or forfeit our fifty dollars and go on away, isn't it?"

"Well, perhaps!" said Jennifer. "But the three blankets are filthy! Of course we have a few along, but we'll need more if it is mountain-cold here the way it was last night."

"Likely I can find a 'washerlady,' " encouraged Jerry. "Suppose I go scouting and see what I can discover. I'll empty the car and take Hazel with me, and Try can stay here with you. Now, what do you want first?"

"Well, a broom and a scrubbing brush, some rags—no, you can't buy rags—cheese cloth! I think that's what to use. Get several yards."

"How many is several?"

"Oh, five yards, I guess. It's cheap, I know."

Jerry went to work.

"Tryon," he called, "spread out those newspapers we got before we left the boat. I haven't even had time yet to read them, but never mind. Spread them on the grass and pile everything that needs to be cared for from the ground on top of them. Empty the car. Then you'd better get your old working togs and put them on. You don't want to soil anything else."

"Be sure to get some soap!" called Jennifer from the upper window.

"There are big brown slippery looking bugs walking around under the sink, awfully fast!" called Heather.

"Oh, let's see!" said Karen and sped on eager feet, with Robin hopping on behind and shouting, "Wes-see! Wes-see!"

"Sister, shall I get some food?" asked Hazel with a grown-up air. "We'll all be frightfully hungry pretty soon, and we haven't anything much left but two jars of jam and some peanut butter."

"Yes," said Jennifer wearily. "Get bread and butter, milk, plenty of it, a glass jar of tongue, a pound of sliced ham, some cheese and crackers, and oranges. There's no use getting anything that has to be cooked till we know how to work that stove. We've got coffee and sugar in the picnic box. You could get some fruit too, whatever looks nice, and a can of cookies."

Hazel and Jerry started off and Tryon and Jennifer organized to clean up. An old floppy broom took the first layer off the floor and frightened the cockroaches away. Jennifer took the dirty sheets from the bed with the tips of her fingers, and dropped them out the window on the grass. Then she sent the dirty blankets after them. She looked with disgust again at the mattresses. How could they ever be willing to lie down and realize that those vile mattresses were under them? How were they going to endure several weeks in this environment? Oh, how silly they had been, to let fifty dollars go away from them so easily without even looking about to see whether this was the right kind of a place or not! Of course mother or daddy would have known at the first look. But maybe she would have known too if it had not been that she was tired and worried. But of course mother and daddy had probably never been in straits like this. They had never been afraid that the police might come after them and drive them into trouble.

And then, for the first time since she had started out on this expedition, Jennifer began to wonder whether after all she had been right to run away from home this way with all the children. If they had stayed at home and gone on from day to day, surely there would have been some way to assert their rights, and decline to have the family separated. Of course it would have been a terrible battle, for Aunt Petra and the rest were indomitable, and it would have been hard for Uncle Blake, for he never had really tried to stand out against those aunts. At least she didn't know that he had. And he might not have tried. He likely had no right to stand out. Why, hadn't he said in the New

York paper that he agreed with them? Practically put his approval as far as that would go, on what they had done?

But Jennifer saw now that it had been a temeritous thing to do, and very likely if she had not been so fearful and so impatient there might have been some other way to accomplish it. Perhaps there had been a guardian, likely some lawyer. What she ought to have done was to hunt him out and go and tell him all about it. Only she hadn't dared.

Well, she didn't, and she was here, and must make the best of it. Probably even this house would turn out to be not so bad when they got it cleaned up. But would they ever get it cleaned so that they wouldn't hate every inch of it, and dread to touch anything?

She could remember hearing daddy and some of his friends tell how they had felt in France when they would get into a dugout to sleep and find cooties infesting the whole place. She shuddered! What were cooties like, anyway?

Then there came another thought. The beds? There were such things as bedbugs. She had heard of them, though she had never met any of them personally. If there should be bedbugs what would she do? There were things they did to bedbugs to get rid of them, but how could she find out?

She put out a shrinking thumb and finger and lifted a corner of the mattress, but dropped it before she discovered anything. Perhaps it would be just as well not to know it if there were any. But oh, the thought! How was she going to be willing to get into one of those awful rickety beds.

By the time Jerry and Hazel were back, Jennifer and Tryon had managed to swab out the terrible excuse for a sink, and to wash off the pantry shelves so there would be a place to put Hazel's purchases, but there was a kind of despair over their faces as the others drove up. They were both tired and discouraged. It seemed to Jennifer that she couldn't lift a hand to do a thing until she had a good night's sleep. Yet she had to go on and work all the afternoon, at hard unaccustomed tasks, and not even know if she was doing them the right way.

Hazel had been smart. She had purchased a dozen rolls of cotton wadding, and when it was opened out to its full width it was wide enough to sheath those awful mattresses. Jennifer took heart of hope and went to work. She and Tryon washed the bedsteads from one end to the other, even the springs had their share of cleansing, and then she shrouded the mattresses in cotton wadding. Hazel had also purchased new sheets. They were coarse and quite stiff with starch, perhaps to camouflage their coarseness, but they were clean and new, and after a little hesitation Jennifer uncompromisingly took the old sheets and tore them into cleaning cloths, which she washed out thoroughly before she used them.

"We can leave these new ones behind in their place when we go," she explained to Hazel, who was horrified that she dared.

So the work of cleaning went on.

They put Robin and Karen to take naps in the car, but all the rest worked, and by night the fire was going briskly—Jerry had asked questions down at the hardware store—and there was a clean table to eat on, a clean chair or stool apiece, and a so-called clean, if somewhat questionable place for each one to sleep. But there wasn't a pillow in the outfit that Jennifer would let any of them sleep on. However, they were too weary to care about that, and after a pick-up supper they went to bed.

The children slept fitfully, tossing about on their unaccustomedly hard beds. Robin moaned in his sleep, and complained sorrowfully in unintelligible language.

It turned out that there were mosquitoes in addition to the other occupants in the house, and there were no screens! Night was their harvest time.

Jerry and Jennifer slept like logs after their hard work, but the children wakened and complained and there seemed to be little peace to be had, even tired as they were.

Moreover the plumbing was atrocious. The water ran continually, filling them with a sense of something decidedly wrong. Jerry tinkered at it and then found he had done more harm than good and so gave up. They didn't want workmen coming into their house to fix things up, and report to the police how many there were of them, but it began to look as if it was going to be necessary.

Somehow they got through the night, though in the morning the children's faces and arms and hands were badly bitten. Jerry confided to Jennifer that he didn't know whether that was all the work of mosquitoes. "You know there are such things as bedbugs, Jen!"

"Oh, do they bite?" she asked aghast.

"Sure they do!" said Jerry cheerfully. "Wait. I'll look. We had 'em at camp one summer when I went out with the kids. I know the signs."

So Jerry looked.

And then Jerry went down to the drug store and bought some deadly concoction that was supposed to kill them. And the next night they essayed to sleep again.

But the army who were supposed to have been poisoned came out in full force and attacked them in their sleep. And when Jennifer turned on the light and saw the vile little creatures walking serenely over the nice new sheet on which she had been sleeping, she uttered a squeal of disgust and decided that they had better move on as quickly as possible.

So quite early in the morning they took their own blankets, and whatever of their personal clothing had been used to supplement the blankets, and hung them out on a line made from the rope that was used to lash their goods to the running board of the car. There they hung in the sunshine, until late in the afternoon, when they started on their way again.

Jerry had asked many questions at the store and filling stations, and had studied maps, so he wasn't altogether without a chart in his mind as he drove away from the little abandoned home.

The agent lived about a mile up the road, so they took the key to him.

"Though there's no sense in locking up," said Jerry. "There isn't a thing in the place that would be worth stealing, except the sheets we bought and are leaving behind us."

But the agent told them he had no authority to give back even five dollars of the rent they had paid. If they were foolish enough to throw up their bargain it was none of his business, and if they changed their minds and wanted to come back by night it was all the same to him. He'd wait three days before he rented it again, but after that they needn't ask to come back.

So they drove away a sadder and a wiser little group, fifty dollars' worth wiser than when they first took that house.

A storm came down and covered the mountains. It slithered down the windshield like suds, and filled the hearts of the little runaway family with despair. How were they ever to find a place to live in a storm like that?

So they plodded on into the night and the unknown roads, and realized that the way ahead looked very dark indeed.

Robin began to sneeze again, hoarsely, and Jennifer's heart was gripped with fear. There was something about that hoarse little voice that awakened memories of nights in which there had been hurrying footsteps, anxious voices breaking into normal sleep. And though she had never taken much cognizance of it before, she now was burdened with the awful responsibility that she had sometimes seen in her mother's face. It had been understood that if those attacks of Robin's were not nipped in the bud, there might be serious consequences, and she recalled the words "bronchitis" and "pneumonia." Oh, if Robin should get sick now! She couldn't call in a doctor if they had no place to call him to, and anyway if they did he would have to know their names and where they lived. Doctors always asked those questions on their first visit.

And they couldn't leave Robin in a hospital alone, it

would break his heart. And of course no hospital would let any of them stay with him. Oh, it was all awful.

Of course if worst came to worst they would have to call up Uncle Blake and ask him what to do. Uncle Blake would surely come to them. But that would mean to fail in their purpose of trying to stay away until nobody had any right to tell them what to do! Oh, if she were only of age right away now, and could take the children to their own dear home and stay there, and tell the aunts please to let them alone and not try to boss them!

With aching arms she held Robin close that night, and soothed him, and began to try to pray in her heart for him. And when the morning dawned they saw a little house, up the side of the mountain, just a tiny thing, with a low curving roof reaching out over a wide front porch, and boxes of flowers around the porch. There were mountain pinks about the doorsteps, and rhododendrons up the mountain side behind the house.

"Oh, if we could just have that!" said Jennifer piteously, lifting a white face from her night's vigil and looking up.

"Maybe we can," said Jerry, hopefully and turned the car up a winding road that apparently led near the cottage.

"It won't be for rent, of course. Such a little gem! It would be snatched up the first thing."

But when they got up there and stopped where the road ended, at the little swinging gate in front of the cottage, Jerry climbed out and went up the steps.

This time it was a brisk little middle-aged woman in a clean blue and white gingham dress who opened the door, carrying an open letter in her hand.

"I suppose this cottage isn't for rent, is it, even for a little while?" There was perhaps a wistfulness in Jerry's tone that arrested the woman's attention.

She glanced at Jerry, looked beyond at the respectable car, and the nice-looking young woman with a child in her arms, and then down at the letter in her hand, a slow, wondering little pucker coming between her eyes.

"Well," she smiled, "to tell the truth, it wasn't five

minutes ago, but—" she looked down at the letter again, "since I got this letter just now I've been wishing I had rented early in the summer and visited my sister instead of coming up here. She wants me to come. She isn't well and her husband's away." She gave Jerry another troubled glance.

"I don't know but I might rent it to you," she said, looking off frowning toward the opposite mountain, "if you are willing to pay enough."

"Oh!" said Jerry with a note of relief in his voice, and then *"Oh!"* anxiety coming to the fore. "How much would you want?"

"Well, I couldn't think of renting it under a hundred and twenty-five at the least. For a month, you know. I couldn't rent it for longer than that. I like to be here myself at the end of the season to close up."

"A hundred and twenty-five," meditated Jerry. "Wait! Let me ask!" and he dashed down to the car and told Jennifer.

The woman finished reading her letter and was ready to talk when he came back.

"Could we see it?" asked Jerry.

"Why, of course," said the woman, afraid now that she might have asked too much, when they saw how really tiny it was.

But there was no question about it in Jennifer's mind when she saw the neatness of the whole place. Not a cockroach nor a bedbug would dare show its face in that immaculate place, and it was completely screened with copper wire so there would be no trouble on that score.

But there were only two bedrooms, a downstairs living room, a tiny kitchen, and the weest kind of a bathroom. For an instant Jennifer hesitated. Could they possibly get along with so little room? Of course! It was bigger than a car, and that was all they had had for several awful nights.

"Can we get along with so little room?" asked Jerry, breathless.

"Oh yes," said Jennifer drawing a deep breath. "We'll manage. It is so lovely up here it will be wonderful!"

Then it developed that there was electric light, and a gas stove, and Jennifer said "Oh yes, they would get along!"

There was no cleaning to be done when they moved into the little house on the mountain side, they had only to contrive how they could sleep, but that seemed a mere trifle considering all they had gone through before.

It was all settled in a little while and soon the good lady had gone smiling on her way to her sister's. Jerry had taken her down the mountain to the station and put her on the train.

When he came back they went around together and surveyed their mansion. They felt as if they had fallen heir to a castle.

"Some of us can sleep on the floor," said Jerry resignedly. "It looks clean enough to eat from."

"Yes, it's clean all right," said Jennifer. "But you won't have to sleep on the floor. Tryon and I have got it all fixed. There are two couches downstairs in the living room, and you and Tryon can have those. Heather and Hazel will take the smallest of the two bedrooms, Karen and I will take the other, and I found a cot in a closet that will be the very thing for Robin. It's evidently been made for a child, for it is shorter than most cots. It has woven wire springs that must have been taken out of a larger cot, and it has a lovely thick mattress pad. It will be more comfortable than most of the beds we strike."

So they settled themselves with delight and were almost as happy as the night they reached the boat. They felt that another month at least was safely planned for their exile.

But that night, in the night, Robin woke up with that sharp bark that meant croup, and fear came and sat in the cottage on the mountain side, where they had all gone so happily to sleep a few hours before.

16

Jennifer arose hastily and tried the few remedies at hand. Some cough syrup. A hot water bag. A drink of hot milk!

But Robin couldn't swallow the syrup or the milk, and the hot water bag seemed only to distress him.

Hazel woke up and came to the rescue.

"Here, I know what to do. You have to have a cold compress. I've fixed 'em for him many a time. Get me a little bit of ice in a cup, Jerry. Jennifer, have you got one of your small handkerchiefs here, and a piece of flannel? You have to fold the handkerchief in a little oblong, and then squeeze it out of the coldest water you can get, and put it at the base of the throat, so, and then you fold the flannel around it to keep out the cold air. Yes, that little wool shirt of his will do. It ought to be wool. Mother always kept a piece. And then every few minutes, as soon as you think the compress is getting hot from his neck you slip it out without letting the air get in, dip it in the ice water again, squeeze it hard as you can, and lay it in again."

Marvelously it worked! The hoarse outcry ceased. Little by little, that whoop that so alarmed subsided, and the household settled into comparative quiet again.

But an hour later there was another whoop, wilder than the first. The flannel cloth had got down and let the cold air in and the child seemed almost choking.

The brothers and sisters gathered around in another

alarm. Poor little Robin, gasping for his breath, crying out, and looking from one to the other in anguish.

Again Hazel did her best, and again there was a little relief, but not so much as the first time, and when morning dawned it was evident that Robin was still a very sick little boy.

Jerry went for a doctor, but the only doctor he could discover had gone off for four days. Nobody seemed to be taking his place. There were doubtless other doctors but this was a quiet district where there were few houses, and the people round about were all tenants, and didn't know the local doctors. The people at the store knew only the local doctor who was away. At Jerry's earnest plea the wife of the absent doctor promised to try to get in touch with her husband by telephone, and Jerry had to be satisfied with that. He hurried back to the cottage, and they waited, and petted Robin till he almost smiled. But still he coughed on, and the cough had a hoarse shrill sound.

Two days went by with no doctor and then Jerry went after him again. But this time the wife was gone too, having left a note on the doorbell that the doctor would return in a couple of days. A casual doctor! Jerry didn't know what to do. It didn't seem right to go off and leave the children all in Jennifer's care, and it would be equally wrong to try to put Robin in the car and drive till they found a doctor.

He went back to consult with Jennifer.

Robin seemed a little better that morning so they wrapped him in blankets and took him out on the porch to lie on Jerry's cot, and he did seem to improve, although the cough still persisted.

The days went by, and at last came the casual doctor. He frowned at Robin, and felt his pulse, and said there didn't seem to be much the matter with him. He guessed he had weathered it, and might as well get up and run around.

So the next day, very briefly, Robin got up, herded back to bed again by Jennifer who felt much worried. But day by day he seemed to improve, until finally he was dressed and out running around with Karen.

They were all much relieved, and began to think they had got through that hard place well, without even having to call Uncle Blake whose weekly bulletins in the New York paper they no longer received of course, because they were sent to Captain Andy, and Captain Andy no longer knew where they were. There was no news stand around their modest little mountain dwelling that dealt in New York papers, so they were again in a world of their own, and didn't realize what anxieties poor Uncle Blake might be going through on his own part.

The housework in their new abode was like child's play, and to the intense delight of the three little girls Jennifer delegated much of it to them, and so had opportunity for a much needed rest herself.

One afternoon she was lying down on the cot on the porch. Jerry and Tryon had gone off to a mountain stream to fish, Hazel and Heather were walking down to the little store on the highway to get some tomatoes to go with the fish the boys would catch. Karen and Robin were out playing by a great tree whose gnarled roots made a lovely playhouse back of the cottage.

It had grown very still and Jennifer sank deeper in her sleep than she had meant to do. She did not know how long she had lain there when she suddenly awoke and looked around. Had she dreamed it, or did she hear a voice of distress up in the woods?

She lay quietly alert for a little, listening. There was no sound in the air but the droning of bees and the chirp of the birds in the high tree beyond the flower beds. There were no voices at all. It must be that Hazel and Heather were not back yet, or else they were at their everlasting reading. Dear little girls! How happy they had been to find that the cottage contained a bookcase filled with sweet old-fashioned story books that they might read. But it must be time that they came in and began to set the table. The boys would surely be back soon.

And where were Karen and Robin? Why, it was strange

she could not hear their voices at all. Where could they be?

She started up, the habit of watching Robin lest he get too tired, still upon her.

And then she heard that cry of distress again, nearer this time. Was that Robin, crying? Why, Robin scarcely ever cried aloud.

She heard it again and started to her feet, looking about.

"Robin! Where are you?" she called, and seemed to hear her own voice echo back to her. And then she heard distinct sobbing, coming nearer fitfully and dying away.

"Robin! Karen!" she called again.

The crying was from up the mountain. Looking up she could see nothing. But she hurried down the steps and up the path that led behind the house, her heart beating wildly. Surely they knew better than to climb up the mountain. She had told Karen very carefully not to let Robin get tired or he might be sick again, but all her calling did no good, and, quite frightened now, she hurried up the mountain side herself, following the sound of crying.

At last she came in sight of a woebegone little figure stumbling down a few steps at a time, and stopping to call, and cry aloud, and then pausing to put his head down in his arms and sob. It was Robin! Poor little sick Robin, coming down the mountain, and just as she recognized him she saw him stumble over the root of a tree and fall headlong, rolling over and over down toward her.

"Robin! Darling!" she cried out, and ran up the hill after him as fast as she could run.

She gathered him up in her arms and sat down on a log, snuggling his face in her neck, and trying to soothe him.

"What is it, Robin, dear? What are you crying about? Did something frighten you?" she questioned.

"I vasn't fwightened," he sobbed out at last. "I vas *tired!*"

"Oh, my dear! Why did you walk so far? Why did you

go up the mountain? You know I told you to stay right there behind the house."

"Wes, b-b-b-but Karen vented, an' I vanted to go! So I vented. But then I got too tired, an' Karen vouldn't come back. Her—her—her sayed Jerwy an' Twyon vas 'tumin' an' ve vould meet them. But th—th—they didn't come, an' I got awful tired, an' I told Karen to c-c-come home, but she sayed it vasn't much farther. So, I c-c-came b-b-back vif out her!"

He stopped and burying his face in Jennifer's arms sobbed again.

"But where is Karen?" asked Jennifer in sudden alarm.

"Her—her—her vented on vif out me!" said Robin solemnly, and then sobbed again.

"Karen!" called Jennifer sharply. "Karen, where are you? You are a naughty girl! Don't you know I told you Robin was a sick little boy and you must take care of him? Karen, where are you?"

But no Karen answered.

Robin lifted his head and looked up.

"Her is vented avay. Her is all gone!" he said. "Her can't hear you. Her is *all gone.*"

"Where has she gone, Robin? Tell me quick!"

"Her is vented vay over the top of the mountain. Her said there vas birds and fairies on the other side, an' Jerwy and Twyon was over zere!" And then he sobbed again at the remembrance.

Jennifer stood up with the sick child in her arms and called and called, wildly, distractedly, but there was no answer, and finally she knew that she must get Robin back to the house and to bed at once or there would be serious consequences. So she started down with him, carrying him, for when she stood him on his feet he swayed and would have fallen if she had not caught him. It was no easy task to get down the steep places in the mountain side with the heavy child in her arms. But at last she struggled down and into the house and laid him on the couch in the living room, tears suddenly springing to her own eyes, she felt so helpless.

Hazel and Heather came up the walk just then and she called to them. They were bringing their purchases and talking gaily.

"Hazel, get a cup of warm milk for Robin. Quick! I've got to get him to bed."

"Why, what's the matter?" asked the little girl aghast. "Robin isn't sick again, is he?"

"I hope not. Karen took him too far up the mountain, and he got very tired. He ought to be in bed at once. And now we don't know where Karen is. He says she went way up the mountain."

"I'll go find her," said Heather briskly.

"No!" said Jennifer sharply. "It's too near dark! You might get lost too."

"Oh, I wouldn't get lost. I know my way."

"No! Don't go!" said Jennifer again. "As soon as I get Robin in bed I'll go myself."

"You carry him up the stairs," said Hazel, "and I'll put him to bed. I've often done it."

"All right," said Jennifer, and lifted the dead weight of the already sleeping child and carried him up the short flight to his bed.

"Now, don't you two girls, either of you, stir a step out of this house till I get back! Do you promise me?" said the older sister. "And if Jerry comes before I get back tell him I've just gone up to the top of the mountain. It isn't far, and besides I think maybe Karen was just teasing that she didn't answer. I'll be back very soon. Take good care of Robin."

Then she turned and hurried down the stairs, and out, up the mountain side.

Jennifer had not returned yet when Jerry came, and when the little girls told him what had happened he dashed into the house and got two flash lights.

"You stay here, Try, and look after the girls and Robin. I'll go after Jen," he said, and dashed away.

Tryon gave a despairing look after him and then turned to the girls demanding to hear the story over again. Then he went upstairs and looked at his little brother, saw the deep flush upon his face, laid his hand on his head.

"He's got a fever!" he said to the girls who had followed him up. "An awful fever! I guess maybe we'd better do something about it. Did you give him anything to eat?"

"We tried to feed him some hot milk, but he wouldn't swallow it," said Hazel with a worried look.

"Well, say, isn't there any witch hazel or anything to bathe his head with? Mother always bathes our heads with witch hazel when we have headaches and fevers."

"Maybe the lady had some in the medicine closet," suggested Heather. "I think we could take some of hers, couldn't we, for a sick little boy?"

They searched the medicine closet and found a bottle with about an inch in it, and Hazel doused it on a handkerchief, and bathed Robin's forehead and cheeks, and he sighed as if it felt good.

"It's getting dark!" said Heather in a frightened tone. "I wish Jennifer would come. Maybe she'll get lost too." She went to the window and began to cry softly.

"Now don't you lose your nerve, kid," said Tryon. "Things are bad enough without you turning on the tears. Mop up and go and set the table. They'll be hungry as bears when they do get back."

"But I'm afraid they can't find Karen," she wailed.

"Well, do you think your tears will find her any quicker?"

Heather laughed nervously, and went down stairs rubbing the tears away.

"Go down and help her get supper, Hazel," said Tryon. "Keep her mind busy. Don't let her cry. I'll stay with the kid."

So the girls busied themselves for a long time setting an elaborate supper table, cutting some radishes they found in the garden, in the shape of little rosebuds, the way the cook at home used to do, putting some mountain pinks in a vase in the center of the table. It was very pretty when it was done, and they went and flattened their noses again against the window pane to look out.

It was quite dark before they came back, those two who had gone on that fruitless errand. They had had a hard time themselves getting back in the pitch darkness, even with the flash lights.

"And, oh, what will it be for Karen? Poor little silly Karen!"

"Now Jennifer, don't you get excited. She'll be all right. She's probably well frightened by this time, and she'll likely get so tired that she'll lie down and go to sleep. We shall easily find her, certainly as soon as daylight comes, and probably right away pretty soon. There's a fellow down at the store who has a powerful flash light that lights up a long way. I'll go right down and get him to come with me, and we'll comb the mountain. It isn't so very big, and it can't take so very long to go over it. Don't get excited now. Take it easy. You know you're the dependence of us all. You're our main dependence. You're the head of this family, the head of the house, and you mustn't give way or we'll all go to pieces."

"Yes, I'm head of this house and I got you all into this awful mess, and I ought to have known better! I ought to have let us stay home, and stood those awful aunts, and waited around till I got older and then got us all back again. But oh, I thought I was doing right."

"Of course you did, Jen. So did I. And so do I now. It's going to come out all right, I know. That fellow at the store will go with me, I'm sure. And he knows every stick and stone on this mountain. He's lived here all his life. Now you go in and look after Robin and the rest. Tryon will stay here with you. And I hope I'll be back in a very short time with Karen. Now, cheer up!"

"Wait!" said Jennifer, her voice trembling. "You've got to come in just a minute before you go. You *must,* I tell you!"

"But Jen, I ought to hurry, you know."

"Just a minute! It's important, Jerry!"

She dragged him inside the door and the others came in from the kitchen, Tryon from upstairs, and looked at them anxiously.

"Come here, all of you," said Jennifer. "You must all be in on this. We've got to pray to God to help us! We've gone on our own long enough and it's time we asked God to take over for us. I don't know that we've any right to ask for help in a hole like this when we haven't paid any attention to God before, but my old nurse Kirsty used to say God loved us, and maybe He'll understand and be sorry for us. But anyway, we've tried our own way and it didn't work, and we've got to ask God. Kneel down, all of you. You too, Tryon, and every one of you have got to pray! If we all talk to Him perhaps He'll do something about it, for we can't do anything about it ourselves. You don't need to say many words for we haven't much time. Jerry has to go. But you've all got to pray. Maybe He'll hear because there are so many of us!"

With a wild pleading look around on them all Jennifer dropped on her knees and began.

"Oh God, we haven't been very good children to you, nor thought much about you before, but now we haven't any mother and father, and we're in trouble. We tried to get ourselves out, and we've done the best we could, but it didn't do any good. And now, God, we're handing our troubles over to you to work out for us. Our little Robin is very sick, and we don't know what to do about it, and our little Karen is all alone out there on the mountain frightened and lost and maybe in terrible danger, or maybe even kidnaped, and we can't do a thing about it, but turn to you. Won't you please take over and make Robin well, and find Karen for us? And if there is anything we can do won't you please show us what it is and how to do it? Amen!"

Jerry followed. "Oh, God! Please lead the way up the mountain. Please send our little sister home, and show us how to take care of them all. Amen."

Then Tryon, quickly, gulping his words.

"Dear God. Please do something about our dear Robin and help him to get well. Please send Karen home!"

And Hazel and Heather prayed quite solemnly, praying into the pillows of the couch where they were kneeling. "Please, dear heavenly Father, help us all!"

They got up wiping the tears away, and Jerry dashed out the door, calling back:

"Don't get worried," and then as a second thought he shouted: "Jen, if Karen gets back get out that old tin horn Tryon found up in the attic and blow it hard three times. Then do it over again, every little while till I come."

"All right!" called Jennifer, and Jerry shot out into the night. But Jennifer went into the house to do the hardest thing of all the hard things that had filled the days since they had first left home: to keep the other children cheerful, and quiet, and make the time go by as quickly as possible for them all, and to look after the little tossing Robin upstairs, hot with fever.

"Now," she said as she came in trying to hold back the tears that would steal into her eyes, "we've taken it to God. We've just got to leave it there, and trust Him. That is the only thing for us to do. We don't want to dishonor Him by crying and holding up our fears to ourselves all the time. Just remember that God is great enough to bring this all out right for us, and there is nothing else we can do but trust Him."

They looked at her in solemn wonder, and tried to smile assent.

"And now, suppose you eat something."

"We're not hungry," said Hazel.

"No, but you'll be twice as fit to stand the waiting if you have something to strengthen you. How about a glass of milk apiece? Each of you take a glass and sit down and quietly talk and drink it, a slow swallow at a time. Then that won't make your stomachs feel badly. Now, I'm going up to look at Robin and when I come down I want to see you all drinking milk."

They smiled assent and went to do her bidding.

Upstairs Jennifer knelt beside the hot little Robin and opened her heart to God again.

"Oh, God! I'm the head of this house, and I don't know what to do. Oh God, please help me to know what you want of me!"

And one by one during that long awful evening each member of that little group sought audience with the King of Kings, and returned among them cheerful and at peace.

17

Karen as she climbed her mountain did not hear her little sick brother fall down after his numerous protests, did not turn around and see that he lay still a long time when he had fallen. She was filled with the exquisite desire to get to the top and see the sunset. Remembering the glory of the sunset at the boat, she desired another, and she knew that it was behind this mountain the sun always slipped away. It had never seemed far to her before, as she looked up to the top. She did not realize that Robin was weak from his illness, and only a baby anyway, and she sped on.

Then when she finally got to what she knew must be the top because the ground began to go down again, there wasn't any sunset there at all. It was all just thick trees everywhere, and she couldn't see through.

She turned back to look for Robin but he wasn't anywhere, and then she thought she hadn't turned all the way around and she turned again, and yet again, because she was quite bewildered about which way was home.

There were dark clouds where the setting sun ought to be, or was that the opposite direction? She didn't know.

It came to her suddenly that it was growing dark and she must hurry. Robin must have gone back and perhaps they would scold her for letting him go alone. So she hurried fast, and the darkness dropped down quickly now. Only when she looked up there was a luminous place where the sky ought to be, and after a while there came a few stars and peopled it sparsely. She grew frightened, for still there were only trees, trees, everywhere! Just trees and darkness!

Then an owl flew up in a tree and hooted at her and she was more afraid. She had never told anybody that she was afraid of owls; she had always hidden her head in her pillow and tried not to hear them, but now the owl was right up there over her head and had her at a disadvantage. She dared not look up lest perhaps the owl's eyes might shine like fire, the way a cat's or a rabbit's eye shone in the road ahead of the car at night, green, or red and kind of horrid. Did owl's eyes look like that? She hid her face, and tried to think what to do. She was afraid to call out, because there was the owl, and he might think she was talking to him, and answer back, and she couldn't bear that, not all alone there in the dark on the mountain!

But after a while the owl went away, and then when she had waited for him to get out of hearing she called aloud: "Robin! Where are you? Robin?" and then a little later she called for Jennifer. But after a while when no one answered she started walking again. She was going down the mountain all the time, so of course she must be going right. There would be a light in the kitchen of the cottage by this time, for they would be getting supper, and she would walk in softly and then jump at them and say "Boo!" And they would jump and then they would laugh, and they would say "Why Karen, is that you? Where have you been? It's almost supper time."

Then when she got to that point she found herself crying, and that wouldn't do! She was too big to cry. So she walked on and on through the darkness, sometimes bumping against trees, and sometimes falling down over a gnarled root, but getting up and going on again because now she must be almost home.

She plodded on, sometimes stopping to rest, for she was very tired and hungry now. But every time she would get up again and go on.

The last of the way was down quite a steep place that she hadn't remembered coming up at all. Had she got out of the way? But it was fearsome and dark up there and she was afraid to go back. At last she reached the road. It seemed a smooth pleasant road, and there was a stream of lovely silver water on the other side of it, and a white bridge in the distance. Perhaps this was the road where the store was, only a little farther on. Perhaps if she went down into it, she could walk back over that bridge and find the store and then she would know her way home!

So she stepped into the road, and started down the way toward the bridge; it seemed the pleasantest.

It was smoother here, and easier to walk, though her shoe hurt her foot a good deal, and she felt her back was aching. She seemed to have come a long way.

When she reached the bridge the water was making a great clattering noise underneath, sort of rattling over stones down there. She looked down once and saw white foam leaping up where the water fell, and it frightened her. She was glad when the bridge was crossed, though the road grew pretty dark again for a little space and she had to hurry. And then out of the darkness ahead came a blinding light. Two lights. An automobile was coming at her, and she didn't know what to do, so she stood perfectly still, and the car presently shot by her. She thought she saw other lights coming, farther on ahead, so she hurried and got past the trees that made it so dark, and found a path at the side of the road. Following it she came out into a wide space where there was sky above with stars, and ahead over at one side there was a great building, bigger than the gymnasium at Tryon's school, oh, bigger than any building she could think of, and on the top there was a great big cross made all of lights, and there were many big bright lights all around. There were words written on the roof of the big gymnasium, and one word she could read. That was "Jesus."

She decided it must be some kind of a nice church with that word and the cross on the top. That must be where the singing came from that she now realized she had heard just after she crossed the bridge. Pretty singing.

If it was a church there would be nice people there, and they would show her the way to get home.

She hurried along and turned into the path that led down to the great building. As she drew near she heard someone talking in a clear nice voice. She was almost running now, and she followed the voice till she reached an open window where she could see in. Then she pressed closer, and slipped up onto a step near the doorway. The great building was full of people, and they were all listening to the man that stood on the wide platform just before her. Suddenly she looked closely at the man, and almost called out to him, for she knew him! It was the man who had helped Jerry fix the automobile the time it got caught on the sharp stones and made holes in the crankcase. And oh! how glad her little heart was that she had found someone she knew who would guide her back to her family. He was all right, she knew. She needn't be afraid to speak to him, for he had been so nice to them all.

So boldly she stepped inside the building among the crowd and strained ahead toward the platform.

They thought she was someone's child who was trying to find her mother, and they gave way for her and let her by, so she reached the broad low steps up to the platform, and mounted them and walked right up to the nice young man. He was talking yet, and people were all listening, but he wouldn't mind stopping a minute to tell her what to do. He had been so nice to Jerry.

So she came and stood close to him and reaching up her hand laid it on his arm. He stopped, surprised, and looked smiling down at her.

"Please," said Karen with a most engaging smile, "won't you show me the way home? I'm kind of lost."

Her voice was very clear and sweet, and the audience was thrilled at the strange interruption.

A young woman who had been sitting at the piano came and tried to draw Karen away, but she drew back from the stranger.

"No," she said decidedly shaking her pretty head, "I don't know you. I can't go with you. I want this man to take me. He knows me and he knows my brother!"

Then the speaker turned and looked at her sharply, for

she was speaking in quite a loud clear voice and the audience held its breath and listened and smiled.

The young man looked down at Karen again, and taking her by the hand he led her over to a chair.

"If you will sit down in this chair for a few minutes, little friend," he said, "I'll be glad to take you home."

Then he turned back to his audience with a smile.

"How I wish there were some in this audience who would ask me the way Home, and start tonight to seek their Saviour!" he said, and a wave of feeling went over the audience. Many bowed their heads and wept as the young preacher went on with burning words, describing how the Lord who had died for them was waiting anxiously for the return of many whom He loved.

And little Karen sat there and began to think how Jennifer would be worrying about her, and how Robin would cry, perhaps, and Jerry would get worried looking. It might be almost as bad back at home as the night the crankcase got torn and had to be mended. And sitting there quite still and listening, Karen began to cry, till the lady at the piano got up and went to try and comfort her, but she only shook her head and turned away.

The meeting was over at last, and crowds came up to the platform to speak to the young preacher, and to get a closer view of the little maid who had created such an innovation in the usual routine of the evening. But the young man swept them all away, and came over to Karen.

"Now, little friend," he said, "shall we go out of this crowd and get into my car and find your way home?"

"Oh, yes, please!" she said with relief and put her hand confidingly in his.

Another young man who had come to the platform watched them an instant, smiling, and then called out as they were going down the steps: "Is it all right with you to take the early morning prayer-group tomorrow morning, Jack?" And the young man with Karen looked back and said yes, and they went on.

"Now," said the young man, "could you tell me the name of the place where you live?"

"Why, it hasn't any name," said Karen serenely. "It's just a place between. It's a cottage high up from the road, with mountain pinks around it, and a store down in the road a little way. Can you find it for me? You helped my brother mend his car!"

A light broke over the young man's face.

"Oh, yes, I remember!" he said. "But that was a long way from here."

Karen nodded.

"But we came a long way since then. This is on the mountain. I was going up above our cottage to see the sunset, and it didn't set. It just got dark and then I turned around some and started back, but when I got down-down-down hill a longer way it wasn't home. And I saw a road, and a bridge, and then I saw a bright cross on a big house, and I came here and found you."

"Yes?" said the young man gravely. "But you don't know how to tell me where to take you, do you?"

Karen looked troubled.

"It's below the mountain," she said, "and there's a store. The man's name that waits on it is Sam. Our home is two houses up from the road. It has mountain pinks all around it and rhododendrons at the back, and we went up above the rhododendrons, and Robin got tired and went back. He's been sick."

"Yes?" said the young man looking troubled, and then he lifted his head and glanced around the circle that stood about them.

"Does that mean anything to any of you?" he asked.

"Mountain pinks!" said one young fellow. "Doesn't that sound like Mrs. Foster's little cottage, and Shufeldt's store down below? Beech Avenue?"

"Mrs. Foster was the lady we rented the cottage from," assented Karen.

"All right, here we go," said the young man, "how do we get there?"

"Cross the bridge and take the highway till you come to the intersection, and ask at the filling station. You turn sharp left and go around the mountain, you know. That's not on this side. She must have come all the way over, and got turned around on the top. Came down the wrong side. Say, you're tired after speaking. Would you like me to take her home?"

A look of instant consternation came on Karen's face, but the young man answered for her.

"Thanks no, I'll go." And then he added with a twinkle, "She knows me, you know, and might not feel so strange."

So presently they were seated in a little runabout and going on their way.

Karen looked back at the bright cross.

"I like that cross," she said. "I didn't feel afraid any more after I saw that, because bad wicked people don't like the cross, do they?"

"I'm afraid they don't," said the young man. "But how did you know that?"

"Well, there are crosses on churches, aren't there? And there's a cross down at the corner where the mission is at home. And then there was that name 'Jesus' on the roof. What else does it say besides 'Jesus'? I didn't know that other word."

"Jesus Saves!" said the young man. "And there's more on the roof. It says 'Christ died for our sins'!"

"Oh!" said Karen. "I don't think I know that one. But when I saw you, and I heard your voice, I knew *you,* because I knew you helped my brother once."

"Well, I'm glad you came to me. I'm glad to be able to take you home, and I hope we shall find the right little cottage. But don't you worry if we don't find it right away. We'll find it somewhere pretty soon. If you walked from there it can't be very far away."

"I guess I'm making you a lot of trouble!" she said with a sigh, primly, in a way that would have reminded her family of the nurse who had been supposed to teach manners and all.

"No, it's not very much trouble, not yet, and anyway I

like to take the trouble, so you needn't worry. You see, you remind me of a little girl I used to know a long long time ago."

"Oh!" said Karen smiling up and showing a sweet weariness in her tired polite little face. "What was her name?"

"Why, her name was Jennifer," said the young man with a reminiscent look in his eyes as if he were thinking back a long long way.

"Why, that's funny," laughed Karen looking up with twinkly eyes. "I have a sister Jennifer. Was this little girl your sister?"

"No," said the young man smiling, "she was just a little girl that came to visit awhile at the house next door."

"Oh! And did you play with her?"

"No," said the young man smiling, "she was a great deal younger than I was, and I had about got through my playing days. But I took her fishing once! And I brought her a little gray kitten with a star in its forehead. Do you like kittens?"

"Oh yes. I like kittens. But our nurse didn't like them. She said they were always getting underfoot, and she really was afraid of them, because she would jump if one came around. She made such a fuss that after a while we didn't have any kitten at all. One morning the kitten was gone, and it never came back! I always thought that nurse scared it away. And now that nurse is gone, and I'm glad. Neither Robin nor I liked her. Of course she wasn't my nurse, she was Robin's, but she acted as if she was mine too, and I didn't like her! Neither did my sisters. Have you got any sisters?"

"No, I haven't. But I think it would be nice to have sisters. Now I wonder if this isn't where we turn? There's a filling station. I guess I'd better ask."

They drove up to the filling station, and asked a few questions and then drove on, and suddenly Karen cried out.

"There! There's the store where we buy the bread and fruit and things. And there! Look up there at that little white house! That's our house! Oh, I just knew you'd find it. I just knew you'd know the way!"

They drove up the little lane that led to the cottage gate and Tryon came tearing down the steps and out to the gate.

"And there's my brother Tryon!" she cried exultantly, reaching out her arms eagerly to him.

"Is that really you, kid?" said the boy peering at her in the shadows of the car. "You bad little kid! Where on earth have you been?" said Tryon. "You've had us all nearly crazy! And Robin is very sick! What did you leave him for? You certainly are the limit!"

Karen's lip trembled and great tears came into her eyes as she shrank back.

"I didn't mean to be bad, Tryon. I didn't really! I just went to see the sunset and it didn't set, and then I got turned around and couldn't find the house. And then—then—I found this nice friend of ours, and he brought me home!"

"Friend?" said Tryon peering into the face of the young man, his tone a severe imitation of Jerry's rage.

"I guess she didn't realize how far she had gone," said the young man looking down at her and speaking in a gentle tone. "She's had a pretty bad scare herself, brother, so don't be too hard on her!"

"Oh!" said Tryon, looking at the stranger. "Why, it's *you,* isn't it? How on earth did she find you?"

"There was a cross, Tryon, a lovely cross of lights, and a big meeting—" and she brushed the tears away and smiled, "and then I heard him talking to the people and I remembered him, and he helped me right away."

"Good-*night!*" said Tryon. "You certainly have given us some scare. I'll say it was great of you to bring her back, and we're all kinds of obliged, of course. Won't you get out and come in? Jennifer will want to thank you. And say! I've got to give the high sign to Jerry. He's up on the mountain with Sam and the flash lights hunting the world over for you! Come on in and I'll blow the signal to Jerry!"

He dashed away from them to the porch and caught up the big tin horn, and in a moment there came forth such a series of horrible sounds as never rent the mountain side before, the old tin horn blowing with all Tryon's might to let Jerry know that Karen was found.

The young man helped Karen out of the car, and Jennifer came out on the porch to see what had happened now. Karen flew up the walk and was folded in her thankful arms, and kissed and hugged; and the young man stood by and watched the pretty sight.

And then quite suddenly Jennifer buried her face in Karen's neck and sobbed aloud.

"Oh, Karen, Karen, we were so frightened!" she said. "Oh darling! Where have you been?"

"I've been to a nice big meeting!" declared Karen lifting her excited little face all wet with Jennifer's tears, and a few of her own, with smiles into the bargain. "And Jennifer, I've brought our friend back with me. That is, he brought me back, I mean," and she slipped down from her sister's arms and went over to the young man and took hold of his hand. "It's our friend, sister! It's the man who helped Jerry mend the car that time in the awful sharp stones. He brought me home!"

Then Jennifer saw the stranger who had once reminded her of some long past pleasant time. But he was standing in the shadow now, and she was in the shadow too, though he could see the sweet outline of her young troubled face.

"How very kind of you!" said Jennifer. "We are doubly grateful to you now. We have been so frightened we did not know what to do. We are strangers here, you see, and we didn't know which way to turn for help!"

"Till we remembered God!" said a solemn voice from the doorway just behind her. And there was Hazel like a little wondering pilgrim who had just seen a light.

"And we all prayed," said Heather stepping out beside her, "and now you've *come!*"

There came a light into the young man's eyes and he said: "Yes, there's nothing like God to help in time of trouble!"

And then that awful horn blew three more terrible blasts, and they all looked toward Tryon and remembered Jerry.

"He's blowing for my brother. He went up the mountain a long time ago to find Karen," explained Jennifer.

"Just after we prayed," said Heather. "He told us to blow and let him know if she came home."

"Do you mean you prayed *for me?*" asked Karen with a wondering smile. "Why, how *nice!*"

"You darling child!" said Jennifer, and stooped and kissed her again. And then suddenly, just as they stood there they heard a piercing shriek behind them, and there stood Robin, tottering on the lowest step, his little hot red face streaming with tears, and terror in every line of his sick little body.

Jennifer turned and ran to him, catching him in her arms, just as Tryon let forth another awful three blasts on the horn, and the little boy screamed and screamed frantically.

The stranger went toward Tryon and put out his hand for the horn.

"Wouldn't that be enough just now, till you can explain to the little boy what it's all about?" he said quietly.

"Oh!" said Tryon turning and hearing the frantic screams, "I forgot the kid. But Jerry told me to call him!"

"Suppose you wait a bit and see what effect this has had. If your brother is anywhere near he must have heard by this time."

And then they could hear Jennifer's low soothing voice as she sat on the stairs with Robin in her arms, and Robin's trembling little frightened tones.

"Fwat is zat awful noise, Jen'fer?" he cried. "Is zat a lion out of my picture book?"

"No, darling. It's just a funny old tin horn that Jerry told Tryon to call him with if Karen came back. We couldn't find Karen, you know."

"Is Karen come back? *Vy* did her go avay and leave me?"

"She didn't mean to go away, Robin. She thought you were all safe with us," said the sister. "She's sorry now, and she wants to kiss you."

Karen came up and put little wet loving kisses on Robin's hot forehead.

"What makes him so hot, Jennifer?" asked Karen shrinking back. "He burns me!"

"Oh!" groaned Jennifer. "He has a terrible fever and I don't know what to do about it. I haven't any medicine! If we only had a doctor!"

"We'd better get to praying again!" said Hazel in a mature, quiet way. "Come, Heather. Come on, Karen! You were the cause of all this trouble. You'd better pray too," and they slipped out into the kitchen and went down on their knees beside the kitchen table.

But Jennifer sat on the stairs with the sick little boy in her arms and did not know that the stranger had stood just outside the door and heard it all. He stepped in now and said quietly:

"There's a fine doctor over at the conference grounds. I could bring him here in a few minutes if you want me to."

"Oh," said Jennifer, "a doctor! That would be wonderful! But I can't bear to make you all that trouble. Perhaps Jerry will be here pretty soon and he could take the car and go."

"He wouldn't know where to find him and I would," said the young man. "Besides, it's no trouble at all. He's a friend of mine, and he's a very noted physician from New York. I'll get him!" and he jumped into his car and dashed off into the night, while the three little girls in the kitchen were praying for help, and Tryon out on the dark back porch was peering up the mountain hoping to see a searchlight.

18

It seemed an age that Jennifer knelt upstairs beside the little Robin before she finally heard a car drive up to the door.

"Oh, God!" she kept praying. "Haven't you heard us? You brought Karen back. Dear little Karen! But Robin is so sick! Won't you please make him well? Aren't you going to send a doctor to us? We can't do anything ourselves. It is the dead of night, and nobody knows us but you! Won't you do something for us? And Jerry isn't here! Oh, God, is Jerry lost too?"

Over and over her heart kept repeating the words until she heard that car drive up, and then she sprang up and slipped noiselessly down the stairs.

Robin was terribly hot. His soft little body seemed to scorch her hand when she touched him! She was almost afraid to take the doctor up there, fearful of what he would say! Oh, was Robin going to die and go to God and mother? Of course that might be better for Robin, but how could she ever stand it? She would feel all her life that she had killed him! The aunts would tell her she was a murderer. They would tell her it was because she had taken him away to a wild uncivilized place and kept him where they couldn't take care of him that he had died!

Tears rained down her face as she hurried to the door to meet the doctor.

The two men stood just outside the door, and the young man introduced his doctor friend. They both saw her tears but they did not seem to see them, and Jennifer was not conscious of them. She led the doctor upstairs and the other young man stayed below.

"I'll be right here if you want me," he said to the doctor in a low tone. "I'll go anywhere on errands if you need anything."

The doctor bowed with a flash of trust in his eyes and went on, and the other dropped down on a chair with his face bowed in his hands. The three little girls had finished their vigils and closed their prayers because they were too sleepy to stay awake, and perhaps they felt that after once stating the case that was all that was needed and they could trust God for the rest. But the stranger now took up the petition, and he was one who was mighty in prayer, a true child of God who had a right to ask and expect to be heard.

Jennifer, frightened, hovered around the little bed while the doctor examined the patient. She was dizzy with fear, wishing Jerry would come. Then after a little she heard low talking under the window, Tryon and Jerry she hoped, and took heart of hope.

But suddenly the doctor looked up.

"You ought to sit down and rest," he said, almost like a command. "You will need your strength later for nursing. Just sit here beside him while I go down and speak to Val. I want him to go for something in my room. He'll know where to find it. Have you any ice? No, don't you go down. I can find a refrigerator if there is one."

He took hold of Jennifer and put her into a chair by Robin.

"I think my brother has come," she said softly. "But anyway Tryon, the younger one, is out there. He will get the ice."

"You haven't an ice bag?"

"Oh, no. I didn't bring it along!" mourned Jennifer.

"That's all right. I have one at my room. I usually cart a few such things along. Now sit right there and if he stirs hold his hand and comfort him."

The doctor went down and was soon back with a bit of

ice in a basin, and a nice clean towel that Tryon had found for him. Then she heard the car drive away again, and soon Jerry stole in silently and stood behind her, looking down at the child, in the semi-darkness of the room. She remembered that Jerry must be very tired and ought to have a cup of coffee or a glass of milk or something, but she couldn't leave just now.

The doctor was passing ice cold cloths over the little hot forehead and eyes, and Robin sighed almost contentedly. Now and again the doctor would put a spoonful of medicine in Robin's mouth and talk gently to him, coaxing him to open his mouth, to swallow the nice cold water.

Then the car came back, and the ice bag was filled and put on Robin's head, and the doctor settled down to watch the pulse and stay with the little one for a time.

"Go and lie down," he told Jennifer. "I'll call you if I need you."

But Jennifer could not go far. She only went out and sat in the dim darkness on the top step of the stairs, with her head resting against the wall, and her eyes closed. Her heart felt as if some great hand had gripped it.

She could hear Jerry downstairs talking to the young man, heard them presently go out to the kitchen, heard the little electric egg beater whirring softly, a bit of ice click, and then suddenly Jerry came with a frosty glass of milk and egg. The stranger must have mixed it, for Jerry didn't know how, she was sure. She drank it gratefully and smiled.

"Did you have some?" she whispered. "You had no supper!"

"I'm all right!" he said staunchly. "I'll get something pretty soon."

But when he went down she saw the stranger there at the foot of the stairs with another glass, and a plate with food on it, a sandwich perhaps. What a wonderful friend he had been! Tomorrow she must find a way to thank him.

She heard the two go out on the porch and settle down

on one of the cots to talk in low murmurs, and then, leaning back her head against the wall in the cool darkness she slumbered fitfully, for it must have been two hours afterwards that she wakened suddenly to see the doctor looking down pityingly at her.

"You poor child!" he said compassionately. "I told you to go and lie down. Well, now, I guess the worst of your troubles is over. The fever is going down decidedly and the little boy is resting well. You can lie down on the other bed beside him there and sleep till morning, I am quite sure. He has broken into a perspiration, and I think the fever is conquered. I'm going to run back to my room for a little while, because I think Val ought to get some rest. He has to lead the early morning prayer service. But I'll be back the first thing in the morning and bring something I want this little patient to have. Give him this medicine if he stirs or wakens, but don't disturb him otherwise. Now you won't be afraid to rest, will you? Because I tell you it is perfectly safe to do so, and I never lie about such things. You may trust me!"

Jennifer looked up with a grateful smile.

"Oh, I'm so glad you came!" she said fervently.

"So am I," said the doctor smiling. "You had a pretty sick little boy here for a while, but I believe he will be much better in the morning."

Then they were gone, and she heard Jerry come up and stand by Robin's bed, looking down, touching the little hand gently, and then looking at her with a wan smile.

"He says he's better," Jerry whispered.

Jennifer nodded.

"You go in the other room and sleep, Jen. I'll stay here."

Jennifer shook her head.

"No! He told me to lie down right here. He told me what to do and all about it. You go to sleep now, Jerry. We'll need you tomorrow!"

So Jerry assented, but before he left he whispered:

"I guess those prayers did some good, Jen!"

"Oh, yes!" she smiled.

It was the doctor who wakened them the next morning. How he managed to drive up to the cottage so silently Jerry couldn't understand. But he did, without wakening one of them. He just appeared among them, there on the porch where Jerry and Tryon were sound asleep on their cots.

"Everything all right above stairs?" he asked as gently as if he had been one of the family and knew what to count on.

Jerry rubbed his eyes and looked sheepish.

"I must have overslept," he said.

"Not really?" laughed the doctor. "It's just that you're still *under*slept. But I had to get up early. Some kid at the conference last night ate too much ice cream for her good and I had to get up and attend her, so I thought I'd just step over and see how you were making out. Heard any sounds?"

"Not a sound!" said Jerry. "I'll step up and see!"

But Jennifer had heard them and appeared at the head of the stairs.

"He hasn't stirred all night," she said. "Or maybe I was too sleepy to know it."

"I guess you'd have heard him if he had made much fuss," smiled the doctor. "Let's take a look."

The doctor's cool practised fingers touched the little wrist, the brow; his head bent down, listening to the breathing and the heart.

"He'll do!" said the doctor. "Now, if you'll come out in the hall I'll tell you what to do when he wakes up."

That was a strange day, when they finally all got up and had breakfast one at a time. Jerry first, and then Tryon, raided the ice box. They took a glass of milk to Jennifer. The little girls were the last to waken, and they got corn flakes and milk and orange juice themselves.

Robin woke a little later and was fed carefully with food the doctor had ordered and superintended. They didn't really all get together until late afternoon. The doctor had been in for the third time, and gone away again, satisfied with his patient and promising to see him again before night. Then they gathered about a late and hastily scrambled together dinner, with gladness in their hushed voices because the doctor had said that Robin would get well. Robin was quietly and coolly asleep upstairs.

The young man hadn't come back. The doctor hadn't explained why beyond the fact that he had to lead a meeting that morning and then had to go away somewhere to lead another.

"His name is Val," announced Jennifer. "I heard the doctor call him so last night."

"No," said Karen very decidedly, "his name is *Jack*. I heard the other man that led the singing call him Jack. He said 'Jack, can I depend on you to lead the early morning meeting?' and he said 'Yes.' Now I guess *I* know."

"Well, anyhow the doctor called him Val," said Jennifer.

"Well, *I* shall call him Jack," said Karen. "He's my friend, anyway. He said I looked like a little girl he used to know and like, and her name was Jennifer, too! He said so."

"Aw, he was stringing you!" said Tryon reaching over for another helping of fried potatoes.

It was a good dinner if they had gotten it in a hurry. Jerry had broiled the steak, and Tryon had fried the potatoes. He had learned how at camp, and he did them well. Plenty of butter and pepper and salt, nice and brown and crispy on the edges. Hazel had cooked the peas. They were her specialty, and she loved them. The little girls had shelled them. Tryon had gone after blackberries and cream. He loved blackberries with plenty of cream and sugar.

"Well, *I* shall call him Jack," insisted Karen. "I tell you, he's my friend. He likes me. He said he did."

"Well, the probability is that you won't have any chance to call him anything," laughed Jennifer. "He's likely gone away to stay now, and we won't see him again anywhere, but he certainly was nice to bring you home at that time of night. Some young men wouldn't have bothered. They'd have taken you to the police or something."

A shadow of fear passed over Karen's face. She was still too near to her awful experience to treat it lightly.

They went to bed very early that night, and the next morning Robin was so much better that the doctor let them read him stories out of the picture books, and cut soldiers out of paper for him to play with.

Somehow the whole terrifying experience had drawn the young family still closer together. They seemed to be glad just to be in one another's presence, and smile, and there wasn't anything too hard or monotonous for any one of them to do for Robin. He was in a fair way to be utterly spoiled if he didn't get well pretty soon.

It was a sad lonely day when the doctor told them good-bye and went away. He said he had a big practice at home waiting for him. After he was gone they drooped a bit, and life in the little cottage grew tame indeed.

But there was one thing the children would never be tempted to do, and that was to climb the mountain. Not even in the daytime would they go off by themselves and climb up where Karen had gone, the night they were afraid someone had kidnaped her. But they loved the little cottage and did not tire of sitting about the porch reading some of its pleasant books, or picking flowers about the dooryard, playing "house" under the trees, or looking off toward the mountains. But the doctor was gone, and the young man who had brought him came no more, and they did not know where he had gone. Even Jerry who had had plenty of time to talk with him during that anxious night hadn't thought to ask his name, or where he lived.

"Well, I'll tell you," said Jerry one night when they had been kidding him about it, "never mind, some day we'll take a little trip in the car, when Robin is real well, and go around to that conference camp Karen is always talking about, and see him! I'd like to have that guy for a friend, I really would!"

But the days went by, and still they did not go.

"We've got to save gasoline, you know," warned Jennifer. "We'll have to travel on all too soon. Our month is almost up here, and Mrs. Foster will be coming back pretty soon."

"Well, can't we go back to the boat, Jennifer?" asked Robin anxiously.

"I'm afraid not, boy, not just yet. I'm not ready to meet Peter Willis yet. But our exile is two thirds over, and won't it be wonderful when we can go home? Then we can go down to the boat as often as we like."

"We'll have to keep it nearer home if we go often," said Tryon. "I can't picture us going all that way! We couldn't spare the time till another vacation, we'd miss so much school."

"We'll see about that," said Jerry thoughtfully. "We'll have some more good times some day on that boat, I'm telling you."

"Maybe Peter Willis will get married to that girl with the painted lips," said Heather. "Then he won't want to come after Jennifer any more, will he?"

They all had a good laugh at that, Jennifer with them, and Jerry looked relieved when he saw that Jennifer wasn't troubled by their nonsense.

Then at last Mrs. Foster arrived, a whole day ahead of her schedule. She didn't stay all night, and she didn't drive them out, but they could see she wanted her house, so they hurriedly packed their belongings and started on the next morning.

"Now," said Jerry, when they were out of sight of the little mountain cottage among the rhododendrons, "how would it be if we tried to find that conference camp before we leave this region, and also perhaps look up our friend? Then I thought we'd stop somewhere and give poor Uncle Blake a call or a telegram or something to ease his mind about us. We've only a little over a month left before we go home now, and it seems too bad to leave Uncle Blake in the dark all this time, with just that last notice in the paper, saying we were all right in a quiet place where we couldn't get newspapers."

"I don't think we ought to run any risks now," said

Jennifer, "even if the time is short. It would just spoil everything. We'll send another notice to the New York paper, and we'll go hunt the conference if you like. I don't believe that young man will put the police on us. He doesn't look like that kind."

"Of course he won't!" said Karen with an air of resentment. "He's a *Christian!* But here, Jerry, here's where you turn around the mountain. That's the way he brought me back."

"Are you sure, kid? I thought he said I took the right fork."

"No, you turn to the left. I guess I know!"

So Jerry humored her and they swept on around a lovely country road with high hills on every side, and a few mountains in the near distance. At last they came to a white bridge over a turbulent little stream with a few mild rapids at one point, and Karen shouted with joy. "Here it is! Here's my bridge! And over there is my big white house with the reading on the roof, and the cross on the top. See, Jerry, it's all white now, it isn't lighted. But can't you see the reading on the roof? That's 'Jesus saves.' Jack told me so. I read the word Jesus all by myself, and he told me the rest. Now, was I right, Jerry Graeme, or wasn't I?"

"Well, it seems as if you must have been right, all right," grinned Jerry. "Now, what do we do, sister?"

"Oh, stay here!" cried Karen. "I want to stay here awhile and go to meeting and hear Jack talk some more. I didn't hear him talk much because I had to interrupt him the last time I was here and make him take me home, but I want to go to a meeting and really hear him again!"

"Well, what do you say, Jen? Shall we try it?"

"Why, if there was any place we could get a little cabin or something, I'd say try it. You know a religious camp is the last place in the world those aunts would ever think of hunting us."

"That's so," said Jerry. "Well, Tryon, you get out and scout around. We'll just draw up here at the side of the road and wait while you see if there's a prospect of any abiding place."

"It would have to be something by ourselves," added Jennifer, "we could never risk going to a hotel or boarding house with a mob like this, you know."

"Okay!" said Tryon and swung off among a group of young people going toward the big building with the cross on the top.

19

A good many of the young people were carrying Bibles.

"That's funny," said Jerry. "Say, maybe there'll be a chance to look into the Bible a little. I've always wondered about it."

"You couldn't learn much in just a few days," said Jennifer doubtfully.

Tryon was gone quite a little while. They saw him walk along with other young people to the great building, and step inside. They saw him come out another door at the side and take a look at the tennis courts, and cross the road and look at the shuffleboards and swings. They saw him go up the hill and enter a big homelike place with wide porches all around.

Then they grew absorbed in listening to wonderful singing that came from the great building under the cross, and forgot to watch for Tryon. Till at last he suddenly appeared among them again, and got into the car.

"It's a swell place!" he announced. "That's a tabernacle over there. They're having a meeting now. They have meetings in the morning and evening and in the afternoon they go swimming in that stream we crossed, and they play games. That's the dormitory up there, at least it's a dormitory for girls, and there are lots of others, and cabins for boys, but they don't allow children here. There's a camp for little girls, and another for young boys, and the rest stay here."

"Oh!" said Jennifer. "Then it's no use! We can't stay! We've got to keep together!"

"Of course," said Tryon. "I told 'em that, and they said there was a little cottage just beyond here we could rent. It didn't have but two rooms and a kitchen, but it had plenty of cots if we wanted to look at it. The people in it are leaving this afternoon. This place closes in another week, so we couldn't stay long anyway. Would you like to drive around and look at the cottage, Jen?"

"Why, yes, if Jerry thinks it's all right," said Jennifer.

"Okay with me!" said Jerry. So they followed Tryon's directions and came to a tiny rough sort of cabin built in the woods. They couldn't go in yet, not till afternoon, but they were charmed with the situation, and the view of the little tumbling stream that sang along below the road.

They drove a couple of miles down to a village and got some lunch, and then they came back and waited until the tenants of the cottage left. Before night they had turned in with glee and were settled and gay as any campers could be. This was a place that the aunts would never, never think to look for them.

That night after the children were asleep, and Jennifer had decided she wanted to get to sleep at once also, Jerry and Tryon went out to the big tabernacle to their first meeting.

Jennifer lay in her cot beside the little girls, and heard the singing, hymns and choruses. It seemed to her heavenly. She thought of her mother and father in the Father's house, and wondered if they were joining in singing like that, and tears stung into her eyes at the thought.

When Jerry and Tryon came back, she slipped out with her dressing gown about her, and sat on Tryon's cot while they told about the meeting.

"It's the greatest thing I ever heard!" said Jerry. "I wish we'd known about this before. We might have been here all summer, and it only lasts a week longer! But believe me we'll all come here next year if we have to build a house just outside the grounds to get us all in."

"But if the children are not allowed how could we?"

said Jennifer. "They have to be our chief concern for the next few years."

"Yes, of course," said Jeremy. "But they are allowed to come to the meetings if some of their folks come with them. It's only that they can't take them in and board them. They couldn't, there would be so many. But if we had a little place just out a ways like this we could go to all their meetings and get the good of it."

So the next morning when they heard the bell ring they all wended their way to the tabernacle and took seats where they could hear everything.

"You mustn't wriggle around or make a noise, you know," warned Jennifer to Robin and Karen, "or they'll not let us stay in this nice place."

So the children sat down with great awe, and listened wide-eyed to all that went on. The singing first, how they all enjoyed it! Even Robin took a book and held it upside down and opened his mouth wide to sing with the rest. And then came prayers, and testimonies of how different ones had been saved here in this wonderful conference. The Graemes learned that to be saved meant to know that your sins were forgiven by God because He punished His Son Jesus Christ for them instead of you.

It was all new to them, though they had been to formal church and Sunday School all their lives. What they had learned there had been mere words, Bible verses and stories that had never been applied for them to their daily living, with its troubles and temptations. It seemed a revelation to them now. Perhaps they were ready to take it in now because from the eldest to the least, they had all felt the need of some Great One who loved them, in whom they could trust. There was a Bible lesson, with a great chart stretched across the platform to make it all plain to them.

When it was over and they were on the way back to their little cabin, Hazel said to Jennifer:

"Why, I didn't know we were all sinners, did you, sister? I thought most of us were pretty good, and it was only the bad people like tramps and gangsters who needed saving. I used to wonder why they wanted such people saved, when they were so bad," said Hazel, wonderingly.

"Well, I guess I never thought about it before," said Jennifer. "I remember Kirsty used to talk about being saved, but I didn't take much notice of what she said. Though she used to be very particular about my saying my prayers."

"Do we get Bibles?" asked Hazel suddenly. "Everybody here has a Bible. I'd like to have a Bible and a pencil and a notebook!"

Jennifer gave a quick look toward Jerry. Could they afford Bibles? Of course they hadn't spent all their money yet, but there was still a time ahead when this week was over, and that must be considered.

But Jeremy's eyes met hers and understood.

"Yes, certainly," he said. "We can go without something else, but everybody here has Bibles and we must have Bibles too. If anybody needs to know the Bible we do."

"Yes," said Jennifer relieved at his decision, "we do! We've got to get something that will hold up through hard times, for there might be other hard things ahead, you know."

That afternoon they went to the little book stand in the corner of the tabernacle and bought some Bibles. Even Robin insisted on having one, so they got him a little red ten cent gospel of John, at the suggestion of the salesman. And thereafter they attended every session of the conference with Bibles in hand.

And when the evening service opened they were on hand on the minute, and joined in all the songs heartily and earnestly. This meeting with hundreds of other young people all intent on the same thing, after their weeks of being cooped up with their own family, was a great experience for them.

But there was one thing that disappointed them, the children at least—for Jennifer would never have owned that she was disappointed—and that was that the young man who had told them about this place, and whose name

Karen still insisted was Jack, was nowhere in evidence. They looked in vain among the audience, and when anyone would come to the platform Karen would stretch her neck and then shake her head toward Jennifer. "Jack isn't here yet," she whispered mournfully. But still they all entered into the services themselves so fully that they presently forgot their disappointment and were happy.

It was a different place from any they had ever been. Everything was unexpected, and wonderful when it came, and they laughed and sang and felt that they were a part of it all. The messages were plain and simple so that even the children could understand. Even Robin didn't go to sleep. It was almost laughable to see him sit up there and listen.

"Well, I'm glad we came here!" said Jeremy when they came back to the cabin and were getting ready for rest. And each of the children voiced their approval in some way.

Day succeeded day in continuous sunshine for which they were thankful, and they grudged each passing day, knowing that this was to end soon.

Without a murmur they trudged the rough paths that led into the grounds. It didn't seem so far when they were to have a good time when they got there. And it was fun coming home all together.

"I think we are all very nice," said Robin solemnly one night as they got him into his pajamas and rolled him into bed. And how they all laughed. Until Robin looked up astonished and said:

"Well, *aren't* we?"

And the days went on, but still they did not see Jack Valiant, nor yet the doctor who had cured Robin.

The older ones went to every meeting, and could not bear to miss a single one, though of course they had to take turns staying home with the little ones sometimes. But the others would take their Bibles and leave the first thing after breakfast, and not come back till lunch time.

The last night of the conference was very wonderful to them all. They had come to feel themselves a part of this great company of believers on the Lord Jesus, to understand that it was their privilege as well as the rest, to have a part in the precious time of fellowship and praise.

The singing had been especially fine. Everybody called out requests for favorite songs. Individuals from the audience were called up to sing or give testimony. The Graemes sat and watched and listened and wished there were some people at home like these, wished that they might hope to have a fellowship in Christ lasting all the year.

Then the young leader whom they all loved and called by a nickname dear to them, came to the front and after a few words of personal thanks and farewell, he said:

"I had a letter this morning from Val!"

A murmur which grew into a cheer of interest greeted this.

"Some of you don't know Val because he wasn't here this week, and maybe you have never been here before. But I'm sure you would love Val if you had a chance to know and hear him as much as we, who have been with him more or less during the summer, love him. Val, as we call him, or Jack Valiant as the world knows him, is a wonderful fellow, a dear servant of the Lord, and a beloved friend of ours. It was our great regret that he couldn't be with us through this last week, but he had other engagements to meet which made it impossible. However, I had a letter from Val today, telling me that he has made definite plans to be with us next summer. He's up at his old home for a day or two now, where he was born, looking after some repairs on the old house and putting it into the hands of a caretaker for the winter. It's up in New England somewhere, I forget just the name—something 'Squam,' isn't it? Or is it near Squam Lake? I never can quite remember the name of it. Kennie, do you remember?" as a young fellow in the front seat raised his hand and then jumped up smiling.

"Yes sir! It's North Benton, I think."

"That's it!" said the leader, "North Benton. I've never

been there myself but since Val was born there I'm quite sure it's worth visiting and I mean to go there some day."

But it was Jennifer whose eyes shone now.

"That's it!" she whispered to Jeremy. "That's where Kirsty lives. *North Benton,* Vermont! Now we'll know how to find Kirsty!"

"So, I'm just announcing to you right now that Jack Valiant will be here at this conference next summer for probably three or four weeks, the exact dates to be announced later, and I hope you'll all plan to come and find out what a wonderful message he has."

But it was Karen's turn to lean over triumphantly and whisper now.

"There! What did I tell you? His name *is* Jack! He just said so, and that's what some of them called him the night I was here first."

Jennifer smiled, but her eyes were dreamy. She was thinking of a boy about fourteen years old who took her fishing when she was nine, and comparing him with a young man who had stood in their cottage the night that Robin was so sick and watched her when the doctor came. Could they possibly be one and the same? The young man who had crawled under their car and helped to mend it? It would be just like the Jack Valiant she had known.

That evening the man who spoke arrested their attention at once.

"I want to ask a question tonight," he said, "that thousands of people are asking: 'Where are the dead?' "

Jennifer and Jeremy gave a startled glance at each other.

"As I would not have the slightest idea where the dead are apart from what God has revealed in His Book, I shall simply tell you what He says.

"In the first place, we understand from the Book that the ones God calls 'the righteous dead' are not in the same place with the ones He calls 'the wicked dead.'

" 'Righteous' ones, dead or alive, are in God's sight,

those who have received Christ as their righteousness. The 'wicked' ones, dead or alive, are those who have not. In the times before Christ came the 'righteous' were those who believed He *would* come to take away their sins. The 'wicked' were those who did not.

"The 'wicked' are not yet in hell, the lake of fire. There is *no one yet* in the lake of fire. And, by the way, if any of you young people have been taught that the lake of fire is not real fire but symbolic, if that is so, *what must the reality be?*"

Although the speaker's voice was quiet and solemn, as though it almost held a sob, the children's eyes were wide with awe.

"But God never prepared the lake of fire for men! It was prepared for the devil and his wicked angels. God does not delight in consigning anyone to that place. It is only those who *choose* the devil instead of Christ who shall have their wish and go there.

"But not one soul is there yet. The place of the wicked dead at present is in the heart of the earth, and always has been ever since the first wicked man, Cain, died. The Hebrews called that place of the wicked dead, 'Torments.' The Lord Jesus Christ Himself spoke of it as such, for there is only misery there. But it is not the lake of fire.

"But 'Torments' is only one part of the great space reserved in the heart of the earth for the dead. That great space is called 'Hades,' or 'Sheol' in Hebrew. Both names mean 'place of the dead.' Hades is divided into two parts and a great gulf lies between the two sections. 'Torments' is one part.

"But while the other part used to be the place of the righteous dead, and was called 'Paradise,' or 'Abraham's bosom,' *it is empty now!* Satan used to hold captive in Hades every soul who died. But Christ, when He died, went down there, and fought with Satan and overcame him, and wrested from him the 'keys' of that place. Remember how He said when He appeared to John years after He had ascended to Heaven, 'I am He that was dead and is alive, and I have the keys of death and Hades'?

Hades is translated hell in our English Bible, but remember it is *not* the lake of fire.

"We read in Ephesians four that when the Lord Jesus ascended to Heaven after His resurrection He 'led captivity captive.' That is, *He took with Him* to Heaven all those righteous dead who had been held captive by Satan in Paradise, the second part of Hades. From that time on their souls have lived in Heaven with Him, although they shall not receive their bodies, glorified, until the day when Christ comes back to take all of His own up from the earth to Heaven, to the place He has gone to prepare.

"We understand from this that Paradise, the place of the righteous dead, has been in the third Heaven, God's Home, ever since Christ ascended. That is why the second section of Hades is empty. We know also that Paradise is up there now because Paul tells us in second Corinthians twelve, that he was 'caught up into the third Heaven . . . into 'Paradise.'

"It is most comforting, isn't it, to know that every person who has received the Lord Jesus Christ as his personal Saviour here on earth goes immediately there, to be with the Lord, when he leaves the body. For Paul said that for a Christian to be 'absent from the body' is to be 'present with the Lord.' Could anything be more wonderful than to look into the face of the One who loved us enough to die for us? And then to live there with Him forever!

"Many people wonder why God has not told us more about Heaven in the Bible. I believe it is because if we knew more we should die of homesickness. David said, 'In Thy presence is *fullness of joy;* at Thy right hand are pleasures forevermore.' Need we know more?

"You say, 'How about *my loved ones?* How may I know that they are there? We cannot always know. But you may know that if they put their trust in Jesus Christ as their Saviour while on this earth they are surely there. And if *you* do, *you* will surely go there too, and shall surely see them again. And even if you are not sure that they trusted Christ to save them, you can be sure of this, that God gave them *every* chance. You cannot know what transaction they had with Him at perhaps the very last moment. Surely you can trust them with Him. If you cannot trust the One who died for you, who can you trust?"

Jerry cast a radiant look at Jennifer and saw quiet tears of joy on her face.

And then when it was all over, how they lingered, and hesitated to go away and leave that sacred place where they had come so near to God, and had begun to understand His Word. They wandered into the book stall and bought a book or two by some of the speakers. They bought a few pictures, and trinkets, and reminders, some framed Bible verses to hang on their walls; for Karen a tiny gold cross on a little chain, in remembrance of the cross that led her to a friend who took her home when she was lost.

"And now I'm *saved!*" she said with shining eyes. "I'm not lost any more, because I have Jesus!"

20

The Graemes had forgotten all about precautions. In this heavenly atmosphere it did not seem possible that policemen could pursue them and herd them back to Aunt Petra. They sat among the happy throng and did not fear. They smiled and talked to the rest as if they were a part of one big happy family. They forgot to guard their names from being heard. They even gave their home address to some new friends they had made during that wonderful week at the conference.

And then to crown it all they went fearlessly to the conference dining room to take breakfast with those who had stayed over. For the ban against children had been raised, because the conference was over, and all who were left might join them.

Robin was so intrigued with the sight of all those people at the many tables that Jennifer could scarcely coax him to give attention to eating.

And when they packed up and drove away at last there were still some with friendly faces who stood about and waved their hands and smiled for farewell, saying: "See you next year!" and the Graemes nodded and called back "Oh yes, we'll be here!"

And so they started on their way.

Their time of exile was almost over, and now they had but to make the pilgrimage to the one place Jennifer had had in mind when she first started out to get away from her relatives. They were going to find Kirsty if they could.

And it seemed strange that not until the night before had they known where even to try to find her. But here they were on the way to her at last!

They didn't realize that the children had taken in where they were going until, on the second day of their journeying, Karen said happily:

"We're going to see Jack pretty soon now. Jerry, how soon will it be that we shall find Jack?"

"Why, kitten, I don't know that we'll see Jack Valiant this trip at all. I'm pretty sure from what the fellows said at camp that he isn't where we're going now, any more. They said he was going to be up in Canada speaking, that he just went to Vermont on business. We're not going to see him now, you know. We're going to find Jennifer's old nurse, Kirsty."

"But I wanted to see Jack!" said Karen with a hint of wailing in her voice. "Why can't we go to Canada? Why can't we go and find Jack?"

"Not now, Karen," soothed Jerry. "We're going to visit Kirsty if we can find her."

They took the journey slowly, stopping at tourist inns on the way, just homey little old-fashioned quaint houses with pleasant rooms and nice homelike meals. They seemed to have forgotten their fear of being followed. They talked much on the way about the things they had heard at the conference, until one afternoon Hazel said thoughtfully:

"We're all different, aren't we? I wonder what the aunts will think about it when we get home. Because, you know, they all go to different denominations, and I don't believe any of them ever read the Bible."

"Oh, Hazel, don't talk that way. We'll have to live the new Life we have found," said Jennifer, "and then perhaps the aunts will want to be different too."

"Oh yeah?" said Tryon. "Well, we'll have to be going some if we're aiming for that result. Personally, I think it would be easier to try to convert the heathen, than Aunt Petra."

They smiled at that, and then they began to talk about

the differences there ought to be in their lives if they were really going to witness for Christ as they had started out to do.

They talked about that more or less every little while that day and the next, and when they were not talking about it, most of them were thinking about it.

It was toward night and growing dusky in the twilight when at last they reached North Benton. And partly by asking, and partly by what Jennifer could remember, they at last drew up in front of Kirsty McCarra's little plain house on the hillside above the road.

It was Kirsty herself who came out to see who they were, thinking they were strangers in need of direction. Then it was Kirsty who came flying down to the road to look in their faces and hear for herself just who this was that had come to see her.

"Oh, Kirsty, Kirsty dear!" cried Jennifer, her voice full of happy tears. "To think I am really seeing you again, here in the dear little hillside house that I loved so much! And you haven't changed at all, except your hair is a beautiful silver! Oh, Kirsty! Don't you know me? Don't you know Jennifer Graeme? The little girl you took care of so long ago?"

Kirsty's face lighted up and she cried out, clasping her hands to her breast. "Oh, and is it wee Jennifer Graeme? Indeed I have no forgot ye, my wee little girlie. You've grown big and lovely, and opened like a flower. But I would have said this one was my wee Jennifer—" and she pointed to Karen, and then looked first at one and then at the other.

"But you'll be coomin' in the noo, and let me be lookin' ye over. And who are these?" She looked at them all curiously. "The big's one's like yer mither, he's that good lookin' an' with her eyes, and the laddie,"—pointing to Tryon—"is yer feyther over again. And the ithers, I kin see a little of both the feyther an' mither. The wee one's got his mither's smile."

Robin was looking at her with solemn eyes, and suddenly he broke out:

"Is that your Kirsty, Jennifer? Why, I *wike* her!" and his own radiant smile came forth like sunshine.

Kirsty made them get out and come in, and when she got them all seated she went from one to the other getting acquainted, then turning to hug Jennifer again, and looking back to Karen.

"You're just like my own wee girlie!" she said, and brought a happy smile to Karen's face.

"I like to be like my sister Jennifer," she said. "She's a good sister!"

"But listen, Kirsty!" said Jennifer suddenly. "I've got to tell you how we came to get here. We've run away! Daddy and mother were killed in an airplane crash, and we found the relatives were going to try to separate us, so we just ran away till I would be of age and could have a right to manage them all and keep them together. We would have come right to you only I couldn't remember where you lived, and we've only just found out."

"Rin away! And the blessed mither and feyther gane! You poor wee lambs! But wasn't there a guardian?"

"We don't know," said Jennifer laughing. "We didn't wait to find out. We were afraid it might be Aunt Petra, so we hurried off before they knew we were going, and they don't know yet where we are. There's only a little less than a month left now till I'm of age. Can you take us all in, Kirsty, until the time is up and we dare go back? We've got some money and we can pay our way, and we'll work hard so you won't find us a nuisance. But we do just long to be near someone we can trust and love. Would we be in your way?"

"In me way! You blessed lambs! You couldn't be a nuisance! But it's only of you dear childer I'm thinking. I've such a wee little humble hoose, and you with your grand mansion! You couldn't stand it, my dears! You'd have ta hev some braw place like you're useta. Let me think what we cud dae."

Jennifer laughed.

"You don't know how we've been living the last two months. The first days we spent on a small boat that daddy owned, and then some people came down that we knew and we had to run away from there quickly before they saw us. And next we took an awful little dirty shack. You should have seen it! And when we left that we got a tiny house on a mountain, and Karen got lost, and Robin got very sick and almost died, and when we left there we were in a tiny cabin of two rooms. So you see we're used to roughing it. But if we'd be a nuisance or you think it wouldn't be good for your sick sister, we'll get a tent and put it up out on the hillside somewhere till the time is up and we can go back."

"Oh, my dearie! But my poor dear sister is gane to live in Heaven the noo, just twa short weeks ago, so she'll not be troubled by any noise any more, and you're welcome to all I hev, but there's little and poor picking for the likes of you!"

"And where do I come in?" asked a voice, and they all turned and there in the doorway stood the strange young man, Jack Valiant, smiling happily at them all. "I'd have you know that these are *my* friends, Kirsty!"

"Oh, and away wi' ye!" said the old Scotch woman with a happy smile. "And when did ye coom? Now you're here all will be well, I suppose. I thocht ye was away ta Canada ta stay awhile."

"Yes, but I've come back, Kirsty. And what's ta hinder me taking Jeremy and Tryon over ta my hoose? An' then the rest of you girls can have a happy time thegither!"

He said it with a perfect Scotch accent, and they all laughed.

"Awa' wi' ye!" cried the old woman. "Ye'll nae tak my bairns awa'; I want them all mesel'."

But that was the way it worked out after all.

Jack Valiant's house was a stone's throw up the hill, and there was plenty of room for the three boys. Kirsty had no trouble in getting the rest of them in her own little house, with Robin in a lovely little crib in which his sister Jennifer had slept so long ago when she stayed with Kirsty that summer.

Jack Valiant was off here and there speaking occasionally, and when he went usually he took Jerry and Tryon with him, much to the sorrow of Karen, who seemed to think she had special rights in the young man because she had discovered him one dark night when she was in trouble.

But the days were wonderful golden autumn days, and the woods were turning crimson and gold. The nuts were falling, the apples in the orchard were ripe. They had wonderful times together going out up the mountain on delightful expeditions.

And one day they went fishing, up where Jack Valiant had taken Jennifer so long ago. And while the rest roamed around here and there, Jack and Jennifer sat down on the great rock where they had sat to fish and began to talk of those other days just past when they had met, till Jack Valiant was possessed of the whole story, and knew how they had found the Lord.

How his face lighted as Jennifer told him the story of their week at the conference after he left. And suddenly he put out his hand and laid it on hers, as it rested on the rock beside him.

"Little Jennifer," he said, "I can't tell you how happy that makes me. You don't know it, but I've never forgotten you, the little girl that went with me fishing. I've prayed for you all these years since you went away again out of my life. Oh, I know you were only a child, and so for the matter of that was I. But I was a lonely boy, and you were a sweet little companion, and I prayed for you. What do you think of that? It was while my mother was with me that I began to pray for you. Do you remember my mother?"

"A little," said Jennifer. "I thought she was very sweet. She gave me cookies sometimes. I used to think my mother would like her."

"Well, I asked her one day after you had gone away if she thought it would be all right if I were to pray for you, and she said yes, of course. So I kept it up. And after she left me and went to Heaven, I somehow kept it up because it was one of the sweet things connected with my mother and my childhood. I didn't know where you were, but I knew God did, so I prayed for you!"

"Oh, I think that is very beautiful!" said Jennifer, and she let her hand lie still under that other strong hand that covered hers for just a minute. It seemed a very sacred time, and not at all like the times other boys—including Peter Willis—had carelessly caught her hand and caressed it.

When the others drew near and he lifted his hand to adjust his rod, their glances met and he smiled, and it seemed that a ray of sunshine had gone through her soul.

And one day, when he was going away for a few days, and it was almost at the end of their stay, he took her for a walk up the hill to a little grove far behind his own house, where his mother and father were buried beneath softly growing hemlock trees. There they sat down and he told her that he loved her.

"Perhaps I've no right to say this now, when you have not known me very long," he said. "Perhaps I should wait till we are better acquainted and know each other's background better. But somehow I feel I cannot go away, nor let you go away without telling you of my great love for you. There may be no opportunity like this again, ever. And so I thought I might tell you of this love and let you take the knowledge of it with you when you go back to your home, to let you see how it will fit into your life. Then if you want me I can come to you when you send me word. But, on the other hand, Kirsty tells me that you are very wealthy, and live in a grand house, and I am only a poor man. Perhaps I should not even have told you of my love. You perhaps belong in another world than mine. A social world that would not recognize me."

Jennifer was still for a minute and then she looked up.

"*That* would make no difference," she said, "for I have been born again, and belong to the same royal family with you. Classes and wealth of this world do not matter. We mustn't think about that. In fact, I don't know yet whether we have much or little. But I am very glad you have told me you love me, for it has given me great joy. I love you, too. I think I have loved you since you were a boy and I was just a little girl. I used to find, when I was growing up, that I was comparing all the boys I met with you—and none of them came up to your standards."

"Dear!" he said. *"Dear!"* and put his arm about her, drawing her gently, reverently, close to him.

"But listen," she said drawing back a little. "There is something else. I must not let this get possession of me, much as I want to, because, you see, I am the oldest. I am the head of this house, and have the responsibility of bringing up my brothers and sisters. I could not desert that for the dearest love on earth. It is something God has given to me, and I cannot run away from it for my own happiness."

"Dear!" he said and drew her closer. "Of *course* not!" And he stooped and laid his lips on hers. "If in the future days you should ever see your way clear to trusting me enough, and loving me enough to let me share in your beautiful task, I should be the happiest man on earth! I would love them as if they were my own. I do love them now very dearly!" And then their lips met and it seemed as if heaven itself had come down to seal their love.

"But—I would have to see how they felt about it," said Jennifer after a little. "I couldn't do anything that would make them feel unhappy."

"No, you couldn't," said Valiant gently. "We'll just ask our Heavenly Father to work that out for us in His own way, shall we?"

"Oh, you are wonderful!" murmured Jennifer softly as he looked down into her eyes, and she smiled. "It would be such a wonderful thing for us all to have a head of the house like you! If it's right to do, I should be very happy."

"My dear, I feel most unworthy for such an exalted position. How would it be if we made Christ the head? We'll pray about it, little Jennifer, and if God wills we'll work it out together, with Christ, *our* Head."

Her eyes lit then with a great joy. "Oh yes!" she said.

"My precious one, it is so wonderful to have you feel

that way! I'm afraid I've rushed you too much to speak about this yet, but this spot seemed almost sacred to us, because it was the beginning of our friendship, and because you are going away so soon now. And I *had* to have your permission to come and see you soon, you know."

Jennifer's face was radiant.

"Oh, you will come soon, won't you?" she pleaded.

He drew her close again as he answered:

"I'm going to bring Kirsty down as soon as she has finished packing up, you know."

"Oh, I'm so glad! I didn't know you had promised her that. I've been worrying about how she was going to get along on the train. She isn't used to traveling alone, you know."

"Of course! I couldn't let her go off alone. She's been a second mother to me since my mother died. She and mother were very close. And now since her sister has gone she's bound to feel these last days here are very forlorn. I'm so glad that it should have been just now, in the beginning of her loneliness, that you should have come, and asked her to go home with you."

"Ah, but you don't know how glad I am that she is free to go. I had it in the back of my mind when I came off here a-searching, but I didn't even know whether she was living herself, nor whether she would ever be free to come to us if she was. It seems too good to believe that she is willing to come. It's going to be great for the children. I can't think of anything better that could have happened for them. I know what she was to me when I was a child, and I crave that for them!"

"You're being a great little mother to them," said Valiant tenderly. "If I thought I should ever in any least little way interfere with that in you I'd run to the ends of the earth and never see you again!"

"Oh—" cried Jennifer. "Don't do that, please!"

And then Jeremy walked into the scene and flung himself down at their feet.

"I've been over the earth to find you two," he said. "What's the idea of coming off here toward dark? You haven't got fishing rods along, and anyway you're not togged out for fishing. I should think you could find cheerfuller places. There's a gorgeous sunset over in front of the house. Why don't you come back and see it?"

"Perhaps we will," said Valiant thoughtfully. "How about it, Jennifer?"

"Lovely!" said Jennifer, and he reached out his hand and caught hers, lifting her to her feet.

"Well, I like that!" said Jeremy crossly. "I come out here to find you two, and you get up and go off and leave me. Oh, I say, Jack, I wish you'd go home with us. I don't see how we're going to get along without you. You're just what we need. I wish you lived at our house."

"Well, now that's a wish I've had myself a number of times. I'd certainly appreciate it if you would intercede with your sister for me, Jerry. I understand that she is head of the house, or will be on the fifth, about the time that you get home."

Jeremy frowned at his sister, and looked from the one to the other.

"Well," said Jeremy, "all I've got to say is she is a fool if she doesn't see it that way. I certainly wish you'd come. It might drive away some of the undesirables that flood the land occasionally. There's one named Pete that gets my goat. He's too rich and too pretty and too stuck on himself. He thinks he owns my sister and it gives me a pain in the neck!"

Valiant gave Jennifer a quick deep look and she flamed up scarlet with an annoyed look at her brother.

"Jerry! For sweet pity's sake don't bring that up again. I should think after the experience we had down at the boat you would know he'll not be likely to come around again."

"Oh, won't he? My sweet little sister, just wait till we get home and dear Aunt Petunia gets in a little of her nice work. He'll be around as engaging as ever with a cart load of orchids and a few diamonds and things. Just wait! Jack, I'd give you almost anything if you'd cut him out. I don't see how I'm going to remain a Christian if that chump keeps coming around."

"Well, now, Jerry, I might consider your proposition if you would offer me inducement enough," twinkled the young man.

And then deliberately Jack slid his hand within Jennifer's arm and drew her close to him, and walked along with Jerry on the other side, whistling softly one of the choruses they had sung at the conference.

As the song came to an end they heard from the little front porch a sigh of relief and a shout of contentment, from Karen and Robin. It was Robin who put their joy into words quaintly:

"Oh, zere tum zose free dears!" he said. "Aren't ve *glad?*"

Valiant and Jennifer looked at each other suddenly, and his hand grew closer on her arm.

"There are only three more to be heard from," he said in a low jubilant tone.

And then from down by the gate where Hazel and Heather were swinging gently back and forth, Heather called out:

"There they come, Tryon! Go on and ask Jack if he won't come home with us, and everything will be just perfect!"

And Hazel added, "Yes, Try, why don't you? He likes you, and he'll do what you ask. It will be heaps of fun."

"That settles it," said Valiant with a wide grin at Jerry, as Tryon came toward them through the dusk, and all the others came flocking.

The evening ended in a general time of joy and laughter, and then Jennifer herded the little ones to bed, for they were planning to start quite early in the morning.

And when the morning came, with a clear sky and good roads ahead, and a hearty breakfast inside, they kissed Kirsty good-bye and went on their way. But it was generally understood that Jack Valiant would be coming to them soon, and they went away quite happy, because he seemed a part of them all now, and he was going to bring Kirsty with him. None of them noticed the glad look that passed between Jennifer and Jack, as they shouted themselves hoarse with good-byes, and waved as long as they could see the two beloved people standing there together at the little white gate.

It was in the first little town they came to that they stopped at the drug store to telephone to Uncle Blake. They had been putting encouragement into the personals of the New York paper for the last three weeks, so Uncle Blake was prepared for their voices as they sounded out over the wire. Every voice of the whole seven was represented in a sentence, even down to Robin's "Uncle Bwake! Ve have had a svell time, and ve are tuming home! Aren't you *glad,* Uncle Bwake?"

Then they got back into the car and started on their happy way home, for their exile was over and Jennifer would be of age tomorrow. She was now head of the house and could decide what they all should do, and they were *not* going to be separated!

21

The Graeme children had been home a whole day and two nights before Aunt Petra found it out, and then it was only by accident that it came to her knowledge.

They had arrived quite a little after dark, and telephoned Uncle Blake, who came over post haste and welcomed them with open arms. They sat late and talked, and Uncle Blake had real tears in his eyes. Tears of joy, as he sat in a big chair and cuddled the sleeping Robin in his arms. But he hadn't said a word to the aunts yet.

"Let 'em find it out themselves," he chuckled. "It will do them good."

So he said nothing to them. But just a little after dinner time that second night a curious neighbor hied herself over to Petra Holbrook's to call, and almost the first word she said was "Well, it's good to see the Graeme house lighted up again, isn't it! I declare I have missed the brightness of that house more than you'd imagine."

And Petra Holbrook never batted an eye, though she did catch her breath a little before she replied calmly:

"Yes, I suppose you would miss them. All that time. It was ridiculous! They had no business to be gone so long! That's all a part of making an old man their guardian. If Miriam had asked my advice I surely would have urged against it. But John was so set in his way, you know, and Blake is getting a lot of pleasure out of it of course, just having things his own way."

The woman stayed and stayed, hoping to get what

Tryon would have called "a rise" out of Aunt Petra, but Petra Holbrook never let anybody get a rise out of her.

It was too late when the neighbor went home to go right over and give those impudent renegades a piece of her mind, but she lost no time the next morning.

Jennifer caught a glimpse of her driving in at the gate as she sat at the dining room table peeling a pear for Robin, and she said in a low voice:

"There comes Aunt Petra, children, and you'll have to behave wonderfully, do you hear?"

They looked at her aghast. The tone she was using was the same tone wherewith she had warned them to close the curtains on the boat when Peter came in sight.

Robin looked at her in horror.

"Do we scwam?" he asked, his pear poised in his hand.

"No, you don't have to go to bed this time, but you must each do what I tell you right away. Robin, you may go out on the back steps and sit there till you finish your pear. Then go quietly into the kitchen and ask Hazel to wipe your face and hands with a wet towel. After that you and Karen may go out to your sandbox and play, but don't make any noise, and be very careful about everything till Aunt Petra's car goes away."

Then she turned to the little girls.

"You three may clear off the table as quick as you can, and try and get everything into the kitchen, and the table empty, before she gets in. Then you go into the kitchen and wash the dishes. Karen, you can help too, and all of you be quiet about it. Then Hazel and Heather can go upstairs and make *all* the beds, just as smoothly as you did your bunks, and if she isn't gone yet you can sit down and read. Tryon, suppose you open the door when she rings the bell the second time, that will give the girls time to get the last dish out. Be sure to shake hands, and say, 'Why, how are you Aunt Petra?' and don't for anything call her Petunia! Take her into the little reception room, and tell her you will call me. Then skip out and warn Jerry in the garage. Now, *scram!* There goes the bell!"

They scrammed to good effect, so that by the time the

second bell rang Robin was sitting calmly on the back steps licking his pear; the girls had hustled every dish from the table, wiped the table off, and departed to the dish washing.

Tryon came with all the grace and ease of Stanton to open the front door with a flourish. Jennifer in the upper hall giggled to herself over his effusive tone. Then as he came up grinning to inform her of her caller, she straightened out her smile and went promptly down, quiet and assured, and greeted Aunt Petra as if she had been a dear distant neighbor who had been absent on a long trip.

"Oh, Aunt Petra! So nice of you to come over. You're looking awfully well. I hope you've had a pleasant summer!"

Aunt Petra's rage rose and her eyes began to snap.

"Well, if I'm looking well it's no thanks to you!" she retorted. "Such a summer as you've led us through! I thought I never would survive it. What in the world did you think you were doing, anyway, running off in that style?"

"Why, Aunt Petra, I'm sorry you have been sick. We certainly had no idea of troubling you. But we've had a delightful time, and all got quite rested. I felt that it was really essential for the children's sake that we get entirely away from all reminders, and it's really done us a lot of good!"

"But why did you have to do things in such a dramatic way, if you wanted to go away? You and your silly old Uncle Blake, as if the rest of us were a lot of snakes that you had to run away from!"

"Why, really, Aunt Petra, you don't quite realize the things you all said that made us feel we had better get away out of your sight. Can you imagine how my mother and father would have felt if they could have heard you plotting to separate us? That was enough to drive any family into exile. But now that it's over, Aunt Petra, suppose we forget it all and be good friends. We'll say no more about it."

"In*deed!*" said Aunt Petra. "You are still as impudent

as ever, aren't you? Well, I'll say what I please about it as often as I choose. And to begin with, what do you think poor Peter Willis thinks of you?"

"Peter Willis?" said Jennifer, her eyes opening wide. "Why, I don't know that it matters what Peter Willis thinks of me, does it? He is nothing to me. We used to be friends, that was all. I never liked him especially."

"The very idea of your talking that way, Jennifer Graeme! When you know that he wants to marry you, and he offered to take you to Europe and get you out of all this trouble with the children! He told me himself that he offered to marry you at once!"

"Oh, really, Aunt Petra? And did he tell you that I refused his offer? Well, I did. I told him that if I ever married anybody—which I didn't expect then because I felt my duty was to my brothers and sisters—but if I ever should be married it would not be to him. Aunt Petra, I'd hate to tell you some of the things he said about my brothers and sisters! And I'm simply done with Peter even as a friend."

"Jennifer Graeme, have you taken leave of your senses? To talk that way to a wealthy good-looking fellow like Peter who adores the very ground you walk on? You needn't think that you can string him along till you get ready to take him over. He's much too high-spirited for that. You'll lose him if you carry on like this!"

"Aunt Petra, he's no loss whatever, and if he were the last man on earth I would never marry him."

"So, you think you'll be content to go unmarried all your days, do you? You'll be sadly disappointed when you find no man wants you at all. You'll get old and shriveled, and then what will become of you?"

"Why, Aunt Petra, you are old, but you're not shriveled. I think you are rather pleasant to look at when you're not scolding someone. I don't see that you are very unhappy just because you haven't any husband any more. I certainly would rather go alone all my days than marry Peter Willis. However, I'll tell you for your relief that I'm not going to go unmarried after all. I'm going to be married one of these days to a perfectly wonderful man!"

Aunt Petra rose in horror.

"Now Jennifer Graeme, what on earth have you been doing this summer? What would your poor mother say if she knew that you had turned down a marvellous man and picked up some nobody out in the wilds? Oh, I just knew that Blakefield Graeme would rue the day he let you naughty children go off by yourselves. Who is the man you have engaged yourself to marry, Jennifer? As if *you* knew whether he was wonderful or not. Who is he? Somebody who will disgrace the family?"

"Oh no, Aunt Petra. He's not like that. Why—he belongs to a royal family!"

"*Royal* family!" snorted Aunt Petra. "As if I'd believe that! You haven't been over in Europe rampaging around, have you? And picked up some worthless second son, or some penniless count?"

"Oh, no, Aunt Petra! Nothing like that. He's a splendid man, and I mean it. He belongs to royalty. His Father is a King!"

"His father a *king!*" screamed the outraged aunt. "*What* king?"

"The King of Kings, Aunt Petra. I mean that he is a servant of the Lord Jesus Christ, he is a child of the King, and that has come to mean to me the greatest thing of all. For I've taken Christ for my Saviour too. I am glad of this opportunity to talk with you, for I wanted to tell you that. And I thought you would like to know, too, about my engagement. I went away to get ready to be head of the house myself, but I'm happy to know that God has sent us somebody a great deal more worthy to be head of the house to us all. I hope you'll like him when you see him, for everybody does."

"No, I shall *not* like him!" stated Aunt Petra inexorably. "I shall *never* like him. Some poor whining illiterate missionary, I suppose, who is marrying you to feather his nest. Oh, what would your poor mother have said if she could have known about him?"

Suddenly Jennifer laughed.

"Why, she did know about him, Aunt Petra. For, you see, we've been friends a very long time, only I didn't know until this summer that he loved me. But mother would have been so glad to have me marry him. You see she never quite liked Peter Willis, although she didn't dream that anybody thought there was anything special between us. But I know she would be glad with me, and so would daddy. And now, Aunt Petra, why don't you take off your hat and stay to lunch with us? It won't be very elaborate, of course, because Hazel and Heather are getting it, but it will be very nice for you to stay and eat with us. Won't you stay?"

"For pity's sake, Hazel and Heather getting lunch! Why, where are your wonderful servants, I should like to know? I don't wonder they got other places if you sent them flying like that without any notice."

"Well, you see we've only just got here, and we haven't fully made our plans, so I haven't sent them word to come back yet. I'm not just sure how many of them I want back. Stanton, of course, was the best of the lot, but I found a letter here from him that his old mother is very sick with a lingering illness and he feels he should stay with her for the present. The chauffeur had a chance to get another job and I told him to take it. We don't really need a chauffeur anyway. Jack and Jerry and I can all drive, and it won't be long before Tryon is driving too. And as for the nurse she was simply impossible. I don't want her back. I'm not sure about the cook. She was rather grumpy at times. I may get her later, though. Just for the present I've engaged the gardener's wife to clean for us, and we're doing the cooking ourselves, as we have done all summer. I think it's really good for us all!"

"Cooking! Well I guess you'll need somebody to clean after you children have been cooking! I think you're all stark staring crazy and you need a nurse, every one of you, and especially your daft old Uncle Blakefield!"

"Oh, we're going to have a nurse," smiled Jennifer. "My old nurse, Kirsty McCarra. Do you remember her?

We've been up visiting her a few days, and we're bringing her down to stay. Her invalid sister has recently died so she is free to come again. Do you remember her?"

"Was she that queer foreign-sounding woman with such a thick speech like a crooked thistle? Mercy, I hope you won't keep *her!* She was very religious, I remember, and she was a great stickler for having your bottles washed so clean she made all your mother's cooks angry till they left."

"Why, we all love her, Aunt Petra. We're so delighted she would come. But aren't you going to take off your hat and sit down till lunch time?"

"No, I certainly am not. I should have indigestion if I did, eating things those wild young ones had cooked! And having to sit and listen to all the crazy things you are planning to do. I'm really sick at heart and I'll have to go home. Royalty *indeed!* A pretty head of the house a man like that will make! And to think you chose him instead of Peter Willis! Now I'm going home and I wash my hands of this family for good and all! If you are determined to go to destruction you'll have to go, that's all!"

Aunt Petra walked out of the door with her head up and her chin in the air. But when Jennifer heard the wheels of her car going down the drive she sat down in a big chair and covered her face with her hands and laughed till the tears came.

"Poor Aunt Petra! And she didn't know what it meant to be related to the royal family, and be a subject of the King of Kings!"

BRING ROMANCE INTO YOUR LIFE

With these bestsellers from your favorite Bantam authors

Barbara Cartland

☐	11372	LOVE AND THE LOATHSOME LEOPARD	$1.50
☐	10712	LOVE LOCKED IN	$1.50
☐	11270	THE LOVE PIRATE	$1.50
☐	11271	THE TEMPTATION OF TORILLA	$1.50

Catherine Cookson

☐	10355	THE DWELLING PLACE	$1.50
☐	10358	THE GLASS VIRGIN	$1.50
☐	10516	THE TIDE OF LIFE	$1.75

Georgette Heyer

☐	02263	THE BLACK MOTH	$1.50
☐	10322	BLACK SHEEP	$1.50
☐	02210	FARO'S DAUGHTER	$1.50

Emilie Loring

☐	02382	FORSAKING ALL OTHERS	$1.25
☐	02237	LOVE WITH HONOR	$1.25
☐	11228	IN TIMES LIKE THESE	$1.50
☐	10846	STARS IN YOUR EYES	$1.50

Eugenia Price

☐	12712	BELOVED INVADER	$1.95
☐	12717	LIGHTHOUSE	$1.95
☐	12835	NEW MOON RISING	$1.95

Buy them at your local bookstore or use this handy coupon for ordering:

Bantam Books, Inc., Dept. RO, 414 East Golf Road, Des Plaines, Ill. 60016

Please send me the books I have checked above. I am enclosing $______ (please add 75¢ to cover postage and handling). Send check or money order —no cash or C.O.D.'s please.

Mr/Mrs/Miss____________________

Address____________________

City__________ State/Zip__________

RO—2/79

Please allow four weeks for delivery. This offer expires 8/79.

Novels of Enduring Romance and Inspiration by

GRACE LIVINGSTON HILL

☐	11762	TOMORROW ABOUT THIS TIME	$1.50
☐	11506	THROUGH THESE FIRES	$1.50
☐	10859	BEAUTY FOR ASHES	$1.50
☐	10891	THE ENCHANTED BARN	$1.50
☐	10947	THE FINDING OF JASPER HOLT	$1.50
☐	2916	AMORELLE	$1.50
☐	2985	THE STREET OF THE CITY	$1.50
☐	10766	THE BELOVED STRANGER	$1.50
☐	10792	WHERE TWO WAYS MET	$1.50
☐	10826	THE BEST MAN	$1.50
☐	10909	DAPHNE DEANE	$1.50
☐	11005	STRANGER WITHIN THE GATES	$1.50
☐	11020	SPICE BOX	$1.50
☐	11028	A NEW NAME	$1.50
☐	11329	DAWN OF THE MORNING	$1.50
☐	11167	THE RED SIGNAL	$1.50

Buy them at your local bookstore or use this handy coupon for ordering:

Bantam Books, Inc., Dept., GLH, 414 East Golf Road, Des Plaines, Ill. 60016

Please send me the books I have checked above. I am enclosing $________
(please add 75¢ to cover postage and handling). Send check or money order
—no cash or C.O.D.'s please.

Mr/Mrs/Miss______________________________

Address______________________________

City________________State/Zip________________

GLH—10/78

Please allow four weeks for delivery. This offer expires 4/79.

Bantam Book Catalog

Here's your up-to-the-minute listing of over 1,400 titles by your favorite authors.

This illustrated, large format catalog gives a description of each title. For your convenience, it is divided into categories in fiction and non-fiction—gothics, science fiction, westerns, mysteries, cookbooks, mysticism and occult, biographies, history, family living, health, psychology, art.

So don't delay—take advantage of this special opportunity to increase your reading pleasure.

Just send us your name and address and 50¢ (to help defray postage and handling costs).

BANTAM BOOKS, INC.
Dept. FC, 414 East Golf Road, Des Plaines, Ill. 60016

Mr./Mrs./Miss______________________________
(please print)

Address______________________________

City________________ State________ Zip________

Do you know someone who enjoys books? Just give us their names and addresses and we'll send them a catalog too!

____

Mr./Mrs./Miss______________________________

Address______________________________

City________________ State________ Zip________

____

Mr./Mrs./Miss______________________________

Address______________________________

City________________ State________ Zip________

FC—9/78